To Noel and Jessica. Just because.

This is not the story that was leaked to the press.
This is how it happened.
This is how the Batman died.

PROLOGUE

Nine months earlier...

He watched the attendants hoist the body onto the metal mesh and it landed with what would have been a painful thump had the bastard been alive, but, unfortunately, he wasn't. Still, that carcass of meat and madness deserved any shame they could give it. They looked up to James Gordon, Gotham City's police commissioner, watching from the second-level balcony. He shook his head ruefully as if to say, *We're not him. Let's get it over with.*

With a grimace, they shoved the corpse's arms to its side and straightened its legs then stepped back, checking with Gordon again.

"We're done," a cop said. "*He's* done. Any time you're ready, sir."

Gordon nodded and pressed the small red button. He had expected to feel more, perhaps anger, definitely the urge for revenge. But he didn't. Burning up what once had been a human being, if only in the loosest terms possible, was as simple as "press and wait." The end of a life—good or bad—should be more dramatic or at least sad. But not in this case.

Hundreds of blue gas flames suddenly burst into life around the remains. Steadily the gauge recorded their heat rising to a scorching 1,800 degrees Fahrenheit. Normal cremation rules demanded that the body be placed in a container or casket, but the governor had waived the rules for this… removal. Everyone wanted to watch this body burn, right down to its ashes. Everyone wanted to make certain there was no chance he would rise again.

Even dead, he scared the shit out of them.

Gordon stood by the red button for nearly two hours as the body was slowly, excruciatingly reduced to its component parts by heat and vaporization. He would wait there until he was certain it was done, and that Gotham City's seemingly endless nightmare would end once and for all.

Finally all that remained of the body was dust, and that was humiliatingly flushed down a dozen different toilets to further make certain his various parts would never be able to reconstitute.

Was it outside of the prescribed law? *Possibly,* Gordon mused. *Primitive? To be certain. Vindictive? You bet.* But this corpse deserved nothing better. He waited until the final flush swirled the last of the ashes on their journey into the ocean, then gave a faint smile to the other observers. They responded in kind, although there was no joy—this was pure relief. He left knowing that at long last the Joker, that self-proclaimed Clown Prince of Crime, was well and truly gone.

* * *

Gordon watched as the attendants slapped each other's backs while grinning and laughing. The Joker was gone and would never return, and if that long pent-up relief wasn't reason enough to raise a glass, nothing would ever be.

They asked him to join their celebratory dinner, but Gordon turned them down, preferring to be alone. It was true that Gotham City would never have to deal with that grinning madman again, but Gordon never wanted anyone—especially his fellow cops—to celebrate death, not even the Joker's.

The end of any life, he thought, *should be a solemn event, not an excuse for a party.* But as he watched his fellow officers treat the moment as if it was New Year's Eve, it appeared to him that civilization hadn't progressed all that much in the last ten thousand years.

Here, in Gotham City, it had probably regressed.

The commissioner's office at the Gotham City Police Department was as sparsely decorated as Gordon could manage. On his desk were three framed pictures of his daughter, Barbara—two of her alone and one she had taken with him and one with his son, James Jr., taken long ago and in better days.

On the wall hung the mandatory professional certificates, and a few photos of him receiving awards of some sort from one mayor after the other. But little else.

Generic Gotham City lithographs, circa the 1930s era, had been hung on the walls by his predecessor. He'd have taken them down, but that would have left blatantly discolored gaps where they had been hanging, so he didn't bother. The rug—threadbare for several decades—had been laid down by his predecessor's predecessor's predecessor.

When Gordon took the job, he believed that making the office his own would lead to him spending his entire life, twenty-four–seven, in this twenty- by twenty-six-foot prison. On the other hand, if it was spartan to the point of discomfort, he thought he'd have more reason to go home at night to his wife and family, and try to maintain the illusion of a life.

Good plan. Lousy results. Except for his daughter, his family had long ago scattered to the winds.

So much for a "life."

He collapsed into his chair, a new and extremely comfortable ergonomic model and his only extravagance, which he paid for himself to help support his bad back. He swung around to stare out a grime-smeared window looking over the Gotham City skyline.

Staring at its beauty from so high up and through the nearly opaque glass, he could fool himself into thinking there might have been a time when Gotham City had offered hope, and not despair. If it ever existed, those days ended with the murders of the city's greatest benefactors, Thomas and Martha Wayne. The bandage had been pulled loose, revealing the festering wound that lay beneath.

Even Bruce, their son, had proved unable to heal it.

Reluctantly, Gordon accepted that the Joker was dead, and that his particular brand of homicidal mania had ended. But he knew there were dozens of other psychopathic wannabes, salivating to claim his throne. Even before the body had been officially identified, the Riddler began shouting from the rooftops that Gotham City was his.

"Riddle me this," he'd bellowed into his amplifier. "Who's as insane as the Joker, but still breathing?" Someone had been stupid enough to reply, "You are," and he'd put a bullet through the poor sap's head.

"No, you idiots," he shouted to the heavens, "it's the Bat. But he won't be breathing for long."

The Riddler may have been a showman, but Oswald Cobblepot—better known as the Penguin—preferred a more surreptitious approach to accumulating power. He quietly organized Gotham City's criminal gangs, choosing to stay under the radar and rule the streets one crumbling corner at a time.

If Gotham City's shadowed alleyways belonged to the Penguin, however, its underground was the domain of Killer Croc, an atavistic freak of nature who more resembled a thickly scaled reptile than a man. Gotham City's sewers extended in all directions, undermining nearly every square foot of the city, providing unrestricted access to any place Croc wanted to go. As long as he had that sort of access, no one was safe.

The list went on and on. There was going to be a gang war—Gordon knew it with a certainty. With the Joker dead and a vacuum to be filled, there was no way to avoid it.

Any day now mob leader Carmine Falcone would decide it was time to take on Harvey Dent, the former district attorney now known as Two-Face. Or gang boss Sal Maroni might decide that if he waited any longer, Rupert Thorne would try to move into his territory. So Maroni would strike first and hard, and there'd be blood.

Hush, Bane, Poison Ivy, and Scarecrow. The Ventriloquist. Mr. Freeze, Hugo Strange, and of course Catwoman—depending on which side of the law she favored on any given day. They all saw Gotham City as a promised land where crime reigned eternal, and its advocates ruled supreme.

The war was coming. Somewhere one of the loose cannons was going to fire the first round. And the police, already woefully undermanned, would crumple in the onslaught. Months. Weeks. Days. Hours.

It was only a matter of time.

The war never came.

There were skirmishes, some more significant than others, yet for nine months the city experienced relative peace.

Nevertheless, Gordon never allowed himself to exhale. This was, after all, Gotham City. And as far as he was concerned, she was genetically incapable of sustaining hope.

1

Maggie placed Tuesday's meatloaf special on the counter in front of Scott Owens, six months a proud officer in the Gotham City Police Department, then poured his second cup of coffee. Because she knew he was on a diet, she'd already replaced his potatoes with mixed vegetables and the cornbread with a side salad, light ranch dressing in a small cup to the side.

He'd lost fifty pounds, and she was determined to help him lose his last ten any way she could.

Owens barely paid attention to the food, forking each bite out of routine and not hunger. Donna was going to have to quit her job to have the baby, so he was trying to figure out if he could support the three of them on his rookie salary. Half of their income would be disappearing in four short months, even as their expenses increased exponentially.

Lost in thought, he didn't feel fingers tapping at his shoulder until they became insistent, and a frightened voice drew his attention.

"Officer? *Officer?*" The words became louder, more strident with each repeat. The man tapping him was in his thirties, dressed casually, and looking very worried as he pointed to the far end of the diner. "Do you see it? Do you see them?"

The person sitting there had his face turned away, buried in a newspaper, and his attitude was strange enough that Owens decided to check it out. The young officer walked over, stepped in front of the man, and recoiled with instinctive shock.

He wasn't looking at a man. If it was a male, he wasn't even human.

Owens stumbled back. What he was looking at was some sort of impossible nightmare. He turned to scan the rest of the diners...

What the hell?

...and suddenly realized there were no longer any human customers, but other things, moving—some even slithering—as if nothing unusual had occurred. He rubbed his eyes, certain it couldn't be real. Yet when he looked again, the shapes were in front of him.

One by one they turned to stare at one another, as if noticing—and finally, comprehending—what had taken them over.

Pauli's Diner, established in the mid-1950s by a former city mayor, loved by the locals as much for its amply portioned home-style dinners as its low prices, was filled with... monsters!

And as one the monsters screamed.

"Dispatch, Scott Owens, badge number 47532. I need immediate backup. Pauli's Diner, Fourteenth and Moldoff." Pause. "No. I can't explain why. You have to believe me.

And for God's sake, please hurry." Officer Owens reached for his weapon but his hand had been replaced with lobster claws which couldn't hold the gun.

The shapes rushed back and forth in chaos. Their arms—sometimes only tentacles—flailed mindlessly, lashing out at anyone, any*thing*, that came close. And the screams grew louder.

Then the shapes were over him, screaming at him. He tried to tell them he was a policeman, but his own words sounded—even to him—like the growling of a wild dog.

Fists and tentacles slammed at him. He felt his face being cut, warm blood spurting from the wounds. The monsters began piling on top of him, first one, then more, fists hitting him, sharp teeth—no, they were fangs—biting into him even as he bit back, sinking his own teeth into the arms or whatever were holding him down.

Owens could never remember being so afraid. Every time one of the things moved, no matter how slightly, his heart raced, his chest pounded, his skin was covered by a slick sheen of sweat. In his college days he had climbed mountains. He fell once, and his injuries kept him in the hospital for almost four months. But even as he fell, he hadn't felt this kind of dread. It was pervasive and it controlled him and he prayed for death rather than suffer it for even another moment.

He twisted and like slime he seemed to flow through the gaps between the other beasts. His claws became flippers and he used them to push ahead. The diner door was only feet away, but it might as well be on the other side of the planet. There were monsters blocking every escape route.

Still he struggled through the mob, and realized these creatures were as confused and terrified as he. They weren't trying to kill him. They were trying to escape, to protect themselves from harm.

Suddenly the front door seemed to explode. Monsters pounded at it, shattering its glass, then pulling their way over the shards and other creatures as they escaped from what had to be hell. Owens was carried along with the others and found himself outside, on the street, his flippers reforming into fingers attached to hands, part of a body that was—thank God—human again.

He fell face down in the gutter. Looking up, he saw a dozen men and women running from the diner as if they still were being chased. A few lay on the sidewalk, or even the street. Some of them looked pretty bad. But there were no other monsters.

Somehow, the threat that came out of nowhere was gone.

Yet the fear was still there.

Owens reached for his phone and tried to call his precinct dispatcher, but he was unable to control his voice. His words still sounded like the howling of a wild animal. And even if he could speak, he couldn't imagine that they would believe him when he said that he had barely escaped with his life from a diner filled with demons.

His hands trembled and he dropped the phone. He tried to pick it up, but it suddenly vibrated. Startled, he dropped it yet again.

One of the fleeing customers stepped on the phone, crushing it. Owens felt utterly alone, and the fear spiked. Like the others, he wanted to run away, and began to pick himself up, but his legs collapsed under him and he was unable to move.

He lay there waiting for death.

But he didn't die.

What he had seen could not have been real, no matter how true it felt. Was it an hallucination? Mass hysteria? If so, did everyone see the same monsters? How was that even possible?

Across the street from him stood the Gotham Triangle Building, home of the *Gotham Tribune*, a newspaper that in its heyday had boasted a daily readership of three million, but in the internet age barely sold a third of that. Raised high on the front of the building was a giant projection screen which scrolled the news in a small banner that ran along its base, while commercials filled the rest of the screen.

On the giant screen were the images of beautiful women in just about legal-sized bikinis, running along a beach, while some feminine product unknown to Owens was being hawked. Suddenly the women pixelated into static and disappeared, replaced by an interior shot of the diner.

For several minutes Owens stared at the images. The restaurant patrons were running wild, striking out, mindlessly biting each other. Then he saw himself slithering across the tiled floor, grabbing the others and viciously pushing them aside as he pulled himself to the door in a desperate attempt to escape. He stared at his own image, huge on the screen—not the monster he thought he'd become but violent and mindless—and he was sick at what he had done.

But then he thought of something else, something so

frightening it made his stomach churn and his skin turn cold. During all the madness, someone was filming the scene and he never saw it. *What the hell kind of cop was he?*

As he stared at the screen, it began to flicker again. His image was replaced by a face covered in a brown hessian sack that appeared to be stitched to the wearer's face. Dark, hollow eyes burned with fire and he gestured with hands that had syringes where fingers should have been.

Was this another hallucination?

Words scrolled across the screen where the news had been moments earlier.

IT IS TIME TO OBEY

The bony figure spoke in a deep, raspy, guttural voice that barely sounded human.

"Gotham City, I am taking over all your television channels, so look at what I have done," he said. *"This demonstration used only five ounces of my latest toxin. Tomorrow this will seem like child's play."* Owens read the crawl again, and stared at the image, recognizing him from one of the daily briefings. That was the criminal known as Scarecrow. *"Gotham City, this is your only warning."*

That hideous face seemed to stare directly at him, causing the blood to pulse in his veins. The huge screen crackled again with static, and then died as if the plug had been pulled.

Our only warning?

What the hell was coming next?

2

Scarecrow's threat worked.

The lines of cars heading to the Mercy Bridge was backed up for more than five miles, some all the way to Memorial Park in City Center. From the bridge one could see City Island and Lady Gotham rising from it, torch held high, standing tall and proud. The great statue had been constructed decades earlier as a beacon, shining a light on Gotham City's hopes and dreams. Sadly, over the years, that light had dimmed, until it illuminated little more than its endless failures.

Police on motorcycles and horseback corralled the lines in a near-fruitless attempt to keep calm those desperate to escape. Repurposed school and city busses were packed to the bursting point and helped alleviate some of the traffic but ultimately they, too, were caught in the endless wave of frightened, fleeing humanity.

Gordon orchestrated the city's exodus as best he could from the back seat of his squad car. He was a blur of motion, switching between a half-dozen cell phones that connected him to his captains covering Gotham City's key districts. The car drove most of its winding path on the sidewalks, its whooping blare of sirens sending already frightened citizens running to avoid being hit.

"*Sir.*" A frightened voice came over one phone. "*My men have cleared about a third of Miagani's population, but there's no way we'll reach everyone in time.*" Jerome Finger, a twenty-two-year veteran of the Gotham City Police Department, was captain of the Fifth Precinct, and he was obviously afraid. But he was also struggling to maintain control. "*I don't know what to do, sir. We really need some help here.*"

"Wish I had some to give, Jerry," Gordon replied. Finger was one of the first cops he met when he came to Gotham City. There was no better or more honest officer anywhere, which is why he had been promoted to captain only three years later. "We're down to a token force. I need you to get out everyone you can."

"*What about those we can't, sir?*"

Gordon hated the answer, but there simply was no other.

"We can only do what we can do." He clicked off the phone before Finger could respond, dropped it to his side, and exhaled. This job was impossible at its best. Today it was even worse.

He watched as several school busses slowly edged past his car, filled with kids junior-high-school age and younger. They were heading north toward Mercy Bridge and Bleake Island. From there they'd go west and, if luck was on their side, they'd be out of Gotham City an hour or two later. The kids looked frightened, and they had every reason to be. This was, without doubt, the most chaotic event they'd experienced in their short lives. Sadly, Gotham City had a way of leaving its mark on even its youngest.

"It always comes down to the children, doesn't it?" he said to Bill McKean, his driver. "I can't even imagine how frightened they are. I see those kids and remember what it was like when James Jr. and Barbara were that age."

McKean nodded. "Yeah, but you know something, Commissioner? Twenty years ago madmen like Scarecrow never existed. Today, they're almost a dime a dozen. I can't even count how many there are." He shook his head. "I think these kids are growing up knowing way too much about how low humanity can get. Without realizing that life doesn't have to be a cesspool, that this isn't what's supposed to be normal.

"That's the real crime, you ask me."

Gordon felt his stomach tighten. "So how do we make it better?"

"Okay, you asked. This is me, remember, but I think we need at least a hundred more Bats. And we tell them to pull out all the stops." His voice became louder with each word. Then he took a deep breath, and added, "Like I says, just my opinion."

"Batman's good," Gordon agreed. "Maybe even vital. I know that, Bill. But no matter how valuable his contributions have been, you know as well as I do that we can't survive forever under vigilante justice. Ultimately we need law—rules and order. The people look to us to protect them, and they have to believe that we can do the job, and that we don't need outside help."

"Agreed, sir," McKean said. "But until that day, he gets the job done."

"Trouble is, he raises the stakes. And the bad guys keep matching him."

"I know, sir. But if you're so much against him, why do you let him do what he does?"

"It's what you said, Bill. He gets the job done. And it's not Batman I worry about. He's a good man, maybe the best I've ever known. But it's those who follow him. The copycats. They might not have his unwavering sense of justice. They're the ones who frighten me. Yes, it's working for now, but I still keep praying that one day my officers will be all Gotham City needs."

"Your lips to God's ears, sir." McKean pulled the car to a stop. "Oh, we're here. Ground zero."

Where it began.

Across from Gordon's car stood the shattered remains of Pauli's Diner, its windows broken, its door pulled from its hinges, its tables and chairs overturned, its stovetops and ovens smashed beyond repair. Seventy years of history, gone in less than four hours.

"Bill, you know, just yesterday there were six point three million people living and working here in Gotham City." Gordon got out of the car and stepped over the debris, avoiding the carpet of glass shards, and entered the empty diner. He looked around staring at what were now only bloodstained memories.

"Today, not so many."

He picked up a child's stuffed bear lying under an over-turned booth, straightened its overalls and cap, and carefully placed it on a countertop, hoping it would eventually find its way home. He would probably never know what happened to the child who owned it, whether it was a boy or girl, or if he or she had managed to get safely out of Gotham City. Some questions would never be answered, and for a man who lived for answers, that deeply bothered him.

He stared out of the diner, past the cracked pavement badly in need of repair, to the vast emptiness—and thought for a moment he saw a black blur swing past.

"Yeah," he said aloud but to himself, "he gets the job done. And God do we need him now."

3

He was perched on a cracked masonry gargoyle two hundred twenty-seven feet above the sidewalk, scanning the horde of running figures. Thousands of men and women, dragging their crying children with them, panic distorting their faces, all hoping without any real hope that they'd be able to get out of the city before the deadline came.

Living in Gotham City always meant living with fear. And soon, unless something was done, there would be nothing else left *but* fear.

Unless something is done, he thought as he saw a policeman here and there break from crowd control and join the fleeing mob. *Unless I do something.*

Batman fired a grapple line across the wide street to the Groiler building and leaped off the stone grotesque, his cape spreading as he glided over the panic below and landed on the golden building's eighth-floor balcony.

Smoke and the glow of flames could be seen a scant dozen blocks away. Fire engines tried to make their way through the crowd, sirens blaring, but they were stuck in the stampede, unable to move.

Batman leaped, once again letting his cape spread wide,

encouraging the air to rush under it and push him up, enabling him to glide over the crowd, past the fire engines, and then around the block. He felt the wind dying and he began to dip, so he fired his grapple again, up to the fourth story of the Kane Building, an old apartment house built in 1940 for Gotham City's elite. Once used to house the wealthy, like so much of city, it was terribly deteriorated. Today it sheltered the poor.

The grapple lifted Batman's arc and sent him soaring up again to where he caught a new gust that took him another two blocks, past Stagg Towers, before forcing him to repeat the process. Most of the people below were so intent on finding their way out of Gotham City that they didn't waste time looking up, so he was able to glide several blocks before a runner noticed him. And even then, before the person could be certain, Batman sailed around another corner, disappearing from sight.

His gauntlet began to vibrate. *Cell call. Audio, not video.* Tim wouldn't call—not now. And Dick barely spoke to him anymore. So it had to be James Gordon, Alfred Pennyworth, Oracle or Lucius Fox. With his hands being used to maneuver through the city, he sent the call to his ear comm.

Alfred was on the other end.

"Sir, to let you know, Mr. Fox is working on the new uniform, as per your request."

"Good to know, Alfred," Batman responded. "But that's not the reason you're calling. Fox would have sent a comm when he was ready."

"Very perceptive, sir," the butler responded. *"The*

computer has picked up a fire alert in Old Gotham City. I recognized the address. GPS indicates you're only two blocks away, and traveling in that direction."

"So?"

There was a pause, then Alfred continued.

"*With all the problems the city is undergoing,*" he said, "*I have to ask, sir—why would you be making a detour there? The building has long been abandoned. No lives are imperiled.*"

"Fires can spread, Alfred."

"*But were that to happen, you know you're not equipped to stop it. The Fire Department will put it down before it spreads to any other buildings.*" Another pause. "*You're going there because of what it was, not what it is… sir.*"

No answer.

"*Sir? In the greater scheme of things, you know that building is not important.*"

"It might be ready for demolition today," Batman replied, "but fifty-seven years ago that building was a showcase. It was also where my father was born. He bought it before he turned twenty, and often brought me to it as he attempted to buy the entire block, planning its renovation. When he… when my parents were murdered, I… I didn't follow through, and I should have, Alfred."

"*I understand that, sir. But why now?*"

"Although it's little more than a metaphor, I can't stand by and watch the city my father tried to save be destroyed by fear." His jaw tightened, and his voice became harder. "This fire wasn't an accident."

"*Sir?*"

"Are you picking up the five heat signatures directly

below me? They're torching this block—and God knows how many others—with Molotov cocktails. They appear to be doing it for fun."

"*Understood,*" the butler said. "*I'll alert the commissioner to have several cells prepared.*"

"Thank you, Alfred. We can't protect our future by viciously razing the past."

The leader of the five appeared to be no more than twenty-four, a smallish punk, thin, wearing jeans and a blue T-shirt with a design on it representing a popular TV cartoon character. He stuck the alcohol-soaked cloth into a glass bottle filled with gas mixed with motor oil, then lit the makeshift wick. When the bottle was smashed it would release a sudden, deadly fireball.

If Batman let him throw it.

The caped figure fired a grapple cable, snagged the punk, then yanked him halfway up the building, locking the grapple into position and leaving him hanging twenty-seven feet off the ground. As the would-be arsonist jerked to a stop Batman dove, cape wings spread, and caught the falling bottle bomb. Then he hurled it over the street toward Gotham River where it safely sunk out of sight.

He landed in the midst of the other four, taking down the largest one with a crushing kick to his jaw. Blood shooting from his mouth, the creep buckled and fell.

The other three were gangbangers who expected their victims to surrender to their combined and overwhelming strength, with only a frightened mewling indicating any complaint. The store owners they terrorized rarely fought back as the punks aimed their weapons at them, threatening to blow them to hell if they didn't fork over the contents of a cash register.

But Batman wasn't planning to mewl *or* surrender. He was going to teach them a lesson they'd remember, no matter how long they were jailed.

He thrust a hard fist into the gut of the closest punk, then used an elbow to smash him on the back of his neck. The punk gasped and crumpled, but—fool that he was—he tried to reach to his waist to grab his gun. Batman's boot smashed the gangbanger's hand and he could hear the bones crack and snap. The thug howled with pain. In six or eight months, when he recuperated, he'd be able to use his hands to feed himself, and perhaps even cut his food, but little else.

His criminal days were over. Batman stared at the downed hoods and chuckled. They wouldn't be causing further mischief any time soon, he thought. He laughed again, and then suddenly stopped as he saw punk four try to run. A minute ago he might have tried to cripple him, but that blood-spawned anger was now gone. He removed a collapsible Batarang from his belt pouch and threw it. Fifteen seconds later he saw the thug fall, and stay down.

Punk five was smarter, or at least he had learned from his friends. He fell to his knees and snapped his hands behind his head, interlocking his fingers as he'd undoubtedly been ordered to do many times before. Maybe this one would learn his lesson when he got out of jail. Batman hoped so, but sincerely doubted it. He activated his comm and keyed it to Gordon's frequency.

"Commissioner, I've got five punks trussed up on Robbins south of Moldoff. Fire-bombers. Someone should pick them up."

"I don't have anyone to spare, Batman," Gordon said, sounding tired and frustrated but trying to hold it together. *"We need to vacate a city of six point three million frantic and frightened people with fewer than a thousand cops. They're trying their best to keep some semblance to order, but there're simply not enough busses and trains to help even a quarter of them. So thieves, arsonists and all the other goddam gutter rats that're out there, they're not on our priority list today. I'm sorry, Batman. It kills me. I'm really sorry."*

"Where are you now, Jim?"

"Most of those left on the streets are the sort that enjoy the chaos," Gordon continued. *"Scum. Criminals and worse, and there's not enough of the good people left to stop them. So I'm heading back to the G.C.P.D. I think my time's better spent planning the evac of the good people who want to get out. Speaking of which, you and I should coordinate—there are some things we need to go over."*

Batman turned back to the five captured punks, all secured with black plastic zip ties.

"I'm not letting them free, so I'll be there with them in fifteen. Twenty max. The usual place?"

"I can use a friendly face right about now. So sure—see you then."

Batman stared into the dark skies and shook his head. Before the Joker died, he had injected his blood into

Batman. Now it was trying to take him over. It almost made him take a life. He had to stay in control, but that wasn't going to be an easy task.

Still, he had no choice.

Batman didn't kill… and he never would.

4

"Penguin? It's Louie. I'm on Seventeenth and Grant. I met with the Newton boys like you said, only they had a change of mind. They don't want to sign with us against Scarerow. Newton, he said these days it's every one for himself."

"And how do we respond to treachery, Mr. Ross?"

"But they confiscated my weapons before I met with them, and they didn't give 'em back when I left. I mean, hell, boss, I was happy to get out of there in one piece. Maybe you can get me some backup?"

"Mr. Ross, I sent you to deal with a situation. I expect it to be dealt with. Solve your own problem, or perhaps Mr. Newton will allow you to become a member of his entourage. You know how much he values… loyalty."

"Yeah. Uh, right, sir. I understand, sir. I'll deal with it. Don't you worry none, boss."

"I never worry, Louie," the Penguin said. "I pay others to do that for me."

Louie Ross heard the phone go dead, and felt his throat go tight. He had no choice. There were seven of them inside the office building, including Newton. The question was, could one man take them all down… one man without a gun?

Sadly, he knew the answer.

Hell no.

When he'd turned nineteen, Louie W. Ross was without many job prospects. He barely graduated junior high and flunked out of high school in the eleventh grade. One of the few jobs he could do back then was be a runner for the Maroni mob.

But he hadn't been very good at it. Just shy of a year later he moved over to Falcone's mob, then to the Ventriloquist's gang, which led him to the specials—the gangs whose primary objective was the extinction of Batman. He tooled between gangs, sticking with each one until they threw him out. Then four months earlier, he'd finally joined up with the Penguin. His problem was, if he failed again he knew he couldn't just join yet another gang.

The Penguin didn't respond well to failure.

Louie looked down the block and saw several cop cars parked there. The cops weren't in them—they were probably clearing the block just like they'd been doing since Scarecrow made his announcement. The street was littered with debris, including a crowbar half lost in the bushes. Louie knew he wasn't the brightest bulb working for the Penguin, but given the opportunity and the incentive of staying alive, he was fully capable of putting together two plus two.

He grabbed the crowbar, looked around to make certain he wasn't being watched, then smashed in a window on one of the police cars. Glancing around again he reached inside, unlocked the door then scrambled inside. There had to be a weapon here somewhere.

As he rooted through the back seat, he didn't see the taxi pull up beside the car. His fingers closed around a shotgun, and he pulled it free from under a blanket.

Bingo!

He stared at it—not the best weapon, he knew. He would have preferred an automatic. But this was better than nothing.

"Hey, creepo. What do you think you're doing?" The voice came from the cab.

"Who the hell are you?" he responded, not really caring. He tightened his grip on the rifle and raised it so his annoyer could see it. "Or maybe you should just get the hell out of here."

The figure in the taxi leaned to the window and Louie gasped. He knew the face… or maybe it would be better to say he knew *both* of them.

"Two-Face?" Louie could barely spit out the killer's name. Everyone knew Harvey Dent, formerly Gotham City's crusading district attorney—the once great hope of the city. But that was before acid was thrown at him by one of the mobsters he was trying to put behind bars. Half of his face was burned to the bone. Strips of flesh dangled from the few patches that were still in place. From one side he looked like the worst monster from the most disgusting movie ever filmed. From the other side—the side not hit with the acid—he still looked like whatever handsome actor they had cast in the hero's role.

"You were saying, creep?" Two-Face grinned a sickly smile.

Louie didn't know how to respond. The mob boss had a

special dollar coin he loved to flip. Both sides had a face on them, but he'd taken a knife and gouged one of the faces. Now his coin looked like him.

"Please, Mr. Two-Face... Mr. Dent... I didn't mean anything. I thought you were a cop. I was just mouthing off."

"Shhh." Two-Face put a finger to his lips. Then he held up the coin, and flipped it into the air. As of that moment, all that mattered was which side of his coin would come up once it landed. Perfect head, you were allowed to live. Scarred head, you died. All the pleading, all the prayers, they all meant nothing. Your life, your future, was left to a coin toss.

The coin flipped six times up, six times down, then landed in Two-Face's hand. He looked at it and smiled. Instinctively, Louie smiled back.

Before it could register, the former Harvey Dent squeezed the gun's trigger, and fired.

Blam!

Louie flinched, and thought he might have pissed himself. He was waiting for it to register that the bullet had gone through his brain, and that he was dead.

That moment never came.

He was still alive.

Yet there was no way Dent could have missed him, not from less than five feet away. He looked up incredulously, and Two-Face nodded past Louie, making the thug turn.

Behind the police car he saw a freshly dead cop, probably the cop in whose car Louie was sitting. He had been coming back to reclaim it.

Two-Face had saved him.

"Thank you, sir," he choked. "Thank you."

Without a reply Two-Face turned his head to show his monster side, where his flesh was ripped away from bone and he grinned a revolting smile. He wasn't looking at Louie, but at his own taxi driver.

"What are you waiting for?" Without warning the engine gunned, the car took off and rounded the corner, moving quickly out of sight.

Louie took another minute to calm his wild breathing. The coin must have come good side up. He'd been half a flip away from dying. But he was okay now. He was better than okay. He was alive.

Then he remembered the shotgun in his hand.

He still had Newton and his men to deal with. His night wasn't over. Indeed, it was just beginning.

Harvey Dent stretched out in the back seat of the taxi and grinned another of his nauseating grimaces. He knew the effect he had on others, and he enjoyed playing the game. If he liked you, he'd angle his face to show his demon side. If he didn't, you'd see how movie-star handsome he once had been.

Keep them off balance, he always said. *Never let them know which side you're coming from.* He laughed, showing his fellow passenger his monster face.

The Penguin wanted to vomit but knew that wouldn't be the best tactic when working with a new partner.

"When you squeezed that trigger, Ross probably pissed

his pants," Penguin said, and he laughed with a perverse squawk. "He's a bloody waste of flesh."

"So why do you keep him, Oswald?" Oswald Cobblepot was the name Penguin had been given at birth. There was never any question why he'd changed it.

Penguin laughed. "Everyone needs expendables."

Two-Face roared with laughter, and it again made the Penguin want to throw up.

Gordon walked across the G.C.P.D. rooftop to where the Bat-Signal was mounted. It had taken him three years and countless fights to get its installation approved, but here it was. Either he'd worn down City Hall with his endless memos, or the city's aldermen had decided to indulge him a bit, on the likelihood that Gotham City's criminals would eliminate the vigilante—and possibly Gordon, as well. Then they would hire a new police commissioner—one who was more... pliable.

Not gonna happen. Gordon hoped the signal would help usher in a new Gotham City. That it would fulfill the people's need to put a face on their heroes. Under Gordon's leadership, Gotham City would *not* be business as usual.

Gillian Loeb and Jack Grogan were Gordon's predecessors, and they'd depicted Batman as nothing more than a dangerous vigilante with an unknown agenda. The problem was, Batman worked on his own, outside the law, and often overstepped the basic rights of citizens.

Criminals, yes, but still citizens.

Gordon didn't want to admit, publicly or even to himself, that he felt there were times the law and its necessary restrictions proved ineffective. That the police could be helpless, even when hell itself was about to swallow them whole. Lots of cops privately believed that was the case—the honest ones, at least.

Dangerous situations could bring out the worst in anyone. All too often shortcuts had been taken to solve problems, "in the name of public safety," but those shortcuts just made things worse. And so rules had been put in place, to prevent such excesses. Restrictions that all too often handcuffed the police in doing their jobs.

It was a contradiction that couldn't be dodged, and it led directly to the Batman. Defending him caused Gordon no end of problems, but in a city like theirs, where law enforcement was hamstrung by judges who had been paid for long ago, the caped vigilante's litany of victories made the citizenry shout their support.

Save one or two innocent people and you'd be forgotten by the next news cycle. Save an entire city—time and again—from the most insane of madmen, and the people began to look to his appearances as the only measure of security they might ever hope to get. Knowing he existed gave them a tangible measure of comfort. Knowledge that there was at least one man out there who would fight for them, no matter the risk.

There were still politicians who demanded that the police stop Batman any way they could. Many of them were crooked, but there were honest politicos who still chastised his methods. Gordon couldn't argue with anyone who truly believed in the law above all, but in his heart he was thrilled that the people of Gotham City had a savior to call their own. And that their hero always towed the line.

God willing, he silently prayed, *he always will.*

"Jim, I've seen you look better," Batman said, walking up from behind. Gordon nearly jumped out of his skin. As always, he hadn't heard the man approaching.

Shouldn't that cape at least make a sound? he thought irritably.

"Been up thirty hours straight," Gordon said. "I think I'm pissing caffeine."

"Not an image I'll easily forget." Batman peered at him. "How is the evac going?"

"About how you'd expect. Riots break out every time a loaded bus leaves the station without the thousands of people who had to be left behind. The train tracks out of Bleake were sabotaged about an hour ago, so that cut off another avenue of escape. We've had more desertions, so I think I've got no more than eight hundred cops, give or take. That's barely enough to patrol a single neighborhood, let alone the entire city. And you?"

Batman looked past the rooftop and out over the city he'd pledged to protect. It was hard to believe Gotham City had rebuilt itself, for the most part, after the devastating earthquake that hit it several years earlier. But the city was back, and it was just starting to recover.

Then this had to happen.

"Don't know if you heard," Gordon said, "but the power grids were attacked, and they're down. Here and there we've got some lights, but it's not good."

Even from the rooftop Batman could see candles flickering in the growing dark. Scarecrow said he wanted fear. Forcing the people to live in an uncompromising night fit right into his plans.

"Truth to tell," Gordon said, "I'd hoped once the Joker was gone that the other madmen who had followed him to Gotham City would leave, too. You know, maybe move to Coast City or Central City—or better yet Metropolis. Let the alien deal with them. It didn't work out that way."

"I had that dream, too," Batman admitted. "Then I woke up."

Gordon forced a fake smile. "There is some good news, believe it or not. I'd say about seventy-five percent of our people made it out of Gotham City. That's a lot of people we won't have to worry about. The last bus should be crossing the city limits within the hour. Personally, I'm just happy that Barbara got out of the city in time. If she'd been trapped here, stuck in that wheelchair, God knows how long she'd last." He paused, then added, "It's another reason I so looked forward to pushing that red button, and sending the Joker to the hell he deserved."

Batman felt his comm vibrate. Ironically, its particular pattern indicated that a call was coming through from Barbara Gordon. Despite the commissioner's belief and desires, Barbara was still in the city, ensconced in the Clock Tower, doing her job as Oracle, monitoring the city for any—she called them—"aberrations."

He couldn't tell that to Gordon, though. Both he and Barbara thought the truth might kill him. At the very least, it would cause irreparable harm.

MARV WOLFMAN

"Everyone should be safe, Jim," he said. "That's what we're working for." Then he turned back to face the commissioner. "Why did you ask me to meet you here?"

Gordon shook his head and gave an embarrassed grin.

"Right. Sorry. Family worries have to be put on the back burner." He held up his phone and quickly entered some data. "I'm sending you a file. We're tracking an unknown military vehicle that's speeding through Chinatown—we have reason to believe it belongs to Scarecrow. It's not much but it's the only lead we've had all night. Trouble is, it gave us the slip. I don't have the manpower left to look for it. I was hoping—"

"Already on it, Jim." Batman held out his glove. A series of hologram images rose from the gauntlet. He scrolled through them until he reached the photos. "A word of caution," he said. "If your men find the tank, tell them not to engage. I'll handle it."

"You know, with all the desertions, it seems as if you're the only one I can count on. Thank you."

"You don't have to thank me for doing my job."

"A job, should I remind you, that you're not paid to do. Anyway, between the two of us, is Scarecrow truly so insane that he'd detonate a chemical weapon in Gotham City?"

"I won't let that happen, Jim." Batman reached into his cape and pulled out a small cell phone, handing it over. "In case you need to reach me. It's going to be a long night."

Gordon took the phone and looked down at it, then back up. But Batman was already gone. He shook his head and gave a tired smile.

"Every damn time."

5

As the Batmobile roared through the city, autopilot guiding its way, Batman tapped his gauntlet, activating its holo screen. Barbara Gordon's image flickered into view.

"I've been wondering when I'd hear back from you," she said. *"That chemical data arrived—I'm working on it now. So, what's the latest?"*

"Your father and I were talking. He's gotten reports that an unmarked military vehicle has been spotted in the Chinatown area. Can you set up a trace?"

"Yeah. Heard the report on the police band. Hold on while I patch you into the GPS tracker." A moment later she added, *"So tell me, how is he?"*

"Holding up."

Oracle smiled. *"Somehow he always does."*

"He's a good man, Barbara," Batman replied. "Perhaps it's time to confide in him."

"You first, Bruce," she countered. *"Seriously, after all this time, I'm not sure what his reaction would be. He still blames himself for what happened to me."*

"He had nothing to do with it. That was the Joker."

"I know. You know. But he feels that if he had been

doing his job right, the Joker would never have been given the opportunity..."

Even over the low-res holographic image, Batman could tell she was looking at her legs, tucked onto the wheelchair footrest. Unmoving and useless as they'd been for the past several years.

"You have to understand, Bruce," she continued. *"Guilt explains why he insisted on igniting the crematorium flames himself. Somehow it seemed as if burning up the Joker's body would bring him, I don't know, maybe peace."*

"I hope it did. He deserves peace of mind, more than anyone else I know."

"Hey, I agree. Which is why telling him I'm Oracle, that I keep the entire city—his city—under surveillance, that I work with you..." She shook her head. *"More than that, admitting that I used to be Batgirl—hell, it's a litany of lies. Do you really think he'll take it in stride? I think it would tear him apart even more than what the Joker did. Do you really want to deal with the backlash from that?"*

"Then maybe it would be for the best if you became what your father thinks you are," Batman said. "Give up being Oracle. Go back to being Barbara Gordon."

"The action librarian?" she said, and she shook her head again. *"Not going to happen, Bruce. Despite what he did to me, I am not going to allow my limitations to be an excuse. If we intend to save this city, we have to be prepared to fight the tyranny of madness, no matter what shape we're in."*

"I'm the last person in the world who would argue with that, but—"

"Bruce, hold that." Her holo image looked off to the side.

"*I've got the coordinates. Forwarding them to the Batmobile.*"

"Got it, Barbara. On my way."

"*Be careful.*"

"Always."

Minutes later he was in the center of Chinatown, speeding through its narrow, twisting streets. This eclectic neighborhood had been cobbled together in the late 1800s. Unlike the rest of Gotham City, its streets didn't conform to any pre-established grid, but instead seemed to turn in and around themselves like a maze, making navigation difficult in the best of times.

Chinatown's founders had well remembered the many attacks their villages suffered before they left their home country, and they were determined to make access to their new homes as difficult as possible for any enemy that targeted them.

They more than succeeded.

"*I'm picking up several blips,*" Oracle said. "*Two tanks ahead on Pel.*"

A half-dozen armed militia mercs blocked the street in front of Batman.

"Barbara, it may take a few more minutes to get there. I'm facing a phalanx of soldiers, more or less."

"*Soldiers. How nice. You giving them a parade?*"

"No. Just the fireworks." Batman tapped the car's computer screen, scrolling to his front weapons system, then tapped the red "armed" icon. With a subtle *whirr*, the weapons swiveled into position.

The Batmobile's side fenders slid back, revealing weapons array 1-A, complete with a half-dozen heat-seeking missiles. *No need for the heavy artillery,* he thought. As the array retracted back into the car, it was replaced by a non-lethal system.

"More like it."

The soldiers were armed with anti-materiel, anti-tank rifles and high-powered carbines. They were prepared to deal with anything the G.C.P.D. could throw at them, and a bit more.

But they weren't dealing with the police now.

Batman slipped his night lenses into position in his cowl as the Batmobile opened fire. The space between the vehicle and the soldiers exploded with blinding, pinwheeling light that instantly blinded them. While they flailed helplessly, the canopy opened and he sprang to the street.

He felt his anger starting to grow. It was the Joker's blood again, trying its damnedest to exert control. But it wasn't going to work this time, he thought as he fought back. He couldn't let it. Not ever again.

He landed and rammed his fist into the throat of the closest soldier, immediately knocking him to his knees, and then he drove his elbow to the back of the man's neck. He wouldn't be waking up for at least twenty minutes. Batman moved quickly to the next soldiers. They were still blinded, but the effect would be wearing off soon.

The blood was making him angry. He was lashing out in blind rage. He had to control it before it controlled him.

He took down two more without meeting resistance. Three more to go. He allowed himself a smile—he was in control of this takedown. The soldiers were fighting Batman, not the Joker's spawn.

One of the soldiers was rubbing his eyes, clearing away the haze. Before he could, Batman slammed his foot into the man's face. He whirled and quickly took down another.

Now only one remained.

The soldier was tall—he had almost two inches on Batman. He looked strong and moved efficiently. This one was a professional. Batman lunged for him but the man sidestepped and grabbed Batman by the wrist. Batman tried to pull loose but he held on. Then, with his free hand, he grabbed Batman by the neck and pushed him into the side of a building.

"Gonna choke the air right outta you, Bat. You're gonna die in a whole lot of pain."

Batman felt himself gasping for a breath that wasn't coming. If he hesitated this soldier was more than capable of killing him. Batman rammed his knee into the man's solar plexus. The soldier grunted but continued to squeeze his throat. Batman kneed him again, then forced his legs up until they were around the man's head. He pushed back, forcing the soldier to release his grip.

As the merc did so, Batman pulled his legs back and twisted, sending the soldier crashing into the wall against which he had pinned Batman. Regaining his footing, he clasped his hands together and rammed them into the soldier's gut.

His opponent collapsed.

Batman stared at the six soldiers, all downed and defeated, and allowed himself a momentary smile. He then activated his gauntlet comm and opened a channel to Wayne Enterprises CEO Lucius Fox. What he needed next would require more than surveillance.

"I've been monitoring the GPS all morning," Fox said. *"I gather you're involved in some manner of fracas. As always."*

"You might say that, Lucius," he replied as he moved back toward his vehicle. "A half-dozen armed mercs, probably working with Scarecrow."

"Probably?"

"It's difficult to interrogate a suspect when he's unconscious. Besides, I've got bigger fish to fry."

"Right. The tanks." Instantly Fox was all business. *"As I say, I've been monitoring your GPS, and the police radio, as well. It's the next best thing to participating in a ride-along."*

"Only a whole lot safer," Batman said. "Can you get someone to round up the soldiers? Check with Barbara. Her contacts may include babysitters."

"I'm assuming you mean the kind that plays with automatic weapons, not chew toys."

"You assume correctly. Have them store Scarecrow's boys in one of our holding facilities. And if they're up to it, perhaps they can ask a few questions. Maybe learn where Scarecrow has set up his base of operations."

"That can be arranged," Fox confirmed. *"Which holding facility? Old Gotham City MTA, Panessa Studios, or Crime Alley Storage?"*

"Let's go with the old MTA building. It's bigger. They can be locked up separately, in different rooms. Makes for better interrogation." He paused, then added, "As always, no excessive violence. Crane leaves behind bodies. We don't."

"Consider it done."

"Later then. And thanks, Lucius."

Batman climbed into the Batmobile and checked his radar. He saw two flashing red dots indicating locations only a couple of blocks away, as Barbara had warned him. He tapped his gauntlet and reconnected with her.

"The old soldiers' home has gotten more crowded," he said. "Anything new on your side?"

"You might say that," Barbara replied, and she laughed. *"In the darkness that is forever Gotham City, I'm about to give you one splendid moment of light. The lead tank is an unmanned drone. The second tank has a pilot. It's still a block away but it's moving in."*

"I can bring out the big boys then."

"Only for the lead."

He tapped the Batmobile's touch screen and switched out the non-lethal array, replacing them with his heat-seekers. No life on board meant he could go full throttle. He paused for another second, checked the radar for the lead tank's heat signature to be certain it was unmanned.

Can't be too careful, he mused. *In and out as fast as possible.*

In order to focus his attention on the manned tank—the more difficult challenge at hand—he needed to quickly get rid of the drone. Trying to keep opponents alive was always harder than simply serving them their just deserts. But Batman had been born in a crucible of killing. Murder was not something he would ever pay forward.

He rounded the corner, gunning his car to alert the drone's sensors to his approach. In case anything went wrong, he wanted the tank to fire in his direction, not into Chinatown's center. Sure enough, its turret swiveled into position, and Batman released his first missile.

Three seconds later, the drone exploded.

Immediately, the second tank rumbled toward him. He scrolled through his touch screen and bypassed all lethal weapons. He found twin M87 conversions which were designed to shred armor. It was accurate for nearly 1.5 kilo-meters, and if he took care in aiming it, he could blow out the tank's treads without severely damaging its turret. The driver would be shaken, perhaps even wounded, but he'd also be alive. And any disorientation would be to Batman's benefit.

He gunned the Batmobile and shot past the tank, circling around behind, forcing it to readjust. As he circled, however, the tank fired, aiming ahead of him. Batman slammed on the brakes and spun the car away.

The missile missed by inches.

He pushed the car into reverse, backing away from the tank while continuing to face it. The tank accelerated and followed. Just as he'd hoped.

A block behind him was a wall, coming up fast. Batman hit the brakes and stopped dead in his tracks before slamming into it. If he wanted to accurately calculate his attack angles, he needed to be motionless. Any movement could affect his weapon's trajectory. With a life at stake, he had to be careful.

That made him a very tempting target.

The tank closed in, its turret swiveling into position, the 75mm gun lining up to point directly at Batman. If the driver fired first, the Batmobile would be little more than twisted, melted steel.

Batman waited.

One more second.

He locked the trajectory and fired two missiles. The first hit the tank's front drive sprockets, and the second shattered its treads. The impact almost sent the tank hurtling to land upside down, but it righted itself, shuddered, and stopped. It wasn't going to move again soon. So Batman fired a third missile and that took out the tank's 75mm guns. By the time he was done, this beast that could have demolished a good portion of the city was little more than an oversized doorstop.

"Batman, I was able to clone his command codes." Barbara's voice came over his gauntlet comm. *"Unlocking the hatch now. The driver must be pretty badly shaken. Be nice to him."*

"No problem," he answered. "You know what a people person I am."

"Yeah, that's what everyone says about you."

He sprinted to the tank and found, as Barbara had said, that the hatch was open. The driver was inside, trapped in a twisted tangle of damaged electronics. Batman's aim had been off by less than a degree, but the driver would still be able to walk, eventually, and most likely with a limp.

"Focus through the pain," he said. "It's for your own good."

The driver nodded vigorously. "My leg... I... I think it's dead. I think they're going to have to amputate or something." He looked up, his eyes wide. "You gotta help me. Please help me."

"Your leg doesn't have to be amputated," Batman said.

"At least not if we can get you to a hospital—sooner, rather than later. Preferably one out of the city. When Scarecrow's deadline runs out in six hours, the last place you'll want to be is in Gotham City."

That's it… give him some incentive. He watched the man try to fight through his agony, but he was failing. Another moment or two and he'd admit to starting World War Two if it meant stopping the pain.

"Now, I can say goodbye and leave you here," Batman continued, "but I doubt you'll be able to worm your way free—and even if you do, with your leg the way it is, I don't think you'll make it off this street in time. But if you give me one piece of information, I can arrange to have you transported out of here by helicopter before Scarecrow's fear gas is released.

"Talk to me or you're on your own."

"Whatever you want," the man said, paling as shock set in. "I'll tell you anything. Just *help me.*"

"Good. Tell me where Scarecrow is hiding, and you'll make it out of this with all your original parts—banged up, but intact."

Batman climbed back into the Batmobile and opened his comm channel to Barbara.

"Scarecrow's got a penthouse on the other side of Chinatown," he said. "It's at 357 Lee Street. Can you pull up its schematics?"

"Silly question. Already done. Uploading now."

6

Scarecrow chose his home well—a modern five-story high rise with an open-air rooftop Chinese garden. Armed mercenaries continuously circled the building, positioned to make certain any approach would be protected by at least two of them at any given time. Oracle uploaded her sensor readouts to Batman's gauntlet comm, revealing additional heat signatures on all three stairwells leading to the penthouse floor. Two mercs manned the elevators while two others perched on the roof. Scarecrow didn't want any surprise company.

His bad luck.

From a rooftop two blocks away, Batman tracked the mercs circling the perimeter, marking the time it took for them to cross the ground level before the next set of soldiers appeared. The timing was impressively precise—there was only a nine-second gap between the moment when the first set of soldiers turned a corner and the next set appeared.

Nine seconds.

The timing sucked, but it would have to be enough.

He silently moved into position across the street. One set of mercs disappeared, and another took their place. This time it only took seven seconds. Timing was getting worse.

He waited and saw the next set of soldiers amiably chatting to each other as they walked, moving slightly slower, increasing the gap to ten seconds. Batman smiled— he'd wait for them to come around again, and when they rotated back, he would make his move.

Two groups of mercs passed in front of him. He silently began his countdown.

The next duo that appeared around the corner would be in front of the chatty guards—that would buy him valuable seconds. He sprang out of hiding and soared across the street.

Nine… eight…

He unfolded two Batarangs stored in his belt pouch and carefully aimed them.

Seven… Kick… left jab… the mercs went down.

Six…

He had five seconds to hide them before the next set of soldiers rounded the corner. Large concrete plant stands circled the skyscraper. Most would have thought them to be a decoration, but they were, in fact, utilitarian. They were spaced close enough together to prevent cars or trucks from smashing their way into the building, assuming any of Scarecrow's rivals had the nerve to even think about starting a war with him.

He dragged the two unconscious mercs beyond the stands, out of sight of the next set.

Three… two… and one.

The guards appeared as if on cue. Batman hunkered behind one of the stands and waited for the three sets of soldiers to complete their rounds. When the final duo turned the corner, he stepped into the open, fired a grapple to the rooftop, and was snapped upward a full second before the next set of mercs appeared.

He reached the roof and fired yet another line, this time snagging the legs of the two mercs stationed there. Before they could register surprise, he pulled the line and knocked them off their feet. They tried to stand up and fight, but he was on them. A moment later and both were blissfully unconscious. Moving to the door that led into the building, he quickly disabled the lock.

Batman tapped his gauntlet comm and Oracle appeared.

"I'm in. But I don't have much time," he said. "I need the lay of the land."

"Not a problem," she replied. *"I tapped into the building's digital phone system and am using it like a series of microphones. Oh, and I located Scarecrow. He's definitely in the penthouse. You can't miss that voice. I'll patch you in."*

There was no reply. Batman was already on the move. He started down the stairs as he listened to Scarecrow, somewhere in the penthouse below him.

"Listen to me carefully then answer my questions. Failure to do so will only end with your loved ones screaming as they painfully, agonizingly, die. Do you understand me? Speak to me. Do you?"

"Batman," Barbara Gordon's voice interrupted, coming through the inside of his cowl now, *"who the hell is he talking to?"*

"I'll worry about that later. I've got company just ahead."

He reached the penthouse landing, and his heat scanners revealed a half-dozen armed mercs making their way up the stairs from the floor below. Someone must have found the goons he'd taken down outside. Fortunately, the stairwell was narrow. It would be difficult for the men to open fire without getting in one another's way. Difficult, but not impossible, and Batman never relied on luck.

They were on the floor below him and once they reached the landing they would see him. At best he had a three-second advantage, and he had to make the most of it. He counted down again and jumped even as the first of the armed soldiers appeared. His weight and momentum forced the lead merc to fall back into the others, tumbling them like bowling pins, knocking the wind out of them. His advantage, but it would be fleeting.

Instantly, they were scrambling to their feet.

He wasn't dealing with amateurs.

"Why are you, in all of Gotham City, immune to my fear toxins?" Scarecrow's voice continued to drone inside of his cowl, still complaining to his unknown companion. *"What is your secret? Tell me now."*

Batman drove his fist into the closest merc's face, shattering his nose. The man yelped with pain as his blood splattered in all directions, looking far worse than the damage actually caused. Perfect. His first strike was designed to elicit a moment of terror that would give the others pause, if only for a moment. And with the numbers against him, he needed every advantage he could take.

"Do you want me to dissect you? Do you want me to make your death, and the deaths of your loved ones, painful? You know you can relieve them of their agony. Tell me how you resist my power. Tell me now!"

Who the hell is he talking to? Batman grabbed the

stairwell handrail and used it for leverage. He spun and smashed his foot into another merc. The man fell back, tumbling down the stairs, crashing into the landing below.

He didn't get up.

Through his comm Batman heard another voice. A woman's, and instantly he knew.

"My plants are eternal, Scarecrow. Nature has been with us from the very beginning, and will outlast us all. There is no poison made by man that she cannot resist, and then provide to me, her very own beloved daughter."

Poison Ivy. Scarecrow was trying to intimidate Poison Ivy.

Fat chance.

As Pamela Isley, she was one of the world's foremost environmental terrorists, targeting anyone who caused eco-damage to the planet. It was never certain if Ivy was insane, though, or operating on a different level than everyone else. But Scarecrow didn't have a chance in hell of scaring someone who believed herself to be the living incarnation of Mother Nature.

Batman drove his elbow into the gut of another merc, but the man refused to fall. As Batman grabbed the merc's arm and prepared to elbow him again, two more thugs ran up the stairs toward them, pistols in hand. They opened fire, not caring if they killed their own man as long as they offed the Batman, as well.

He reacted instinctively, twisting the merc aside to narrowly avoid the bullets and tossed him back, away from harm. Then, in a single, fluid move, Batman somersaulted down the stairwell, slamming into them both.

The fight is taking too long, he realized. Every delay

meant more of Scarecrow's men would join in.

"*Unless you tell me what I want, I will see your forest burned to the ground. Your plants will cry out in agony. I will make certain you watch all of them die. Or tell me what I want to know and I will make their deaths swift and painless.*"

"*Then there's nothing left to talk about,*" Ivy replied, and her voice rose. "*You have declared war on planet Earth. May she have pity on whatever has replaced your soul.*"

Batman slammed past the final merc and pushed open the door to the penthouse floor. There was another soldier inside. The guard stared, realizing that somehow Batman had made it past the others. Then he opened fire.

Batman dove to the floor and spun, his legs slammed into the man, toppling him. He dropped his gun as he fell, then scrambled to retrieve it, but Batman was already there. He kicked the gun aside, then turned to the merc, now both weaponless and powerless. The thug held up his hands to surrender.

"First smart thing you've done today," Batman said as he drove a fist into the man's face. The merc crumbled unconscious to the floor. "Unfortunately for you, you still have a lot to answer for."

There was only one apartment on the penthouse floor. Batman sprayed the lock with explosive gel, then detonated it, causing it to erupt with a muffled impact.

"Oracle, I'm inside," he said. "What are you seeing?"

"*Picking up two heat signatures… no. Make that one. The second one has left the apartment.*"

"He didn't come this way. There must be a back door."

"*There is. It's a hidden stairwell. According to the building's* blueprints it connects to a panic room behind the bedroom."

"Panic room? Okay, this may add another wrinkle. Can you find out if the apartment belongs to Scarecrow, or someone else. If it's Crane, there's no telling how many hidden traps he's built in."

"*Checking now, but it could take a few minutes to hack into the city housing plans. By the way, according to the news, my father and his men rounded up Victor Zsasz and Hugo Strange. They were attempting to blow up Gotham Central Station. They failed.*"

"Good for your dad. We need every victory we can get. And speaking of your father…"

"*Not again, Bruce. This city needs me. Hell, you need me.*"

"Barbara, I agree. Oracle is indispensible—but you can be my eyes and ears from anywhere. All Oracle needs is her computers and a Wi-Fi connection."

"*I'm staying, Bruce,*" Barbara said. "*Please don't insult me by asking again.*"

"I won't. But if we can't stop Scarecrow, and if he unleashes his toxins, this city is done for. If the worst happens…"

"*Bruce, we'll just have to make sure it won't. And we'll do that together.*"

"Are you prepared for your father's wrath when he finds out?"

"*I think I'd rather face Scarecrow than him. But yeah, if he finds out.*"

"You won't have to do it alone. I'll have your back."

"*Never doubted that,*" she replied. "*Ahhh. Okay. Just hacked into the city files, so now it's a matter of systematically going through them. I'll get back to you as soon as I root out the intel. Be safe. Oracle out."*

Batman entered the penthouse suite. A long wood-paneled foyer led to the living room, which was spacious and beautifully appointed with antiques that were old when the Victorian age was still young. Intricately carved wooden tables depicting foxes and hounds made Batman think of an eighteenth-century English hunt scene.

The tables flanked a large, plush couch with curved armrests and lion's-claw feet. Whoever lived here obviously enjoyed hunting. Scarecrow had never shown any inclination as an antiques connoisseur, but anything was possible.

The expansive chamber held four more couches, each set up with facing chairs, creating a series of small sitting areas ideal for simultaneous conversations. Stunning stained-glass lamps—the real thing, rather than knock-offs—sat on each table. Wayne Manor was equally beautifully decorated with irreplaceable antiques, but they had been bought by Bruce Wayne's mother and hadn't been changed or added to since their murders. He always had more on his mind than house decoration.

"Batman." Barbara Gordon's voice pulled him from his thoughts. *"The apartment is owned by Dr. Frank Adams and his wife Tatjana. They left for a month-long vacation less than a week ago."*

"Good. That means Scarecrow is a very recent addition. He probably hasn't had time to set up many traps."

"Or he thought he'd only be using the place for a short while, and didn't take the time."

"Either way it makes my job a bit easier. Thanks."

He made it through the living room and found himself

facing another long corridor with rooms branching off it on both sides. The heat signature came from a room at the end of the corridor, so he didn't bother looking into any of the others. He was there for a reason, and it wasn't a tour.

The door was locked—it was the only one that wasn't already wide open. He could blow it off its hinges but decided not to cause any unnecessary damage. Instead he removed a pick from a pouch pocket, inserted it in the keyhole, and jiggled it until he heard the lock click into place.

The door opened and he stopped in surprise. He'd expected more antiques, but the room was devoid of furniture—it was empty, except for a half-dozen large steel-bar cages, six feet tall by four feet wide. They were one-person prison cells, and the bars were thick enough to hold in an elephant.

It was overkill.

Only one cell held a prisoner.

Poison Ivy.

7

Ivy was draped with a vine that disappeared out a shattered window on the far side of the room. She was petting the plant, humming to it, and it seemed to vibrate with every stroke. The scene was so intimate that he hesitated, but then moved quickly to the cage lock. She gave no indication that she noticed him until he swung the door open.

"I could have escaped without your help, you know," she said, still petting the throbbing vine. "Nature won't be contained when she doesn't want to be. By the way, what are you doing here?"

"Why did Scarecrow lock you up?"

"What? No hello?" She frowned in mock indignation. "You're getting rude in your old age."

"Ivy, I asked you a question," he replied. "Please answer it."

"And what if I don't want to?" she said, smiling seductively.

He stared at the vine sensually twisting around her arm and waist. "Do not make me repeat myself," he said, anger edging into his voice. Batman didn't know if plants understood human language, but it looked to him as if the vine suddenly shrank. It pulled away from its host, and disappeared back outside the window.

Ivy's smile turned to an expression of anger.

"You *are* rude." She exited her prison and walked to the room's balcony, stepping outside into the night, where she breathed deeply of the cool air. "Ask any plant and they'll tell you that it's so much better to be outside than cooped up in a human's apartment." She leaned over the edge, and he followed her gaze. They watched her vine retract back to ground level, then she turned to Batman, once again smiling.

"You see? You scared her away. You know you're no better than him. He threatened my children, too." From atop the balcony railing, Ivy picked up a small potted plant that looked as if it hadn't been watered in the week the home owners had been away. It was limp and pale. She tenderly gave it a playful kiss and it reacted, growing from a sagging stub, circling her arm and briefly grazing her lips, returning her kiss.

"Ivy..." She nodded, and they headed back into the cell room, then out to the hall.

"All right," Ivy said. "You're a tough man, but you've never been a mean one." She stopped and looked up at him. "You want to know about Scarecrow? Well, it started with a meeting."

"What meeting?"

"Don't be so impatient. Stories, like plants, need to grow and can't be rushed. Take it easy and smell the roses. You'd be surprised how much you can learn from them."

"Ivy, time is running out. If Scarecrow wins, Gotham City will die, your plants will die, and I won't be able to save them."

He could see her face contort, as if she was trying to understand his words. Finally, she gave him another smile.

"Yes, of course. Now, he *is* a mean man, and I believe he'd slaughter all life if given the chance—plant, animal, and human. Anyway, the meeting. Everyone was there. Penguin, Two-Face, Riddler. Even poor Harley. That dear dimwit actually believed she had a chance at a life with her... Puddin', but then of course, *whoosh*. He gets himself toasted, roasted, and finally mulched. She was bereft of her usual élan."

"Ivy. The meeting."

"Right. Of course. The meeting. Scarecrow said he had a plan. That together we could take you out, and Gotham City would be ours."

"Over my dead body."

"I believe that was the idea." Her smile turned sly. "The old notions are still the best, you know."

The small potted plant was still growing. Thorns emerged from its stems. The once-tiny flower was no longer cute. It looked as if one wrong word would send it on the attack.

"Anyway, I told him I wasn't interested in his pathetic human games. I mean, how could destroying a city—even one as life-stifling as Gotham City—help my plants?"

"And his response?"

"Well, if he had one, I never heard it. All I remember after that moment is blackness, then waking up in that room, in that cell. He came and babbled some insanity at me, then heard something—probably you—and fled. I sat there trying to formulate a plan when you interrupted." Her look was coy. "You know the timing between the two of us has never been good."

"That's everything?" he demanded brusquely.

Ivy looked like she was trying to give him an answer as she walked from the room, still carrying the potted plant. She made her way to the elevator, humming again along the way, pausing before each dying plant in the apartment, taking a moment to revive it.

"Ivy," he said, "I asked if that was everything."

The elevator door beeped, and a moment later its door slid open.

"Pretty much. I told him it was a shame for him that his vile toxin had no effect on me. I seem to remember that he didn't laugh very much at all. Hmmm. Do you think that's why he did what he did to me?"

She paused, pinched a small piece from the plant, then set the pot on the floor. She stepped inside the elevator and pressed a button. He moved to follow as the elevator door began to slide shut again. Ivy smiled and blew him a kiss.

The potted plant's stem grew longer, erupting upward and circling Batman, squeezing his chest, pressing in harder and harder until he could no longer breathe.

"Nature always wins."

He was gasping for air as the plant yanked him back, out of the elevator.

And then the doors closed.

"Will he ever learn?" Ivy looked at the cutting in her hand. She stroked it, and it quivered with life. Muzak played as the small car descended to the lobby. Plants loved this music, and so did she. Its quiet rhythms seemed to put her at ease, and with the myriad stresses in her life, she welcomed whatever calm could be found.

The car jerked to a stop as it reached the first floor. She waited for the doors to slide open again. Next stop for her was the botanical gardens. Those gardens truly scared Scarecrow; so where better to go to produce even more of her toxin repellant?

The door opened, and Ivy gasped. Batman stood directly outside, dead plant growth strewn across the ground, lifeless brown vines dripping off him.

"My children!" she shrieked. "You killed my children!"

"No," he said, and the word was like a slap. "You did, by pitting them against me." He grabbed her by the arm and pulled her out of the elevator, then slapped handcuffs around her wrists. "You're coming with me."

She smiled and gave him a fake pout.

"You only had to ask."

Scarecrow wasn't happy.

As the prominent psychologist Dr. Jonathan Crane, his job had been to help people rid themselves of their deepest fears. He reasoned that fear kept people from becoming their best, and by minimizing those dark terrors, an individual could achieve peace.

Crane spent years researching fears—why people had them, how they manifested and grew stronger, and finally, when he learned everything he believed he needed to, he began to experiment on how to eliminate them.

Over time he came to believe that to fight fear one needed

to create and instill a substitute fear. Firemen fought fires by building a firewall to prevent the bigger blaze from moving forward. Doctors fought many diseases by injecting their patients with small doses in order to build the antibodies necessary to resist the main infection. He believed if one substituted a lesser, more governable fear, it could replace the overpowering dreads that paralyzed his patients.

And it worked.

He replaced nyctophobia—the fear of the night and darkness, a phobia that crippled so many of his patients every day when the sun went down—with hydrophobophobia, the very rational fear of contracting rabies. He replaced arachnophobia, the fear of spiders, with syphilophobia, the avoidable fear of contracting syphilis.

There were thousands of such fears that could be substituted with thousands of others far easier to treat, and less likely to arise for a person living a reasonably normal life. One could, he realized, avoid almost all situations that generated taurophobia, the fear of bulls, much easier than selenophobia, the fear of the moon.

But with each success, Crane began to relish the godlike ability to enter a patient's mind and to take it over, rebuilding their response mechanisms from the ground up, changing the very way they reacted to the world around them. He enjoyed watching his patients respond to a new series of phobias, and he began to believe that people *deserved* the fears they sought to eliminate. If they were good people, after all, there'd be no reason to fear anything.

Only those with something to hide should ever be afraid. *Send the fear out there,* he thought. *Infect the masses. See what happens to them.* Those who were good would resist his infection. Those who deserved punishment would become victims of their own darkness. What he was doing was right and just.

And well deserved.

Nearly everyone succumbed to the basest fears, which meant he was achieving what providence had meant for him. He was culling the weak. Within a generation only the strong, the pure, his believers, would live.

And that, he decided, was good.

But there were those who disagreed with his mandate and fought him. Most of them he dealt with easily, but not Batman. The Dark Knight always managed to resist.

Scarecrow was on the offensive now. He was going to cleanse Gotham City, and to do that he needed to see his greatest enemy die.

"Batman must be mine," he ordered the criminals. "Defeat him and bring him to me. My champion will be rewarded."

Now he needed to recapture Poison Ivy. She possessed the antidote that rendered his toxin ineffective. He would not allow her to synthesize it—and let the weak resist his warriors. "As for the woman, bring her to me alive, and you will be wealthy beyond your greatest dreams."

8

Batman and Ivy had made it to West Broadway when one of Scarecrow's tanks appeared behind a row of parked cars. With a squeal of metal on metal it reared up, crushing the vehicles beneath its massive treads.

Ivy tried to pull back, away from Batman, as the tank smashed car after car into twisted steel, but he firmly held onto her.

"Did you come here to rescue me or get me killed?"

"Neither," Batman said as another tank rolled into sight. More appeared from other directions, six in all. All of their escape routes were blocked. Then he heard the whoosh of helicopter blades, and saw a police copter hovering above them—he recognized it as a WayneTech-467, designed by Lucius Fox for reconnaissance, not combat.

There were no weapons on board.

Lt. Adrienne Broome, with seven years on the G.C.P.D., was the chopper pilot. She'd flown in the last Middle East war, then retired from the military when the troops were brought home. But Adrienne lived for the adrenaline and after floundering a few years with jobs that didn't come close to being fulfilling, she applied to the Gotham City Police Air Division and was quickly accepted.

The job required constant concentration, and where most found it daunting, she thrived in it.

Below, she saw Batman, headed for the Batmobile, which was parked about a block away. He was pulling a redheaded woman dressed in a tight uniform of some sort. It might have been a trick of the light, but her skin appeared to be... green. The tanks following them were moving closer. Maintaining her calm, she reached for the comm.

"Lt. Adrienne Broome," she said. "Commissioner, I've got six heavily armored tanks on the ground in Chinatown. They're targeting the Bat and a woman I don't recognize."

Gordon responded, and it sounded as if he wasn't fully comprehending what she was saying.

"Did you say tanks?"

"Yeah. Batman and the woman are surrounded. They need backup, with offensive weapons. Armor-piercing weapons. Please advise."

"Sir." Alfred Pennyworth's voice suddenly came in over Batman's comm. *"I thought you should know I'm detecting no heat signatures. I believe those tanks are unmanned, and being controlled remotely."*

Batman let himself smile. "Then I'm clear to engage?"

"Indeed you are, sir."

Batman tapped his glove's control panel, then turned to Ivy.

"Hold on tight, and do what I do."

Broome waited for Gordon to answer, but the comm remained silent. After a long pause, she hit the button again. Its light blinked green—she was still connected to G.C.P.D. HQ.

"Sir, I asked for advice. What do I do, sir?"

After what seemed to be forever but was probably only a few seconds, Gordon responded, his voice soft and his words slow and measured.

"We have to help him. We can't let him die."

"Umm, things seem to have changed, sir. I'm not sure he needs help."

"What do you mean, Lieutenant?"

She stared at the Batmobile, moving toward the tanks even as its parts seemed to shift and change.

"It's his car, sir. It doesn't seem to have a driver inside, but it's heading toward him, and, sir, it's, ummm, transforming."

"Transforming? What the hell are you talking about?"

"I'm not sure I can explain it, sir, but it looks as if it's becoming a tank. And I think the Batman is controlling it." She watched in silence as the vehicle's fenders tucked in under it. Metal sheathing unfolded and slipped over its chassis, covering it, as steel plates lowered to protect its tires.

Damn, we sure could have used that in the war.

While she watched, Batman positioned himself in front of the woman, shielding her as he did something to his gauntlet—it had to be a digital control of some sort. The

7 1

car responded instantly, spinning in place until it faced the closest tank even as its wheels pulled out and revolved.

Sixty-millimeter kinetic-energy penetrator cannons rose from behind the front cabin. To its rear an armor-piercing incendiary Vulcan gun unfolded. Surface-to-air anti-tank missiles were primed to fire a barrage that could simultaneously target and take down up to six hostiles at once. Finally, riot supressor guns flipped into position, ready to fire non-lethal slam rounds at any human attacker.

The Batmobile was now in battle mode and ready to take on all attackers.

Twin missiles exploded from the Vulcan guns and slammed into the militia tank. Batman pushed Ivy to the ground and shielded her with his body. Seconds later the tank exploded and shrapnel flew in all directions. His uniform kept them from being burned as heated scraps pelted down on them.

Keying further instructions into his gauntlet, he spun the Batmobile again and aimed its next two missiles at another tank. As this second tank exploded, he pulled her to him.

"This would be a good time to leave," he said.

She smiled seductively and lifted her hands, which were still handcuffed together.

"The master of understatement, as ever," she said, laughing. "You lead, I'll follow."

They ducked into an alleyway and Batman stopped. He checked his gauntlet display again.

"There are four more tanks to deal with, and it appears

I've only got one more set of missiles. We're going to have to do this fast."

He fired his final missiles, and the third tank answered with a loud, explosive roar. His fingers quickly danced across the touchpad and the Batmobile spun again, but this time it lurched ahead, speeding around the exploded debris and pulled to a rolling stop in front of them.

"Ivy, now! Inside."

The hatch slid open. Batman lifted Ivy and placed her inside. Her seat belt automatically buckled her in, restraining her. For good measure he removed the cuff from his hand and attached it to a steel bar in the car's inner compartment. Ivy wasn't going anywhere. She leaned back and with her free hand slid her finger along the Batmobile's padded walls.

"Wonderful toy you've got here," she said. "What will it turn into next?"

Batman positioned himself behind the wheel, gunned the engine, and the car shot forward, zigzagging to avoid the missiles that arced toward them. Even though she was strapped in, Ivy gripped the seat in front of her for added protection. She squeezed shut her eyes as the Batmobile careened around a corner. Once she felt the car slow down she reluctantly opened them again.

"Who taught you how to drive?"

"Did I forget to tell you to hold on tight?" Batman said. He spun around the next corner and hit the gas, increasing speed, then making another sharp right, and then another, coming in behind Scarecrow's final three tanks. "This is going to get loud," he said.

She stuck her index fingers into her ears and leaned back, closing her eyes yet again. The handcuffs forced her to lean to the left at an awkward angle.

"Do your worst."

The Batmobile stored nearly nine hundred rounds of promethium-coated bullets which, aimed properly, could do significant damage—even against a tank. And all he needed was to slow these juggernauts down long enough for an escape. Anything more would be gravy.

As the tanks began rotating their turrets the 180 degrees they needed to face him, he targeted their optic sensors, external mantlets, and periscopes, then set his guns for automatic fire. The Batmobile's absorption baffles prevented Batman and Ivy from being permanently deafened by the roar. Within seconds the tanks were effectively blind.

He slammed his foot on the gas and shot forward. His gauntlet comm vibrated and a moment later the police commissioner's face appeared on its holo screen.

"I don't know what you did to shake the hornet's nest, Batman," Gordon said, *"but we need more of it. We've spotted a transport deploying more tanks around Panessa Studios."*

Panessa Studios? Batman thought with a frown. *Coincidence, or does Scarecrow know?* But he just nodded to Gordon. "Not to worry. I'll deal with them, Jim."

Gordon responded with an exasperated smile. *"It's been non-stop all day, and I keep thinking everything's getting worse instead of better. It's hard to keep going. How do you do it?"*

"By keeping my eyes on the goal," Batman replied.

"We want Gotham City safe from fear, and if Scarecrow is anything, it's fear. We have to take him down. Everything else is extraneous."

Gordon nodded. *"You know, I never questioned going on the offensive against the Joker. I mean, he was insane, deadly and, God, every bad thing I can put on the list, and then probably more. But even if his tactics were unpredictable, they were still the strategies of a human being. I can't even begin to understand what Scarecrow is about."*

"Scarecrow is human, too, Jim. And we'll stop him the same way we stopped the Joker."

"I know he's human. But his weapons aren't bullets and subterfuge—they're chemical and toxic. Shields can stop bullets. A well-laid-out plan can skirt almost any deception, but how do you stop airborne poisons? It scares the piss out of me."

"I may have the solution here with me," Batman said, turning briefly to Poison Ivy. She was humming that same song again. "And I'm bringing her to you now."

Gotham City lockup was filled beyond capacity. Gordon was used to that. Whenever the police force showed any sign of weakness or discord, the city's worst tended to make an appearance. They may have been cowards, but a lot of them were smart enough to smell opportunity.

Batman held onto Ivy's handcuffed wrist and pulled her inside a large room filled with cops and the few civilian personnel who had decided to stay in the city to help. Working as hard as any of the police, these people were why he continued his mission to save the city. They were Gotham City's hope and future.

Gordon was on the phone, screaming at whoever was on the other end.

"Civil unrest? No kidding! Look, there's a war on the streets, and we don't have the manpower or the equipment to stop everyone everywhere," He paused for a moment to listen. "Vale, you're a damned good reporter, and I know you've got a job to do but so do I. Still, if you want a quote, fine, here's one. 'Against overwhelming odds, the Gotham City Police are doing the best goddam job we can. If people want to help, they should get the hell out of the city before the bad guys close it down, and they're trapped here.' That good enough for you?

"And, Vale, why the hell are *you* still in town?" He slammed down the phone and growled. "Do they really think I'm just sitting around clipping my toenails?" He glanced up and saw Batman walking into the office, pulling Ivy along with him. "Well, well, look who the bat dragged in," he snorted. "One less crazy for us to worry about."

"Is the isolation chamber ready?" Batman asked.

"WayneTech's finest."

Ivy shook her head. "Oh, good. Another cell. I'm sure you'll all feel much safer once dangerous me's been locked away."

Batman returned to the Batmobile and pulled away.

With a little more than five hours to go before Scarecrow followed through on his threat, the city was overwhelmed.

Those who had been unable to leave Gotham City, or hadn't made the attempt, were out in the streets, running wild and directionless. There wasn't a window on Broadway that hadn't been shattered, a store that hadn't been looted, or car that hadn't been overturned then set afire.

The few police who remained were trying to maintain peace, but they only numbered in the hundreds. For every success there were dozens of failures.

Fewer than a thousand firemen patrolled the streets, too, outfitted and wearing their oxygen masks on the chance Scarecrow unleashed his toxins earlier than promised. They managed to extinguish the small fires that could be found on nearly every block, but had to leave the major blazes to burn themselves out. As with the police, there were too few of them to have any real effect.

Thomas and Martha Wayne had loved this city, and used their immeasurable wealth to help make it as great as it once had been. Believing in the fundamental good of mankind, they tried to rescue the city from the hell that was doing everything in its power to claim it. But in return for their charity, they were unceremoniously gunned down by a nobody with a gun.

Their son, Bruce Wayne, couldn't embrace their larger, grander vision. He, too, cared deeply for the city, but he had a different approach. He wanted to eliminate all those other nobodies who carried guns. Long ago, as he stood in that alleyway, in a pool of his parents' blood, he promised himself he would do everything in his power to prevent any other child from suffering as he had.

The mother and father had tried to attain an unattainable perfection. The son only hoped he could help keep the innocent alive.

As Batman sped through the madness, Gotham City was a city that was teetering on the brink—as it had been for more years than he could count. And as he hurried past the shouting crowds of frightened citizens, he feared Scarecrow had finally pushed it over the edge.

He tapped his comm and Oracle's face appeared.

"Any progress with the fear toxin analysis?"

"I wish," Barbara replied. *"It's going to take a little longer than expected. Come by the Clock Tower when you get a chance. I could use some fresh eyes on this."*

"Okay. I'll see you soon. But I can't promise fresh eyes. It's been a long night." Cutting the connection, he took a long, deep breath and hit the gas pedal.

He'd sleep when he was dead.

9

When a cataclysmic earthquake had leveled much of Gotham City, the Clock Tower downtown was one of very few buildings to survive intact.

Its lower floors boasted stunning oversized suites only Gotham City's elite could afford, while its much-desired penthouse, accessed only by private elevator, housed a luxurious living space, and much more. Hidden behind secret sliding panels lay Oracle's headquarters—a multi-room citadel from which Barbara Gordon kept a watchful eye on the city, reporting to Batman all the varied problems that required his attention.

When Barbara chose the Clock Tower for her high-tech base of operations, Bruce Wayne's construction company retrofitted the building to withstand far more than the publicly registered plans recorded, including the most damaging of natural disasters. It had proved to be a fortunate decision for her, as well as the tower's other tenants.

After the quake, Wayne's company used their success with the Clock Tower to bid for multiple city contracts to retrofit the rest of Gotham City's skyscrapers. If all went well, more than seventy-eight per cent of the city's towers would be refitted by the end of the decade. Thus far they were ahead of schedule, and under budget.

But no one could have predicted the current catastrophe.

Batman entered Oracle's computer room, a vast digital complex equipped with technology that exceeded the state of the art. Barbara wasn't anywhere to be seen, so he stepped up to the multi-screen holographic display and began to key in data. The faster he got the answers he needed, the better off everyone would be.

"Excuse me." Barbara's voice came from behind him. He turned to see her rolling her wheelchair into the room. "Do I come into the Batcave and start messing with your stuff?"

"Your DNA hasn't been processed for clearance," he replied. "You wouldn't get past the exterior cave without finding yourself hopelessly trapped behind bars." Then he stepped out of the way as Barbara rolled up to the main terminal and shut down the program load. The computer went blank, then rebooted to a different program.

"First, thanks for the vote of confidence," she said brusquely. "Second, what you initiated was the wrong program. I was trying to re-spark Gotham City's power grid and let in the light. You would have made sure that wouldn't have happened for at least another forty-eight hours. Your bad.

"And third, why isn't my DNA in your system?"

"I've been busy," he said as new data appeared in thin air, then scrolled down, finally coming to rest with chemical symbols categorized under the heading "Fear Venom."

"So have I," Barbara said. The chemical symbols were

quickly replaced with bar graphs.

"I can see that," Batman said. "It looks like you've managed to reduce the compound to its core elements."

Oracle nodded, but didn't look confident. "Trouble is, there's nothing in there we can trace."

"Not in this form," he agreed, "but what if we're looking at this the wrong way?"

"Meaning?"

"You're searching for the toxin. What if we focus on the manufacturing process?"

Barbara's eyes lit up. "That could work... It really could. You know, if I create a simulation mixing the core chemicals I've already isolated, we might be able to get a taggable answer." She shot him a sideways glance. "Not bad thinking for a detective." Barbara grinned as she quickly entered more data.

New images filled the air as the chemicals combined virtually, causing an onscreen chain reaction, visibly creating yet a third chemical in the process.

"There it is," she said. "Why didn't I think of it? You see that?" She pointed to a bar graph that suddenly yielded a peak. "The reaction emitted a unique radiation spike. Very, very good, Bruce. You ever think of starting a new career in science?"

"I'll leave that to the experts," he replied. "Is there any way to track it?"

Barbara stared at the spike and nodded. "I can run a scan of the city, targeting this particular signature. If it exists, it should show where Scarecrow is creating his fear toxin. But before I can do that, I'll need a few hours to bring the satellites into position." Her expression turned grim. "Trouble is, the toxin's set to release in four hours. We don't have the time."

"Maybe I can repurpose the ground-based antennas as a go-around, to allow us to access the info sooner. Could that work?"

Barbara's hands danced across the keyboard, and she grinned as the results scrolled into view.

"It should," she said. "But we'll need you to bring at least two of them online. I know of one—it's employed by Gotham Broadcasting Corporation, at Panessa Studios."

"I know the one," he said. "And is there a second antenna that will do the trick?"

"Not certain—not yet, but I'll figure that out well before you're finished with the first one."

"Good," Batman said. "Time's running out, and if the truth can be told, Barbara, this worries me. Your father said it best. The Joker was a killer we could stop any number of ways, but even if we do everything we can, there's no telling if we can prevent Crane's fear toxin from infecting the city. If it gets into the air, we lose.

"This may be beyond us. Beyond me."

"Then all we need to do is stop him before it's released."

"I like how you underplayed the word 'all.'"

"If I don't keep a positive view," she said firmly, "I'll never find the answers."

Batman nodded quietly and started to leave.

"Bruce?" There was an underlying urgency to her voice. He stopped and looked back. "Bruce, I spoke to Dad," she said, quietly, almost sadly.

"And?"

Suddenly she was fighting back tears, trying to maintain control.

"I hate lying to him. I mean, he'd kill me, or maybe it would kill him if he knew I was still in the city. I mean, he just said it again. He still feels as if any harm that comes to me does so because he didn't do enough."

Batman looked away, and then glanced back at Barbara.

"We'll worry about him after we stop Scarecrow," he said before turning again and leaving. The door slid shut behind him.

Barbara sat alone in the Clock Tower, replaying all the lies she'd had to tell her father since long before she became Oracle. He never learned that she had been Batgirl, who—more often than not—fought on the street alongside both Batman and his partner, Robin.

Gordon never quite realized that by crippling her, the Joker wasn't just sending a message to Gotham City's police commissioner that nobody was safe. He was sending Batman the same message, too. To compound that message, he'd killed Jason Todd, the young man who had donned the Robin uniform after Dick Grayson put it aside to become Nightwing.

Though she was paralyzed by the Joker's bullet, Barbara's need to seek out justice intensified rather than diminished. She created her Oracle guise as a way of protecting the city she still loved, and she wasn't going to give it up now just because some Joker wannabe was out to make a name for himself. Surrender to one lunatic gave an unfettered license to them all.

Yet while she had started down this path to promote justice and truth, instead she'd found herself lying to the one man she loved the most, and who unconditionally loved her in return. James Gordon was more than her father—he was unquestionably the best man she knew, and that included Bruce Wayne.

James Gordon never hid behind a mask. Her father never shirked the public eye, and even his home address was listed in the city's public records. He was too good a man to be treated like this, but Barbara knew no other way around it.

She had long believed she needed to keep secrets from him, in order to protect him. But now, as the city was facing what might prove to be its gravest threat, she was beginning to wonder about the wisdom of her decision. If the worst-case scenario unfolded, if Scarecrow succeeded in creating an entire city paralyzed by fear, she didn't want to die or see him die with any secrets remaining between them.

But how to tell him the truth after so many years of lying?

10

Back in the nineties and right through to the zeroes, Panessa Studios had been a thriving television and commercial advertising facility employing nearly 150 entertainment *professionals*.

By 2004, local crime bosses began levying "protection taxes" on Panessa, and Gotham City's general fortunes started their deep decline south. Studios moved their non-Los Angeles "inner-city" film shoots to New York, Toronto, Detroit, New Orleans, and Vancouver, leaving Panessa bankrupt and deserted.

Wayne Enterprises, using the DBA "PanCo," quietly purchased the studio and its nine acres of warehouses, soundstages, and back lots. PanCo made a small business out of renting it to the very occasional commercial unit that didn't have the finances to go anywhere safer. Yet Wayne's objective for the land wasn't to restart it as a film studio, but to use it for far more private purposes.

While some of the land and buildings still were open for use, the back two acres and former soundstages 35, 36, and 37 were officially closed. "Condemned" signs indicated mold and asbestos complications. Even the local gangbangers didn't try to break in—not that they could have made it past Lucius Fox's security system before the police showed up to arrest them.

Theoretically, if they had tried and managed to get past the system, and if somehow they got to the soundstage, they still wouldn't realize that the facility's inside was significantly smaller than its exterior. Hidden behind false panels, Fox had constructed a series of soundproofed, self-sustaining holding cells that, when required, would be used to contain and interrogate the worst of the city's worst.

Better here than the Batcave, Batman mused as he approached soundstage 37. But he wasn't there to tour the studio's empty cells. The first antenna was hidden in a forest of satellite dishes, all installed in the early nineties to take the studio into the future world of digital transmission. Most were inert, but some were leased out to companies like the Gotham Broadcasting Corporation.

"Batman." Oracle's voice suddenly blared over his comm. "*I've got good news and bad. The good, the studio is a hundred percent clear. Except for you, there are no heat signatures anywhere. I think you're free of Scarecrow's forces.*"

"And the bad?"

"*Power to the entire studio's been knocked out. That means the satellite dishes are little more than hunks of steel.*"

"Not a major problem. I never leave home without my own power source."

"*The Batmobile,*" she said. "*Of course. Okay, you handle that. I'll find that second antenna. Good luck.*"

"We make our own luck, Barbara," he said as he backed the car toward the satellite array behind soundstage 37, former home to Gotham City's News Center-1 team. Setting the proximity alarm to alert him to unexpected intruders, he ran charge wires from the Batmobile's engine to a small generator. It, in turn, was attached to a single, unimposing antenna hidden among the rest.

He set the Batmobile to neutral, then gunned its engine. Moments later the generator hummed with power. Shortly thereafter he reported his progress.

"Oracle, the generator's at eighty-five percent. It should be full charged in less than three minutes." Checking to make sure the generator would run independently, he asked, "Do you have an address for the second antenna?"

"I do, but you're not going to like it."

"Why's that?"

"It's Falcone Shipping."

"Yeah, well, nobody ever promised me that this was going to be simple."

"It gets worse."

"Do tell."

"We have a missing cop. Alan Dini, twenty-year vet—his name came up when the computer gave me the location. He last reported that he was patrolling the docks near the Falcone warehouse, and saw something he thought wasn't quite kosher. Said he was going to look into it. That's the last we heard from him."

"Has the G.C.P.D. sent out anyone to look for him?"

"I checked. With all that's going on, there's nobody available. Besides, they're assuming that he just decided to leave the city, like most of the cops already have. But it's too much of a coincidence—I'm thinking Dini may have seen

something connected with Falcone Shipping.

"Since you're already on the way there..."

"Got it," he replied, cutting her off. "Do you have details on the location?"

"As much as I can get," she said. *"When I first scanned, there were a dozen heat signatures in a supply room in shipping warehouse 15. All but three left, but if I was a betting girl I'd say that's where they're holding him. I'm uploading the warehouse's schematics to you now."*

"While I look in on our hostage, update your antenna readouts and keep me posted. I have a hunch tying into that one won't be the cakewalk Panessa was."

"Speaking of which, Bruce, I've locked onto the Panessa signal and patched into the satellite. Even if the studio antenna gets shut down I'll be able to use the satellite. Now I need a second one."

"Now that's good news. You buried the headline."

"Long as I don't bury you along with it. Be careful. Falcone's tentacles reach in a lot of different directions."

Warehouse 15 was an old commercial steel building, built in the 1940s on Bleake Island's southwest district two. It boasted two rear loading docks that opened onto the Gotham River, and was one of several buildings that surrounded "Falcone Plaza," all situated around a main structure that looked more like a fortress than an administration building.

Ships would anchor outside of the warehouse and use cranes to offload their stacked pallets. Its minimal design was meant to be utilitarian and adjustable, depending on the goods being shipped and—when necessary—stored. Cargo could be loaded by truck, through the front access ramp.

Batman checked his readings and saw that there were still only three heat signatures coming from a small room off the main storage area. One of those pulsing dots had to be Dini, while the other two must be his captors. If Falcone had suspected Batman was coming, there would have been many more thugs on duty.

For a mob boss, Falcone didn't think big.

Warehouse 14 stood approximately fifty yards away from its twin. There were no heat signatures coming from inside. Batman grappled to the roof, then sprinted to its edge. His cape snapped open to form batwings, which allowed him to glide the fifty yards and silently land on warehouse 15's roof.

He paused, entered a gauntlet command, and did another check for heat signatures. *Better safe than sorry.* Two of the heat signatures were walking back and forth across the room, while the third was still. The motionless dot had to be the prisoner.

Batman lowered himself in through an open-air vent and readied his Batarang. He threw it across the room, where it slammed into a wall with a metallic impact. The two goons reacted to the sound and turned as Batman glided down from the vent and slammed into them from behind. Both were down in less than thirty seconds.

Officer Dini saw Batman coming to him, his gloved finger over his lips. The cop nodded, understanding, as Batman picked the chain lock that held him in place.

"Run toward the back," Batman whispered. "Use the

river door and get out as fast as you can, then call for backup. If all goes well, our friends in the main warehouse will be ready for pickup by the time their ride gets here."

"Batman, I thought I was… I was sure they were going to kill me," Dini said breathlessly. "How can I thank you?"

"Do your job. Stay in the city and help the civilians get out."

Dini looked to the rear door, which was open to the river. "I will. I will. I promise."

Batman was gone before he could turn back.

11

Carmine Falcone, referred to by the Gotham City mobs as "the Roman," had been linked to Bruce Wayne years before the Batman made his first appearance. Luigi Maroni, a crime boss and rival to Carmine's father, shot the young Falcone as a warning.

Frantic that his son was going to die, Vincent Falcone brought Carmine to Thomas Wayne, Gotham City's premier surgeon. Not being prescient enough to know the grief this still-young thug would later cause his own son, Wayne saved Carmine's life.

Later still, the Waynes were brutally murdered by Joe Chill—a low-level waste of humanity engaged in a robbery attempt gone bad. Carmine Falcone, who had succeeded his father as Gotham City's crime boss, visited the young heir to the Wayne fortune. Because he owed his life to Bruce's father, he swore to grant Bruce a single unspecified favor—then and there, or at any time in the future.

Knowing that Falcone would never honor that pledge by giving up crime, Bruce had never redeemed the offer.

Carmine Falcone and his rival, Salvatore Maroni, the son of Luigi, fought their way across Gotham City, block by block, until they decided they'd lost enough men to a war that wouldn't end until they both were killed. After a long negotiation they divided Gotham City, each claiming control of precisely designated areas. From then on they remained in their own territories, each rarely infringing on the other.

Too much was at stake to risk another blood bath.

Falcone Shipping looked out onto Lady Gotham with both love and disdain. Vincent Falcone's father, Alfredo Falco, had brought his family to Gotham City from Italy, then promptly changed his name to Al Falcone, which to his ear sounded more American.

He was a butcher in his home town of Padua, but using all the advantages that American freedom gave him, he became a butcher of another kind here, working for one Gotham City mob after the other, rising through the ranks as his merciless dedication to his craft built him a frightening reputation.

He loved what America gave him, but he also despised the cops and feds who relentlessly tried to prevent him from doing what he was so obviously best at. He saw American politicians—who were supposedly elected to protect the common people—get away with crimes far beyond his scope. Over the course of a year or two he might make three or four million dollars tending to his trade, but these white-collar criminals were hiding away a hundred times that, all the while denouncing Falcone and his kind.

On one hand, love for America.

On the other, hatred for its duplicity.

Al's son Vincent understood the American system better than his father who, though feared by nearly everyone, essentially ran a one-man chop shop. Vinnie's son, Carmine, grasped it better than both of his predecessors. He took what was considered to be a mom-and-pop gang and turned it into a major threat worth many times what had been dreamed possible.

Carmine Falcone also owned most of the Gotham City police force, or at least he had before James Gordon became commissioner. Except for Maroni, with whom he reluctantly made peace, he also had no major enemies.

Until Batman appeared.

That pointy-eared shadowy spook caused him no end of financial grief, and Falcone vowed to kill him the first chance he got.

Despite many such chances, he consistently failed to honor the promise he'd made to himself. Yet he never wavered in his commitment. Falcone only had to succeed once. The odds were on his side and he knew, sooner or later, Batman would die.

His death would not be pretty.

12

Batman tapped his comm and connected with Oracle.

"Officer Dini's safe—I'm back at the Batmobile. What's the current assessment from the Falcone antenna?"

The response came instantly. *"Satellite feed is showing armed warriors,"* Barbara said. *"From their uniforms, I'd say they're Scarecrow militia, not Falcone hoods. That means they're probably better trained."*

"This day keeps getting better and better."

"At least it isn't dull," she replied. *"Don't forget you're going to need Fox's power conductor to ignite the antenna's power supply."*

"Already on it," Batman replied, removing the power conductor from the Batmobile's input connector. He synched it with the car's main unit, then took off.

The tower housing the second antenna rose from the center of Falcone Plaza, a large courtyard with high fortress walls on all four sides. Gargoyles, imported from England, protruded from each wall. *"Don't just make your fortress impenetrable, make it frightening."* Words of wisdom from Al Falcone.

According to his heat sensors, there were at least nine

guards patrolling the plaza, each armed with a laser-guided automatic rifle. One of the soldiers—appearing to be a superior—stepped away from the others. He held a voice amplifier to his lips.

"Batman, we know you're here," he shouted. *"We found whatever the hell gizmo you attached to the antenna at Panessa Studios. Don't worry, we dismantled it. Next we're going to dismantle you. Sounds fair, doesn't it?"*

Batman didn't answer. They only suspected he was here, and there was no reason to confirm their suspicions. His fingers danced across his gauntlet as he checked his heat scanners for nearby opponents. None were close. That meant they not only didn't know he was there, but they also didn't know why he'd come.

The tower was nearly a hundred yards away, and the nine mercs not only surrounded it, but patrolled inside as well. He couldn't fire a grapple and zip to it, he couldn't approach by foot, and he couldn't drop down on top of it. Somehow he'd have to find another way inside.

"Batman, we know you can hear this," the soldier shouted into the amplifier. *"Show yourself and you're a dead man."* To prove his point the soldiers took firing position, rifles aimed in all directions.

"Idiot," Batman muttered to himself. *If you knew where I was, the rifles would be pointed at me. This is a duck hunt, not a barrel full of fish.*

He slipped in closer. The nearest two soldiers were fifty yards away. As fast as he was, he couldn't make it across the courtyard and take them down before they'd shoot. Even if they weren't marksmen—and he suspected Scarecrow only hired the best—the odds were against him. There was no way this could be a simple, straight-on assault.

He studied the gargoyles on the walls surrounding the tower. There were at least four of them, one on each wall. He fired a grapple to the closest gargoyle and it snagged the stone beast, then yanked the line to determine its hold. Waiting for a moment when all of the guards were looking elsewhere, he retracted the line, which pulled him silently up to the gargoyle. He scrambled to its top, then looked back to see if there was any reaction from the mercs.

None.

They hadn't heard the grapple mechanism.

Perfect.

Two mercs walked below him, with three more positioned across the courtyard. Their patrols included the wall's lower perimeter. The other four were inside the tower—that's where the antenna controls would be. His timing would have to be precise.

This is doable.

Batman fired another grapple line to a gargoyle across the courtyard. The guards walking the perimeter would arrive soon. If he made his move one second too early or too late, he'd be cut down by a volley of bullets.

Unlike the soldiers outside Scarecrow's penthouse, chatting away when they should have been on high alert, these two were total professionals. As two arrived directly below him, he launched himself from the gargoyle. His descent would take four-point-eight seconds. They would have moved another three and a half yards, which meant he'd be able to take them down from behind.

He landed on the first one and smashed an elbow into the back of the man's head. The sudden shock and pain forced the merc to his knees. Batman slammed his fist into the man's throat, and he went down.

The second one was already turning to him, raising his weapon to fire. Batman crouched and spun, kicking his foot into the merc's stomach. The man bent over in pain and Batman spun again, smashing his foot through the man's nose, shattering its cartilage. As the goon joined his partner in blissful unconsciousness, Batman fired a grapple line to the closest gargoyle, and disappeared on top of it.

Plastic surgery might fix the goon's nose, but he'd be wheezing with every breath for the rest of his life. A good reminder. The man was a killer, and Batman wasn't going to waste a single moment feeling sorry for him.

He fired another line across the courtyard, away from the fallen mercs. Judging from their rate of movement, the other guards would discover them in forty-three seconds. He didn't want to be anywhere close.

Shouting. It had taken them less than thirty seconds. Scarecrow definitely hired top professionals. Now everyone was on the alert.

He winched across the courtyard again, perching on another gargoyle. From here he could see two other mercs join the three who were already searching for him. That left only two inside the tower.

He liked those odds.

Batman pulled a Batarang from his belt pouch and sent it spinning across the courtyard to where he'd been moments earlier. It began its circle back then hit the tower's south wall, as intended. The soldiers heard its *thump* and ran in that direction, scanning the area as they went. Batman already had a second Batarang in his hand, and anticipated that at least one of the five would be slower than the others.

He was right. He sailed the Batarang into the slowest merc, slamming him in the back of his head, dropping him instantly to the ground. The others, running to the south tower wall, didn't look back to see that one of their number was down.

Launching himself silently from the wall, Batman landed near the downed soldier and made certain he wouldn't soon get up. Then he fired his grapple to another gargoyle and took off. Three down. Four outside the tower. Two inside.

Time was running out.

Using the grapple he shot across the courtyard, unseen by the mercs below, and perched on top of the tower. There was an open window fifty feet below the peak. The two thugs inside would see him the moment he entered. His appearance would have to be a surprise.

He hit his comm and spoke to Lucius Fox.

"I'm at Falcone Shipping," he said, keeping his voice low, "and I need a diversion to the northwest. Think you can rig up something?"

There was a moment of silence, then Fox replied.

"Given time, I can accomplish most anything," the man said without a hint of ego. *"How soon will you need this distraction?"*

"What can you give me in thirty seconds?"

A *whooshing* sound came over the connection.

"*Really? You don't believe in making things easy, do you?*"

"If it was easy, anyone could do it." Even as he spoke, Batman prepared himself to move, knowing without doubt that something was about to happen.

"*A flawless reputation gets increasingly more difficult to live with,*" Fox replied. "*But I've had twenty seconds since we begun this conversation, so tell me what you think of this.*"

Suddenly the riverfront lit up with a fireworks display, bathing Lady Gotham in streamers of red, purple, white, and green. Each burst of light was accompanied by the traditional resounding boom. A half-dozen peonies exploded over the water, then a globe of sparkling stars that seemed to envelop the city. Chrysanthemums and willows burned high above, mixed with a barrage of horsetails that rose high then suddenly fell, breaking into a shower of streaming light.

Bright white rings and comets crackled one after the other in a steady, deafening stream. There were repeater cakes and falling leaves, dragon eggs and flying fish.

Batman waited. The mercs rushed to the opposite window to see what was happening, and there they were transfixed by the glittering bombast of fireworks.

"*We set it up last month for this year's Independence Day festival,*" Fox said. "*We'll have to report an industrial accident, but we can always redo it—perhaps even better.*"

Silence.

"*Mr. Wayne? Do you hear me?*"

But Batman was too busy to reply. He jumped from the tower and, once he was far enough out, fired a grapple to the roof. The cord snagged the parapet, tightening, then arcing him back to the window. He tossed a gas grenade inside and lowered his oxygen mask into position a moment before the grenade exploded.

The mercs choked and coughed as their lungs burned hot and their eyes swelled with tears. Batman landed inside the tower and drove a fist into the closest one's chest, taking him out, but not before he fired his weapon. The shot missed, but the explosion would certainly alert the thugs outside.

The clock was ticking.

He whirled, grabbed the second merc's head, and slammed it into the tower wall. The soldier fell unconscious to the ground.

The men outside would be entering the tower. It would take them less than a minute to race up its narrow, winding stairs.

Batman found the control panel for the antenna, attached the Batmobile's power conductor to it, then started the car's engine. Power surged through the cable and into the antenna.

"Oracle, everything's in place, but you need to do this fast. Trouble's coming."

"I can see," Barbara said from inside the Clock Tower, where she would be able to watch the heat signatures climbing the stairwell. *"Unfortunately I can't hurry technology."*

Batman ran to the tower door as the soldiers raced up the stairs. Fortunately, the stairwell was narrow so they couldn't run side by side, and it didn't have a handrail. He'd only have to deal with them one at a time—those behind the leader couldn't fire their weapons.

He launched himself at the first soldier, and the impact slammed him into the soldiers behind. Like a human battering ram he kept pushing at them, forcing them to tumble back down the stairs. Without anything to grab, they flailed helplessly as they fell.

"*Batman.*" Barbara Gordon's voice came over the comm. "*I need another sixty-seven seconds to establish the satellite link. Can you keep them busy?*"

"Do I have a choice?"

"*Not really.*"

"There's your answer."

The hindmost men fell to the first landing, stacking atop each other. One of the goons struggled to pull his gun free, and succeeded. He obviously didn't care who he killed as long as he got Batman, too.

Batman slammed his foot into the top goon's side, forcing him to roll over as he instinctively reacted. That exposed the merc below him as well as the goon with the gun. He grabbed the second merc's head and slammed it into the third one's face. The man's nose exploded in a fountain of blood and he squealed at the sudden pain.

"*Thirty-four seconds, Batman,*" he heard Oracle say. "*You can do this.*"

The lead soldier pushed himself to his feet and grabbed him from behind, his arm wrapped around Batman's throat, tightening, making it increasingly difficult to breathe. The fourth merc watched the struggle and decided to turn him into a human punching bag—his fists pummeled Batman's mid-section with rapid-fire delivery.

His arms held behind him, Batman lashed out with his feet, kicking at anything in their way.

"*Nine seconds, Bruce.*"

He let them hit him. Instead of wasting energy resisting,

he took the punishment. In his head he counted down the seconds. Eight… Seven…

A fist smashed into his face, cutting open his lip.

Four… Three…

Another fist slammed into his solar plexus.

Two…

"Batman, I have it."

This was it. Batman breathed in deeply, the cold air invigorating. He closed his eyes, gathered his strength, then lashed out.

His legs wrapped around the merc trying to strangle him. He twisted and sent the soldier flying down the stairs, into two others. He leaped over the next closest assailant and landed on the three who had fallen.

Three quick jabs made certain they wouldn't get up for at least an hour. He whirled and confronted the final merc, kneed him in the groin, then drove an elbow into the back of his neck.

"Barbara, let the police know they'll need to take out the trash," he said. "I'm out of here."

"Will do. Why don't you come by the Clock Tower? I should be able to figure out where the radiation is coming from while I help patch you up."

"There's no time," he said, heading for the roof. "Besides, I've been hurt much worse than this. But get me the info asap."

"Okay. But hold on. It's coming through. Coming… and there it… Well, look at this. Definitely not a surprise."

"What? Where is Scarecrow's fear toxin being manufactured?"

"*Our old stomping grounds, emphasis on stomping. The Ace Chemicals warehouse.*"

He remained silent for a moment while the information sank in.

"Thanks, Barbara," he said. "I couldn't do this without you."

"*I bet you say that to all the Oracles.*"

"Lucius," Batman said into his comm.

"*I'm right here,*" came the reply. "*What do you need now? Fireworks weren't a big enough show for you?*"

"They were perfect, but we now know where the fear toxin is being manufactured—it's at Ace Chemicals."

"*Why am I not surprised?*"

"Oracle said the same. But it does mean there's a definite danger posed by the toxic radiation."

"*One radiation-resistant suit, coming up.*"

"Am I that obvious?"

"*Let's say I can predict the future. And by that I mean I've already prepared such a suit for you, assuming you'd eventually find the radiation source. A Batwing will deliver it to any location you request.*"

"You're a lifesaver, Lucius."

"*Does your praise also come with a substantial raise?*"

"Let's not get too crazy. Batman, over and out."

13

Jim Gordon tried calling Barbara—for the thirteenth time since Scarecrow issued his threat—and once again the phone answered with a high-pitched whine followed with the by now repetitious drone of, *"All circuits are busy. Please hang up and try again later."*

All he wanted was to make certain his daughter was safe, and yet the technology that she so embraced was preventing him from getting an answer. For a brief moment he thought it would be better if everyone went back to sending smoke signals, but as he looked up at Gotham City's perpetually slate-gray skies, he knew that was implausible. All the sky here was good for was reflecting the Bat-Signal. No matter what time of day or night it might be, there'd always be a dark cloud on which to project it.

When his wife—the former Barbara Kean-Gordon—suddenly and without warning left her husband, their daughter Barbara, and son James Jr., Gordon's world had unraveled. Even in the bleakness that was Gotham City, he had believed that family and love provided the light and hope he needed. As long as he had his family together, anything was possible.

Yet his wife left, and James Jr. fell into a world of darkness, only to emerge in the role of a homicidal killer. Only his daughter remained with him in Gotham City, her wide, honest smile keeping him a believer that things could work out. That life didn't have to slowly and systematically destroy everything that was good.

Now, thanks to a psychopath who sought to displace hope with fear, he was unable to make certain his final hold on sanity was out there, safe and well. Gordon swore Scarecrow would be stopped, quickly and permanently.

Just like the Joker.

A phone buzzed on his desk—the one Batman had given him—and he tapped "receive." Batman's voice sounded urgent.

"I'm heading to Ace Chemicals," Batman said. *"Meet me there with as many officers as you can muster."* The phone went dead and Gordon stared at it. That was Batman. No pleasantries. Here in an instant, then gone just as fast.

Gordon glanced out his office window to the city that was either testing him or destroying him—he didn't know which it was, but thought that ultimately the results would probably be the same. He took out his department-issue cell phone and called Weezie Robbins in dispatch.

"How many officers can you free up?"

"You're joking, Commissioner, aren't you?" Robbins said, her voice soft but firm. *"There is nobody I can free up. Hell, I don't have the manpower to accomplish what I already need to do."*

"This is important," Gordon said. "We believe we know where Scarecrow's manufacturing his fear toxin. If we can contain it, Gotham City might still be spared going through yet another hell. Please, anything you can do, just do it."

"*I'll do my best, sir,*" she replied. "*Where do you want them? And when.*"

"Ace Chemicals. And ASAP."

"*Like I say, Commissioner. I'll do my best. And good luck, sir.*"

"Today we all need that. Thanks, Weezie."

He took a long look at the framed photos sitting on his desk, of Barbara. *If this works I'll see you again real soon.* He left the office and headed down to the garage. His driver, Bill McKean, was already waiting for him. They took off into the endless night.

Something tells me we're going to need a lot more than luck tonight.

Alfred Pennyworth had been with the Wayne family well before Bruce was born, and he had stayed on as the boy's legal guardian after the Waynes were murdered. He was loyal, caring, and patient, for certain, but there were always rumors about his past.

While growing up, Bruce heard a story that when Alfred was younger he had replaced his own father as a fourth-generation major domo to the English queen, until the Waynes managed to hire him away. There was *no* speculation as to how anyone, regardless of wealth, could pry away a loyal servant of the crown.

Another rumor detailed Alfred's life with the UK's MI6, which focused on rooting out foreign enemies. Once again there was a question left unanswered. Why would such an officer allow himself to become a butler?

Long ago Bruce Wayne had decided not to pursue the investigation of the mysteries surrounding his greatest friend in the world. Eventually he decided that Alfred was, after his own father, the best man he ever had known. Whatever he used to be, it only contributed to what he was now.

That was good enough.

Batman's gauntlet comm buzzed while he was speaking to Gordon. Seeing who it was, he cut short the conversation with the commissioner, and picked up the incoming call.

Alfred's face floated above the gauntlet comm. "*Sir,*" he said, his voice calm and controlled, "*the police force is reduced to fewer than six hundred officers. Quite understandably, most of the others fled along with their families.*"

"It's not a valid excuse, Alfred," Bruce said. "When you're a Gotham City police officer, the entire city becomes your family."

"*All well and good, sir, and in your case understood, but one needs to remember that we're talking about an airborne toxin. For all we know, Scarecrow has already unleashed a milder dose, simply to initiate the panicked withdrawal.*"

"You're speculating."

"*Of course I am, sir. But I've been monitoring the roads, and the police officers I've seen, well, they're displaying a greater level of fear than I've seen before. Some of those men must at one point or another have found themselves bravely confronting the Joker. It doesn't sound natural, sir.*"

"Everyone feels fear, Alfred," Batman argued. "I understand that."

"Indeed. You created your entire persona to instill fear."

"In criminals," Bruce added. "But if a person doesn't have anything to fear…"

"Then you become just another person dressed up as a bat," Alfred said, cutting him off. *"Is that what you were going to say, sir?"*

"No, it was not," Bruce replied. It was a moment before he spoke again. "I know fear. I fought through it. Or did you forget the well?"

A strange expression crossed the butler's face, but only for a moment. It had been so long ago, when Bruce was no more than eight, that he had fallen into that long-forgotten dried-up well near the back of the Wayne estate. He lay there on the well's damp floor, lost, crying, darkness everywhere, when thousands of bats appeared out of nowhere and screamed past him, their claws ripping at him as he flailed about helplessly, desperately trying to protect his face.

The young boy, protected by loving parents, had never before felt fear like that, and it seemed to go on forever—though he later realized that it could only have been minutes. Then Thomas Wayne's hand reached down, grabbed his, and pulled him to the surface.

His father held him tight, letting him know that as long as he was with him, he'd never allow his son to feel such terror again. Within a week the boy was back to running wildly everywhere on the estate, causing his usual brand of mischief, eschewing the caution his father tried to drill into him. Life moved on, as it always did.

Yet that day, those few frightening moments, had seared into Bruce Wayne's psyche and never let go. Batman might have been born because of a killer's gun, but even before that, fear had changed the course of Bruce's life.

He wasn't about to let it destroy the city he loved.

"I do remember, sir," Alfred said. *"It's a day I won't forget. But I thought you…"*

"I never forget anything, Alfred. It's my curse. But I also haven't forgotten my father sitting me down in his library that night. The fireplace was lit and the flames, dancing with abandon, were mesmerizing in their beauty."

Alfred nodded but said nothing.

"My father taught me that fear is irrational—it's not reality. Whenever it begins to build, you have to keep reminding yourself that it's only an hallucination. And as with any hallucination, you have to look past it and deal with what's real and tangible.

"He said that once you recognized the difference between what's real, and what's only in your mind, you can learn how to push past the illusion and embrace the real. It's much too easy to miss that difference, he explained. That's when you get lost in your fears."

"Sadly, sir," Alfred started, *"not everyone in Gotham City was fortunate enough to have your father's counsel."*

"I know. I see it every night. And even without fiends like Scarecrow, this city breeds fear. But as my father said, the job of the Wayne family is to help those without our good fortune. Help them to understand how best to deal with what most frightens them.

"God knows, I've tried, and I'm not going to stop."

"Sir, I sense a 'but' coming."

"Yes, and it's a big one. Scarecrow is all about fear, and the kind he brandishes isn't hallucination—at least not in the traditional sense. His chemicals worm their way into the subconscious. It finds your weakness and exploits it. Because it's chemical, it's as close to real as it gets, and it's nearly impossible to stop."

"So, do you have a plan via which you will accomplish the impossible?"

"No..." Bruce answered. "And maybe. You know I fought Scarecrow before, when I was trapped in Arkham Asylum. Scarecrow wasn't even fully powered up, and I nearly succumbed."

"This sounds more 'no' than 'maybe.'"

"Agreed. But the 'maybe' comes from knowing that Scarecrow still isn't fully powered up."

"And how do we know that?"

"If he was, he would have activated the fear toxin right when he made his threat. The fact that he didn't means he needed time to finish its manufacturing, and then distribution. Also, why would he warn the entire city of his plans?" Batman paused, then continued. "There's only one reason that makes sense. He doesn't have enough fear toxin to effectively manipulate six point three million people. He wanted the city reduced to a token force, because that's a number he can deal with."

"So he's limited by whatever process he uses to manufacture the toxin..."

"...and he doesn't want to broadcast the fact that, even if he succeeds now, he could never have taken over an entire city. His failure would embolden his enemies, including those of us who are still here to fight back. And hope is the very last thing he'd want to inspire."

"Well, sir, now that you know, you're in a much better position to resist him. Besides, as you say, you've fought and defeated him before."

"I know. But everyone has fears he can exploit. Even me."

"Your fears, sir? I thought you had long ago conquered them all." Something in Alfred's voice told Bruce that he didn't believe it.

"No, not all," he admitted. "I may know what my fear is, but if he reaches inside me and extracts it, I'm not certain I can fight back."

"What fear is that?"

Bruce hesitated before continuing. It meant revisiting one of the greatest agonies of his lifetime.

"You'll remember that my parents wanted to go to the opera that night. I was the one who insisted on the movie. Since that time, there hasn't been a day when I haven't asked myself, if I had gone along with what they wanted, would they be alive today?

"That's my fear, Alfred. That my selfishness is what killed them. And that's the one fear from which I can't run."

He suddenly clicked off the comm and closed his eyes. He was starting to feel his anger returning. *The goddam Joker blood.* Thinking about his parents, and his part in their deaths, was making him lose control.

His father once told him that when you succumbed to anger you were no longer able to think rationally, and an irrational life was always doomed to failure. Thomas Wayne showed him how to let that anger fade. How to take back control. How to resist the primitive impulses.

His breathing slowly returned to normal. He felt his pulse slowing.

But as the Joker's blood continued to take root, he also knew maintaining control was going to be hellishly impossible.

14

James Gordon's car crossed the bridge and pulled up to the all-too-familiar bright yellow police tape surrounding the large courtyard for the Ace Chemicals lab complex. Bill McKean moved to open the commissioner's door, but Gordon stopped him with a wave of his hand.

"How many times have I told you I can open my own door, Bill?"

"Just doing my job, sir."

"I know," Gordon said. "But that's a perk I don't need."

There were nearly twenty G.C.P.D. officers positioned around the front three buildings. To do the job right, Gordon estimated he'd need at least 150, but he'd been hard-pressed to get the officers who did come, and was grateful for their presence.

Captain Nolan of the Sixth Precinct stood near one of the hastily assembled barricades, on the phone, checking with his people. George Nolan had put his life on the line at least a dozen times before Gordon had promoted him to captain, and the commissioner would've bet a year's pay that he'd be one of the loyal officers who stayed behind, while so many others took off.

"Commissioner," Nolan said. "Looks like the shit hit the fan again. Is this damned city ever going to squeeze out a break?" Nolan, who was born and grew up on Park Row, never tried to shake off his Crime Alley beginnings. His vocabulary was as raw as the day he started working for the force, fifteen years ago.

Gordon laughed. "George, I'd give away half my pension to see that happen, but I'm afraid the luck genie would just look at it and laugh. So," he added, nodding toward the chemical plant, "what do we know?"

Nolan shrugged, and Gordon figured that might be the clearest answer he'd get all night. But the captain continued.

"We know we don't have enough men to stop a greased pig at a county fair, let alone God-knows-how-many armed killers they got inside. I was hoping you had a plan, sir."

"I don't, but I'm praying *he* does," Gordon said, watching as a sleek black vehicle crossed the bridge and pulled to a stop in front of them, its turbine engines shutting down with a piercing whine. A moment later its driver's hatch swung open, and Batman stepped out. It closed behind him and the car automatically initiated its electro-shock defenses to repel any foolish attackers.

The Dark Knight was wearing a different suit than earlier. He frequently adjusted his armor depending on what he was going up against.

"Any word from inside?" Batman asked Gordon.

"Nope—nothing. The facility's locked down—not a door or loading dock can be opened. From what we can gather, and judging from the number of cars in the lot, we believe there's still a skeleton crew of workers trapped in there. We've tried contacting them, but we've gotten no response. We're not hopeful."

"I'm picking up heat signatures."

"We saw them, too, Batman. But at this point we don't know if they're workers or Scarecrow's men. And with all the buildings in the complex, it's difficult to pinpoint an exact location. We're going to have to get closer."

"No," Batman snapped. "Pull your officers back. If the men in there are still alive, I'll find them." Then he added, "When I do, let's hope they can tell us what Scarecrow's up to."

Gordon's G.C.P.D. phone buzzed suddenly and he answered it.

"Gordon. Talk to me." He paused as he listened, and Batman saw his eyes widen for a second. Something startled the commissioner, but he was too much of a professional to show it for long.

He clicked the phone off, then shook his head.

"Just when you think things have gotten as bad as they could…" He looked up. "Scarecrow's sent out a call to all possible allies in the tri-state area. He's asking them to come to Gotham City, promising them the city has become the Wild West, and everything's up for grabs."

"That's nothing's new," Batman said. "The Joker did the same a few years back, and even the Riddler recruited cohorts in his own attempt to become the top dog. Crane's looking for more power players to create a distraction. He wants them to keep us busy while he completes whatever he's planning."

"I know," Gordon replied. "But in the past we always

had a full compliment of cops to show off our muscle. Even when we've faced the 'blue flu,' we've had the essential manpower we needed. This time, based on what I just heard, the criminals flooding into the city already outnumber the rest of us two, maybe three to one."

Worried expressions took hold on the faces of the cops who heard their exchange. Then they looked at Batman, and he saw the hope appear again in their eyes. They were praying he'd be able to rescue the city as he'd done so many times before. So he began walking purposefully toward the factory, then turned back.

"I need you all to stand back behind the lines," he said. "My suit's protected, so once I'm inside it should be able to temporarily protect me from the toxins. Unfortunately, without protection, you'd succumb to his poisons pretty much immediately. So stay here. Please."

He turned back to the factory then stopped again as he heard the roar of helicopter blades above him.

Peering upward, he saw a pilot leaning out of the cockpit—definitely male, face covered in some sort of mask but he was too far away for the details to be seen. The man waved at him, and it wasn't a friendly gesture.

The copter was heavily armed, and its weapons array began to swivel. Cannons shifted into position, and Batman knew from the telltale hum that they were being primed as the craft approached the chemical plant.

If the pilot was going to shoot, Batman didn't want any of the Ace Chemicals workers—if they were still alive— to become collateral damage. He sprinted across the courtyard, away from both the building and the police. He hoped his actions would cause the copter to follow him.

The first explosion hit.

He braced himself. An instant later it was followed by a second explosion, and a third. But he hadn't been scratched. Whoever the pilot was, he couldn't possibly have missed Batman three times. Not with modern targeting guidance.

He looked up.

The city bridge leading to the factory had been blown apart. Cars and busses were plummeting into the river below. Another missile struck the bridge's suspension towers, shattering them. The deck wobbled and swayed, forcing the suspender cables to pull back and snap. Bridge parts, still on fire, fell into the deep waters. Thick black smoke rose from the ruins.

Batman stared at the carnage. Whoever the pilot was, he was sick enough and twisted enough that he was willing to kill hundreds in order to block further access to the island.

Why the hell didn't the bastard just put up a "no trespassing" sign? he thought with dark humor. But nothing about the situation was funny.

The copter swooped low, then banked toward him. This time the pilot didn't wave. He seemed preoccupied. Batman couldn't see what he was doing, but suspected he was locking in coordinates. And he couldn't outrun missiles. Even if they missed him by a dozen yards, the explosions would still consume him.

The pilot's voice echoed from the cockpit, amplified so it could be heard over the screaming blades.

"No more last-second escapes, old friend. No more Utility Belt wonders that pull your sorry ass out of the fire, as

they have so many times before." The copter slowed, then hovered in front of him. The pilot looked up from whatever he'd been doing and stared.

"Remember the Winchester murder? How about the Joker's centennial attack? Well, this time you won't be able to grapple your way out of here, or use your Batclaws to grab my landing struts. You see, old man, you've used up your quota of miracles. You've had a great run, but the ride is finally over. There's a new mask in town, which means it's time for you to be retired."

Batman never expected to one day walk through his front door and quietly and peacefully die at home, but he hoped that when he died it would be while he was helping others live.

Then it hit him. The pilot had mentioned the Winchester murder. That was five years ago, and he and the police had never reported the details. How would he know Batman had used his grapple? And how could he know he'd used his Batclaws to bring down a helicopter with the Joker in it?

None of that was part of the public record.

Who the hell…?

The pilot checked his head-up display and tapped the controls on the copter's keyboard system. Batman's heat signature was locked in. There was no place he could run that a single missile couldn't search out and destroy him. And there was more than one rocket set aside for the task.

He pressed the trigger mech, but the HUD blinked red and the words "System Override" flashed on the console. He pressed it again, but nothing changed.

The goddam missiles weren't firing.

"What the hell?"

His comm system crackled and Scarecrow's raspy voice came through his earphones.

"I will not permit you to kill him, Knight. In death he will have nothing left to fear, while I still have so much more to give. Your only job is to keep him away from Ace Chemicals."

"You swore I could kill him."

"Vengeance will come. When I say so."

He started to shout as he heard the comm shut off. Scarecrow was no longer online.

"Damn!" The Knight slammed the console with his fist, yanked the controls, and the copter banked away. *Another time then.*

It couldn't come soon enough.

The Arkham Knight watched Batman, standing impotently in the courtyard. He turned to speak to Gordon before heading back to the Batmobile.

"Old man," the Knight whispered to himself, "I could've taken out both you and the cop, and it would've been so damn easy. But no. Not yet. Scarecrow wants to play a few more games before then. So go ahead, go inside. See what my men have in store for you. If you survive, fine. If you die, Scarecrow will be pissed, but I'll stand up and applaud. Whatever happens—between you and me, old friend—there's going to be a lot of blood involved. Have fun. I know I will.

"This is going to end sooner than you think," he muttered. "You can trust me on that, Bruce."

15

The Batmobile roared up a ramp toward the cluster of buildings that surrounded the courtyard. Batman tapped his gauntlet comm to connect to Oracle but received no answer. Not a problem—her satellite-connected heat sensors might be more powerful than his portable unit, but his would suffice.

He saw multiple thermal blips throughout the quad. The captives could still be anywhere, and he needed to get closer to find them. He gunned the engine and sped across the campus.

According to his sensors, two tanks were waiting for him, both unmanned drones. If Scarecrow wanted him dead he would have had his goons driving them, forcing Batman, who avoided lethal attacks, to be cautious, slowing him down, making him an easier target to destroy. But it was becoming more and more apparent that Scarecrow didn't want him dead. At least not yet.

That must have been the reason the copter pilot turned away at the last moment, instead of blasting him off the face of the planet. The master had jerked the dog's leash.

Scarecrow only wanted to slow him down.

The obvious question was… why?

The answer, sadly, also seemed obvious. Jonathan Crane

wanted Batman to feel fear before he killed him. Scarecrow needed him to see Gotham City succumb to his toxin, to watch his city descend into a state of primitive dread where its oh-so-valued citizens would see enemies everywhere. Where they would mindlessly attack one another, and destroy those they once loved but no longer recognized.

But most of all, he likely wanted Batman to experience complete helplessness as he failed to save what was most important to him. Scarecrow wanted to destroy Batman's mind before he destroyed his body—neither of which goals the Joker had ever achieved.

It was all too possible. If the fear toxin turned even a thousand ordinary and decent citizens into paranoid murderers who saw demons wherever they looked, those thousand could easily kill many thousands more. And if Scarecrow managed to blanket the entire city with his toxin, nobody would be spared. Driven by inexorable fear, the population of Gotham City would exist for one reason only—to destroy or be destroyed.

They had to stop him.

As the tanks closed in, he ran his fingers over the touch screen and accessed his weapons controls. Twin cannons swiveled into position, their ammo counter indicating that only two missiles were available—one in each turret. There was no leeway for misses.

He double-checked the targeting mech, breathed in deeply, hit the firing icon, and launched the rockets. Nine seconds later both tanks exploded. Perfect hits, but now he was out of major firepower.

The Batmobile ground to a stop, its hatch swung open,

and Batman took off at a sprint toward the closest building, only to confirm that its steel door was shut and locked from the inside. He removed a small canister of explosive gel from his belt pouch and sprayed it on the door hinges. Contact with air hardened it into position.

Batman reached for his detonator when a sudden taser blast sent him falling back, involuntarily yelping in pain. Struggling to his feet, he saw three armed mercs rappelling from the building roof. The foremost one fired, and a new taser hit him in the chest, dropping him to his knees where he fought the compulsion to flail like a marionette.

He writhed on the ground, helpless to stop the barrage of fists that slammed into his face and gut. His stomach was burning and he found it nearly impossible to control his body, still shaking wildly from the taser blast. Focusing as best he could, he forced his legs under one of the mercs and pushed. Surprised, the man stumbled back toward the steel door.

Batman's hand shuddered as he finally pressed the detonator, setting off the explosive gel that was already in place. Even as the explosion took the merc out of the action, it ripped the door's hinges from the wall.

The explosion startled the other two thugs, giving Batman the few precious seconds he needed to gather all the strength he could. He activated the Batmobile by remote, and heard its weapons system power up as its AI scanned for targets.

All he had to do now was survive.

Sadly, that was becoming an increasingly unlikely concept.

The weapons honed in on Batman's signal, then targeted

the figures surrounding him, as per Fox's programming. Rubber bullets slammed into the mercs, leaving the killers unconscious.

Batman stumbled to his feet and through the opened door, and switched his cowl lenses to "detective mode" which could sense heat patterns, movement and sound even through walls nearly a half-foot thick. Though already beginning to recover, he was still trembling from the taser blasts, and knew he wasn't yet capable of taking on trained fighters. Unfortunately, that was exactly what he would need to do in order to find and rescue the captive workers.

He launched his grapple and pulled himself up to the ceiling, then kicked through a top window and climbed outside, pulling himself onto the roof. This building was the tallest on the Ace campus, and overlooked the entire facility. From this perspective everything looked peaceful.

Removing a small device from his belt pouch, he tossed it high over his head. It was a remote scanner that tied directly into his gauntlet communicator. It hovered for several minutes, sending out sonar signals, and then suddenly beeped.

Accessing the campus schematics uploaded by Oracle, he cross-referenced them with the data provided by the remote. There was a pulsing green light over one of the buildings—the one that housed the pump room. That was where the hostages were being kept.

Now he had to get to them. Several dozen armed mercenaries were going to do their damnedest to make certain he wouldn't.

* * *

Bruce Wayne had visited Ace Chemicals many times when he had considered buying the factory and especially the land. He gave up the notion when his geologists reported that the grounds were irreparably contaminated, and there'd be no way to ever cleanse it. Over the course of his research he'd checked out every building and knew their layouts by heart. Despite that fact, he still referred to the floor-by-floor schematic Oracle had provided. It never hurt to have overlapping intel—"belt and suspenders," she'd say.

All Ace Chemicals buildings were crisscrossed with underground tunnels that ran under the campus, accessed through steel gratings. Back in the day, thousands of dollars' worth of liquor and unstamped cigarettes had secretly moved through these passageways or others exactly like them. This factory, like so many of the others built in Gotham City in the mid-1930s, was designed with that era's bootleggers in mind, and they served their masters well.

Constructed for Prohibition, the underground network also stretched into the city, reaching nearly every corner, mostly hidden from view. The maze of tunnels, always dark and somber, provided a physical reminder that the booze-soaked Gotham City skin everyone thought they knew so well only served to hide its diseased bones.

Batman planned to put the tunnels to good use. He pried loose one of the gratings and slipped into the darkness, then pulled the steel back in place. Even if the unconscious mercs recovered, they would have no idea where he'd gone.

Inside the warehouse, he made his way up until he

found himself peering at the steam pipes that vented the heat created during chemical processing. He stared out through a grating and saw a single thug, pacing back and forth. The sound coming from the vents would be loud enough to cover the Dark Knight's movements.

He followed the man's path and took position about ten yards ahead of him, then stood quietly as the merc walked past. In a sudden move imperceptible over the pump's rhythmic thumping, he pushed the grating aside, grabbed the man's ankles, and pulled his legs out from under him. The merc fell and Batman quickly covered his mouth with one hand, preventing him from calling out, while he wrapped his other arm around the man's throat and squeezed until his opponent gasped for air and collapsed.

Incapacitate, don't kill. He was controlling the Joker's blood.

Securing the merc's wrists with plastic ties, he gagged him then dragged him into the tunnels, leaving him there while he moved on to look up through the gratings into the next area, which was also filled with pipes.

Three mercs patrolled this new chamber, talking but still paying attention. They weren't close to one another, so there was no way to take out one without being shot by the others. This action would have to be perfectly timed.

He quickly moved through the conduits until he was directly under one of the guards. The three were still talking about a girl one of them was dating, and it became clear that the conversation was nearly over. Batman waited while they finished, and the other two turned to continue their rounds.

As soon as they turned away, Batman lunged through

the grating and pulled the closest merc into the tunnel with him. He drove his elbow into the man's throat and quickly took him out of the action.

Harsh, but still controlled. He breathed in deeply and moved on.

The merc nearest to the action heard the scuffle, turned back, and saw Batman running at him. It took a moment for him to realize what was happening, but he'd been well trained. Instantly, his weapon was in position to fire, but as he squeezed the trigger Batman jumped over his head, twisted, and slammed the man from behind—both feet hard to the back of his head, smashing him into a power box.

Sparks exploded, the merc gasped, and crumbled to the ground, unconscious.

No sign of the third man.

Batman triggered his comm and spoke to Alfred.

"Oracle's off-line. I need some help. Whoever the guy in the copter is, he's assembled an army. These men are trained pros."

He gave Alfred the best description he could of the man who had piloted the aircraft. When he stopped speaking he could hear the butler typing.

"Master Bruce, there's only one hit. I'm accessing intel on a Black Ops team working out of Venezuela. There's nothing but speculation on their commander, though. The only thing sources agree on is he calls himself the Arkham Knight."

"Fancy," Batman replied. *If not unique,* he thought to himself. Then the third guard reappeared. "Hold on. I've got a merc coming at me who's begging for a lesson in hand-to-hand."

"I'd say be careful," Alfred admonished. *"But when have you ever listened to my advice when it came to war?"*

"More than you'd suspect, Alfred," Batman said, and he laughed.

The third merc took aim, and he had a clear shot. There was no way he was going to miss. Batman dived to the ground and sent a Batarang hurtling toward the killer. It spun past him, and the man grinned.

"Can't aim for shit, can you?" The Batarang began its circle, arcing back, and slammed into him from behind. He fell without a sound.

Batman retrieved the Batarang and folded it back into his pouch. "You people always forget what a boomerang is supposed to do," he said as he dragged the unconscious form over to the other two, and dumped them all into the tunnel safely secured.

He tapped his gauntlet comm and heard Alfred respond.

"Sir, I'm picking up a computer in the room. Do you see it?"

"Give me a moment… yes, I see it," he said. Stepping over to it, he found a twentieth-century keyboard, a massive hunk of metal that other businesses had long ago replaced with aluminum copies or even less-expensive plastic. Data began to appear, and he switched from one screen to the next as fast as the tech would allow. "Alfred, there's a crew of Ace Chemicals workers on site," he confirmed. "I'm one room away from the first of them."

"Good. You can expect to find opponents, as well . There's no way they're going to let you get close to their leader."

"I expected as much," Batman replied, and he reached into his belt pouch, grabbing the Batmobile remote and pressing the override control. "That's why I brought along some backup."

Outside, the Batmobile's lights flared. Gordon turned as he heard its engines hum with life. He looked through the window expecting to see Batman, but there was nobody in the driver's seat. As he tried to open the door, the car roared and took off.

Gordon sighed. "A man and his toys."

Inside the warehouse, Batman checked his remote, then returned to the computer. He found the old control override, and pulled the lever.

"Gates opening," he murmured. "Time to bring in the car."

The massive steel doors leading into the warehouse slid open, and the Batmobile drove up the loading ramp into the vast central storage area. It was the size of several football fields, and through the monitors he saw trucks and forklifts used to move the huge chemical barrels that crowded many of the aisles.

Militia tanks—unmanned—ground their way through the facility, programmed to locate intruders and destroy them. Perhaps these tanks weren't specifically meant to kill him, but that didn't make them any less dangerous, and the collateral damage they'd create in the process wouldn't be pretty. Or painless.

The Dark Knight's vehicle transformed to battle mode and sped toward him. He heard the growl of the engines before he saw it. When it was ten feet away, sensors triggered its sliding roof, opening it wide. Batman leapt, somersaulting into the driver's seat. The roof slid shut and auto-control went to manual.

It felt good to be behind the wheel.

There were at least a dozen mercs between him and the first captive. As he roared toward them they fired, but their bullets bounced off the Batmobile's protective shields. He tagged each of the soldiers and set his firearms to deliver rubber bullets. Laser guidance would guarantee precise hits, so he wouldn't waste ammunition.

Two tanks came grinding in his direction, and he guided the Batmobile to squeeze between the two, firing its Vulcan guns at them. The tanks convulsed with explosions and rolled, slamming into the warehouse wall, bringing it down. Through the hole he saw a smaller room and past that, a window set in a wall.

In that far chamber, chained to a steel pipe, was the first captive worker he had encountered.

Five more mercs opened fire, and now he had a collateral victim to protect. No time for precision. He spun the Batmobile wheel and its weapons swiveled toward them. Nearly three-dozen rubber slam rounds blasted from multiple barrels and thumped into the killers. They were down before they could cause any further damage.

The room was clear.

"Oracle, are you seeing anything?" he asked. "Anymore soldiers?" Barbara didn't answer. "Oracle?" he repeated. Still no answer, and worry began to claw at the back of his mind. He checked his comm. Signal bars were low, but he still should have made it through.

Whatever the problem, he was on his own.

He double-checked his own sensors. Beyond the worker, the closest red dot was at least three corridors away. A stroke of luck—he'd take it any way it came.

The Batmobile hatch slid open and Batman ran through the room to the smaller chamber beyond, and the chained captive.

"You're safe now," he said as he freed the man. The worker was shaking with fear and stammered as he tried to talk. The words rushed from him.

"T-they've been running the plant for hours. They brought in trucks. Weapons. Soldiers. God, so many soldiers. And shipments of hazardous materials. They're mixing them right now. They, they knew exactly what they were doing."

His voice started to break and Batman forced a change of topic, to keep him from dwelling on what they had put him through. *Keep him talking about anything but being a hostage. But keep him on message. Make him part of the team, not just a frightened victim.*

"You did a great job, sir. But I need more information," he said calmly. "What's your name?"

"Name? Cheung. Mark Cheung. I'm the chief chemical engineer here."

"And you're doing a great job so far, Mark. Now I've got a very important question to ask you. Do you know where I will find their leader, Scarecrow?"

Cheung looked as if he was trying to think, but the thoughts weren't coming fast enough. Still, Batman remained silent.

"All I know is his people said he's moving ahead with his plan. He's got a whole freaking army backing him up." His panic started to build again. "They're insane!"

"That's what I needed to know, Mark. Now I can be prepared, so you're doing great. Even better than that, you're safe now, Mark. There's nothing to worry about. We'll get you out of here, and I promise I will stop him."

Cheung's eyes were wide with fear, as he shook his head.

"You can't," he said, the words catching in his throat. "Nobody can. You don't get it. Scarecrow, he's building some kind of bomb that'll cover the entire East Coast with his fear toxin. I mean, my God, his people, they said he's mixing it right now. We're screwed, Batman. We're all totally screwed."

Batman calmed Cheung down, at least long enough to get him into Gordon's protective care.

But the man's words were chilling. A sense of dread began to build in Batman, and he quickly tamped it down. He had work to do—and thanks to Cheung, he knew just where the enemy was located.

"I understand, Mark, but you have to hear me. Whatever Scarecrow seems to be, underneath that Halloween mask and those gimmicky syringe fingers, he's only human." He let that sink in. "Which means I can stop him. You understand what I'm saying? He *can* be beaten. He *will* be beaten. So come with me."

"You're not going anywhere, Batman. Except maybe to hell."

Batman turned to see the door slam shut then heard as it was bolted from outside. Through the window he saw the Arkham Knight, flanked by a dozen armed mercs.

The Knight was covered head to foot, and his armor almost resembled Batman's own, right down to the trademark bat ears. Was it intended as an homage or a parody? Large control pads replaced sleek gauntlets, his face was entirely shielded, and his eye slits glowed a vivid blue. Splashes of red gave the appearance of blood. Weapons hung off his belt, but he didn't draw them.

He stepped up to the window, placed a finger on it and drew a happy face in the dust.

"Good to see you again, Batman. If this glass wasn't separating us, I'd shake your hand. Yours, too, Mr. Cheung."

"Well, that's not going to happen," Batman said. "Tell your men to put down their weapons and give up. Now."

The Knight laughed. "Like you say, that's not going to happen." He turned to his men and gestured. "Keep your guns trained on him. Avoid that bat-symbol. That's a… a little trick."

He turned back to Batman. "Isn't it?" The Knight's voice was raspy but not quite mechanical—it was being electronically filtered. Batman had done the same thing himself, for many years.

With a laugh he turned back to his men. "That area, under the bat, it's been reinforced. It's where his armor is strongest. And because it's placed over his heart, it's a convenient symbol to target—if you didn't know better."

He pointed to various parts of Batman's armor and continued. "Aim for the weak spots at the shoulders, there and there. Coordinate your fire at the points where the plates meet."

Cheung's eyes were wide with fear.

"How does he know that, Batman? Who is he?"

"No idea, but I intend to find out."

"Excuse me," the Knight interrupted. "Did Mr. Cheung say something? Maybe it's something we all should hear?"

"He's an innocent. Leave him out of this."

"C'mon, Batman. Nobody's fully innocent. Haven't you said that yourself, many times? The real question is, how guilty is he? But then, you're always defending the weak and helpless. And truth to tell, that's what I like about you."

"What do you want, Knight?"

"What do all your enemies want? But you know the thing that separates me from the rest of the rabble? I know your next move before you do. I know how you think."

"Do you know what I'm thinking right now?"

The Knight reached for a weapon—a compact device vaguely shaped like a pistol—and pulled it out. He looked at it admiringly and stroked it lovingly with his other hand. "Of course. You're thinking, 'Who the hell is this guy?'"

"Not even close. I'm trying to decide which of you I'm going to take down first."

"Yeah? No. You're not. You're thinking what I said." The Knight pointed the gun at Batman and pressed the barrel to the window. His finger toyed with the trigger. "What to do? What to do?" The Knight lined up the gun sight, targeting Batman's mouth. He adjusted its position until it was exactly where he wanted it.

"You know what I *don't* like about you? It's that you've never had a sense of humor. Everyone should, but you, you only see what's wrong with the world. To you, everything exists in shades of funereal gray." The Knight laughed and added, "Maybe that's why they call you the *Dark* Knight."

"Do I have to ask again? What do you want, Knight?"

"Want? Just so we're both on the same page here, I want… I want to kill you. But first, Scarecrow and I, we want to make you suffer." He gestured to his men to back away, then ran his hand across the happy face and smudged it away.

"But not right now. Later. After you watch the city you love descend into hell. Very soon."

The Arkham Knight turned and walked off, his men following behind.

Batman led Cheung to the Batmobile then slipped in behind the wheel. Activating the ignition, he slammed the gas and the turbos ignited. The car swiveled to face the warehouse door and rocketed forward.

He drove back through the warehouse and down the ramp to the police waiting area outside. The car jerked to a stop and Batman exited, helping his charge do the same and handing him over to Gordon.

"His name's Mark Cheung. He's going to need help."

"He'll get it, I'll make sure of that myself," Gordon promised. "And, oh, great work. I knew you wouldn't let us down."

"We're not done yet. I know where Scarecrow is, and now I'm going to stop him."

16

Batman crossed the campus through its underground tunnels. This took him to the building that housed Ace Chemicals' mixing chamber. Cheung said Crane was preparing his fear-toxin bombs, and this building was the only one where the mixing process could be accomplished.

He checked his sensors and saw a single red blip in the building, in its basement chamber. If Scarecrow was there, then why weren't his mercs guarding him? Crane wouldn't have sent them all to stop Batman—not without leaving behind some kind of auxiliary force.

And where is the Knight?

It wouldn't be wise to enter via conventional means, so before he reached a door he pushed aside a grating, hoisted himself out, and hurried down a deserted passageway. Still no guards. Something was wrong about it, but there was no way he could turn back now.

Especially if Scarecrow was within his reach.

He proceeded to the basement floor and located the large steel doors that led to the mixing chamber. They were wide open, as if waiting for him. Checking his sensors yet again, he still saw only a single blinking red light. There was no way for anyone with a heartbeat to avoid being picked up by the sensors, if Scarecrow was alone, he had to have some sort of plan.

Jonathan Crane was anything but sloppy.

The difficulty with fighting maniacs was reasoning out their criminally insane thought processes. All too often they were crazy for no discernable reason, and with vague and chaotic patterns. It was like trying to find rhyme or reason where there was none.

Batman entered the mixing chamber and saw Scarecrow, his back to the door, pouring the contents of a mixing tube into the large vat built into the room's floor. Automatic beaters were mixing the chemicals already in the soup. They withdrew, a lid slid over the top, and the vat began to shake like a huge paint mixer, blending its contents together.

Scarecrow turned and gestured for Batman to approach. His hideous mask showed that rictus of a grin, while his patchwork canvas hood shrouded his face in stark shadows. Canisters hung from his midsection, and on a bandolier draped over his right shoulder, looking vaguely like bones.

"You spent an inordinate amount of time searching for me, Batman. For your own survival, you should have used the opportunity to flee."

"It's over, Crane. I'm going to shut you down, and then I'll dismantle your operation."

Scarecrow dropped to his knees as if to surrender, put his arms out in front of him, his wrists pressed together, waiting to be cuffed.

"You can try. Here."

Without hesitation Batman grabbed him by the neck

and hoisted him upright until his feet were off the floor, dangling.

"How do I stop your bomb?" Batman demanded.

"You know your actions here make it certain she's going to die."

A chill ran down his spine.

"What are you talking about, Crane?"

"You should have guessed. You should have known."

"No more games, Crane. Who dies?"

Scarecrow's fingers, encased in syringes filled with his toxin, tapped the gas mask hanging to the side of his face, as if trying to sort out what he was going to say. He then gestured to Batman's glove.

"Call her. See for yourself."

"Her? Oracle?" The chill again. "What did you do to Oracle?" Batman activated his gauntlet comm, and this time the holo screen rose from it.

"Wrong question, Batman. Don't talk in the past tense…"

"Oracle, it's Batman. Oracle, are you there? Talk to me."

"The past is over. It's what I am doing now that should frighten you."

Batman saw the camera on Oracle's end jerk to the right. She was sprawled on the floor, her wheelchair overturned, a gag tied tightly across her mouth preventing her from talking—though he could hear her muffled voice. He couldn't tell if she was in the Clock Tower, or somewhere else.

Plastic ties secured her hands behind her back. She was shaking back and forth, trying to pull her bindings loose, but she couldn't. The camera righted itself and Batman saw the Arkham Knight. He waved to Batman as Scarecrow's voice filled the small room, rising in pitch and volume.

"My reach extends far beyond your own. There is nothing you can do to stop me."

"Oracle. I'm going to find you. I swear I'll save you."

But the holo went dark and retracted back into his glove. She was gone. But where?

He turned to grab Scarecrow, to force him into revealing where Barbara was being held, but all he saw was a steel panel in back of the room, closing with a metallic impact.

Crane was gone.

Sprinting to the door, he tried to pull it open. As he did Scarecrow's voice echoed from a dozen speakers scattered throughout the room.

"*Chasing me is a grand idea, Batman, and I strongly suggest you do so. Of course, as you hear this, I'm heading toward a waiting helicopter and in a few minutes I plan to be as far away from this facility as I can. Oh, I neglected to explain why. You see, I've set Ace Chemicals to explode. So you can chase after me, and perhaps even beat Barbara's location out of me, or you can try to contain the explosion, which, by the way, will spread my fear toxin across the city. You have two minutes, ten seconds.*

"*But please, come after me. I so want to see this city driven even madder than it is.*"

There was no time to search for the explosives—they could be hidden anywhere in the room. The lid over the vat opened, exposing the toxin, its deadly vapor rising like steam.

Two minutes left.

Don't react. Take your time. Think.

He turned, his gaze sweeping the room. The walls

were filled with shelves and on each one sat several sealed canisters, all with stickers listing their chemical symbols as well as their commercial names. The first wall had canisters marked as alcohol compounds used to make fuels, solvents, and more.

Some shelves were crowded with canisters labeled Methanol, whole other canisters contained chemicals used in food flavorings and additives, or fluorine, which was used in dental hygiene products as well as in refrigeration units and aerosol sprays. There were still other chemicals, those used in the manufacturing of drugs, disinfectants, perfumes, herbicides, fuels, and more.

There was an entire wall of canisters whose stickers only indicated their chemical compounds, but did not include their commercial names.

When chemicals were ordered, the nine-to-five factory workers who loaded and unloaded the trucks wouldn't be given a complicated list, filled with rows of chemical symbols they likely wouldn't recognize. Their list would consist of commercial names. That there was an entire wall of canisters without such names meant they weren't intended for outside distribution.

Batman activated his gauntlet, punched up its computer, and recited the chemical names listed on the canisters.

"What are these used for?"

The holo-voice took several seconds, then responded.

"They are neutralizing agents used in the dilution of acids and airborne chemicals. Do you require an entire list of uses?"

"No."

The explosion would occur in exactly one minute, thirty-two seconds.

He rushed to the canisters, grabbed two at a time, and carried them back to the vat. He dumped their contents inside, desperately hoping that would dilute the fear toxin before it detonated and spread across the city.

One minute seventeen seconds.

Five more canisters.

He dumped two more into the vat, raced back and took the final three. They were large and awkward, but he had no alternative.

He emptied the contents of the final canister into the vat, then pressed the button he saw Scarecrow activate before. The lid slid shut and the vat began to shake.

He had thirty-seven seconds to get out of the room and clear of the explosion. He raced back in the direction he'd come, cleared the canister room, and sped through the warehouse. The next room was just ahead.

He was going to make it.

The vat exploded.

Fear toxin shot out in all directions. In the moment before the first surge smashed into him, he hoped he had diluted the toxin enough to minimize its deadly effects. At least for those who weren't so close.

The wave of toxins slammed into him, carrying him across the room, smashing him into the wall. His armor cracked, and Scarecrow's toxins began seeping into it. He tried to hold his breath and replace his breather, but a second explosion hit...

...and everything went black.

* * *

The laughing woke him up.

It wasn't the laughter of a comedy club, or when a friend tells a good joke, but a nasty laugh, cackling without humor. Dark. Guttural. The laugh of an animal about to devour its prey.

Only one man laughed like that. No. Not a man. A monster. A beast. A remorseless thing. But it was impossible.

It couldn't be him.

The Joker was dead.

Yet there he was, standing no more than five feet away. Gun in hand. Laughing as if he didn't have a care in the world.

It couldn't be real. This couldn't be the Joker. They had DNA tested his ashes. He was gone. Flushed into Gotham River, and there was no way—not even in hell—that Humpty Dumpty could be put back together again.

This had to be an illusion.

Still, Batman lunged for the mirage. He was going to disperse the ghost as one would smoke. He reached for the Joker. The clown laughed again, then fired his gun. The bullet went through Batman's forehead, through his brain and exploded out the back of his head, taking skin, blood, and cartilage with it.

A moment later, while the Joker was still laughing, Batman crumpled to the ground.

Dead.

17

Seven days earlier...

Helicopter blades shattered the silence of the night. Beneath the copter was the Art Deco Gotham Palace Movie Theater, built in the center courtyard of the once thriving Panessa Studios lot, inaugurated December 18, 1936.

Framed photos lined its walls, depicting celebrities, actors, actresses, sports figures, and even famed mobsters. The Gertrude Lawrence film *Rembrandt* was the first movie shown there to the Panessa execs, so of course she flew in from Hollywood. So did Bette Davis and Jean Arthur and Robert Taylor and Henry Fonda and so many other A-listers. Joe Louis, came with Olympic sensation Jesse Owens. Mel Ott, Lou Gehrig and even "Babe" Ruth flew in from New York for its star-studded showing. Everyone who was anyone wanted to see the film before it was released to the general rabble.

That was the Gotham Palace in its heyday. Today it stood shuttered and peeling, its plush chairs smashed and broken, its gold-foiled wallpaper, flown in from Italy, torn and faded.

* * *

James Gordon exited the copter and walked to the front of the theater. The massive glass doors were etched with scenes from Hollywood's greatest movies. There was Rudolph Valentino romancing Vilma Bánky, and Charlie Chaplin's Tramp looking wide-eyed and hungry. Lon Chaney's Phantom seemed to loom over the robot Maria from Fritz Lang's *Metropolis*, but to Gordon the best of them all was King Kong holding a screaming Fay Wray. He must have seen that movie a hundred times when it played three times a day, every day, on TV's *Million Dollar Movie.*

"Impressive." Batman's voice came from behind. Gordon didn't turn, but continued to stare at the etchings, remembering the films from which they came.

"Yeah. They are. I grew up with black-and-white movies on TV. Hell, although all my friends had one, we didn't get a color set until I was ten. I saw all those great movies that way. They don't make 'em like that anymore."

Gordon turned. "You didn't bring me here to wax nostalgic. And the city's going to hell faster than we can put out the flames. So why?"

"Follow me," Batman said as he led Gordon into the theater. They walked behind the candy counter to a blank wall that suddenly slid open as they approached. Outside, the walls were old and cracked. Inside they were polished and bright. Wallpaper became polished steel. Worn and torn carpets had been replaced by spotless tiles. New computers lined the walls, their screens scrolling past one Gotham City location after another. To Gordon it seemed as if nearly every street was being monitored and recorded.

He wasn't sure what to think of it.

"What is this?"

"A means to keep the peace."

Another door slid open, revealing a smaller room. In its center were five cages with clear glass walls, and four of them housed one person each. One sat cross-legged on the floor in the center of his cage, laughing wildly as if watching something hilarious that Gordon was unable to see.

The second cage had a man standing up, smiling broadly, his arms spread wide as if greeting an adoring crowd like a sleazy nightclub host about to introduce his next act. In the third cage a woman was sitting on a bed, looking frightened. In the fourth cage a man sat alone, looking worried but not acting insane.

The fifth cage was empty.

Gordon wasn't sure what he was seeing, but didn't like what he was thinking.

"What the hell is this place? Who are these people?"

Batman stared at the four in the cages.

"Before it killed him, the Joker sent his infected blood out to all the hospitals in the state."

"I know," Gordon said. "We tracked it all down."

"We missed some."

Gordon looked at him quizzically. He could ask Batman if he was certain, but that would be a waste of breath.

"How?" he said.

"Hospital errors. Transfusions that went unrecorded. Five people were affected. Untreated. The blood's gestated too long. It's altering them. They're becoming…"

Batman couldn't bring himself to say the obvious.

Gordon watched the nightclub host, laughing and greeting

his invisible audience. The man's eyes were glowing green. His lips were twisted into a grotesque smile that seemed to grow larger and wilder with each passing moment.

"The Joker? They're becoming the Joker?" Gordon said, not actually believing what he was saying.

"His name's Johnny Charisma, your cliché nightclub barker," Batman said, nodding toward the second containment unit. "What's happening is akin to a form of Creutzfeldt-Jakob disease, but it's mutated beyond anything on medical record."

Johnny Charisma sat on the bed, tapping his feet, laughing as if everything he saw was hysterical.

The man who'd been sitting cross-legged stood up and began pacing his cell, coughing and hacking. His eyes were also glowing green, his mouth beginning to curl in a twisted rigor grin.

"He calls himself Big Al," Batman said. "Full name Albert Christopher Rogers. Shot in an attempted robbery. Was given the Joker's blood during a routine transfusion."

"And what about her?" Gordon asked, pointing to the woman sitting on her bed, alone and frightened. Her eyes were brown, but beginning to show flecks of green.

"Christina Bell. Mother of two. Her husband died three months ago. Stroke."

"And him?" Gordon was looking at the fourth man. Gray hair. About sixty-five. His eyes were clear blue, and he seemed physically fine, though clearly frightened.

"Henry Adams. He's been infected the longest, yet he's symptomless, somehow immune to the Joker's blood. I've got Robin running tests to find out why. One thing's certain, Henry's immunity is the key to all of this."

Adams stood up and walked closer, placing his hands on the glass wall. To Gordon he appeared genuinely afraid, and he had every reason to be.

"Batman, come on," the man said. "Let me go. I've cooperated with you. I've done everything you asked. You said—you *swore*—this would only take a few days. Please. My wife's probably scared out of her mind."

"Henry, I told you—she knows you're fine. My people are making sure she has everything she needs."

"She needs *me*. I need her."

"It'll only be another couple of days, Henry. I promise."

Gordon stared at Adams, then finally turned back to Batman.

"You know what you're doing here, don't you?" he said, trying to remain calm. "You can't hold these people here against their will. Especially him. You said it yourself, he's not affected."

"We're close, Jim," Batman said, his voice soft, filled with concern. "We can't let him go until we save the others."

Gordon turned back to the cages and stared at the empty one.

"Wait. You said five people were infected," he said. "You only have four. There's one missing."

Batman stared at the empty cell and shook his head.

"He'll be here soon, Jim."

Gordon saw Batman's reflection in the glass cage, and for a moment he thought Batman's eyes were green. He looked again and realized there was no way to know what color his eyes were—the lens set into Batman's mask blocked any view.

"I had to do this, Jim. I had no other choice."

As Batman led Gordon out of the room he hit the wall plate by the door and turned the lights off.

The world went black.

18

The present

The black seemed to linger forever before it was shattered with loud bursts that forced his eyes open. He wasn't sure where he was, but he recognized the shape dancing in front of him, gesturing wildly and cackling like the madman he was.

The Joker was still holding the gun with which he'd shot Batman. The source of the bullet that penetrated his skull and emerged from the back of his head. But that was impossible. The Joker was dead. Dead. Batman pinched his arm and ran his fingers across the back of his cowl, searching for the point of exit. There was none. Of course there couldn't be one. He was alive.

Yet the Joker was still standing in front of him, waving his gun, shooting it off like he was playing one of those crazy cowhands in a Wild West show.

"You thought you bought the farm, didn't you?" The Joker said, and he laughed. "Or rather, that I bought it for you. But you're still here, and I guess so am I. But am I really? One of us is dead and the other, well, let's chalk it up to a condition in flux. Not quite dead, but maybe soon to be."

"You're not here," Batman said. "Go away."

"Who's more twisted, old friend? The man who sees mirages, or the man who talks to them expecting an answer? But you look like you *want* to talk. So pull up a chair and let's chat."

The sudden bursts were growing louder. Were they... explosions?

"Hey, I'm talking here, Bats. Eyes on me. So, there's something I always wondered—does that armor you wear breathe, or does it get sweating hot in there? And how the hell do you go to the bathroom? I mean, it's gotta take at least—what?—an hour to peel it off, and another to put it back. By that time the bad guys probably made it all the way to Central City."

They are *explosions.*

Why are there explosions?

"Excuse me. Talking. We're having a conversation. Anyway, I've been wondering. How's your little pal, Robin? Not the dead one I bludgeoned, but the still-currently-alive one who I still need to kill. He feeling good? His head ready for some two-by-four action? By the way, have his parents ever put two and two together, and figured out that he puts on a mask and fights crime at your side? I'm betting they'd be pretty pissed if they knew."

There shouldn't be explosions, unless...

Batman's eyes opened fully. He was standing, and he recognized where he was. This wasn't a movie house. He was in a warehouse. The Ace Chemicals warehouse. He had never left.

Another explosion. Closer this time.

He began to run. The Joker was still standing in front of him but Batman smashed through the illusion and picked up speed when he saw the Batmobile parked in the courtyard beyond, its motor running, waiting patiently for him.

The explosions were louder and coming closer.

Batman remembered pouring the neutralizing chemicals into the vat of fear toxin. If it worked, the toxin would be so diluted as to be minimally effective.

If not...

The Batmobile's sensors detected him coming closer, identified him for who he was. Its hatch slid open and the gears shifted from park to drive. Batman jumped and somersaulted into the driver's seat.

"Go. Fast. Now."

The vehicle roared with power and lurched forward, building up speed with every passing second, still running on autopilot, its AI avoiding collisions. Through the rear-view mirror he saw the explosions closing in behind him.

"Faster!" Taking partial control, he pressed the gas pedal as far down as it would go.

Walls fell behind him, shattered in the explosions that were taking down the warehouse. Debris rained on the Batmobile, obstructing his view, but he pressed on, urging it ahead, trusting in its ability to maneuver. He saw something in front of him and remembered there'd been large doors meant to let in sixteen-wheelers filled with cargo. But the doors were closed now. Scarecrow meant to lock him in and blow up the place around him.

"Armor bullets... six degrees east. Prime and launch. Now!"

His cannons opened fire. Dozens of armor-piercing bullets obliterated the doors that were meant to seal his doom.

Not today.

The car raced through the doors and sped down the ramp. Behind him, one by one, the row of warehouses that had been Ace Chemicals was consumed in a ball of bright blue flames.

He punched his comm and left a message for Gordon to meet him at the G.C.P.D. lockup, then he switched the car back to full auto-pilot, leaned back, closed his eyes, and breathed in deeply. The trip to lockup would take approximately fifteen minutes. The last few hours had been hell.

He could use a few minutes of down time.

He cast his thoughts back to better times, back when his parents were alive, when they'd take him on vacations to Gotham City's Gold Coast resorts. But his mind kept returning to the chalk-white face of the Joker. Instead of hearing the calming calls of seagulls, all he heard was that madman's insane cackling.

What the hell was his nightmare all about? He knew the Joker was dead. DNA analysis proved it was him. His flesh and bones were incinerated. He may have been insane, but he was still human. Flames dealt with him as they would with flash paper.

The cackling stopped, and the Joker's grinning maw disappeared. The rational Batman accepted that the Joker was gone for good. So why the hallucination?

He wanted to avoid the answer, but his analytical nature—that thing he so depended upon—wouldn't let him. Batman's nightmares were the result of being infected by the Joker's damned blood. He was the fifth victim, and the nightmares he was experiencing were the beginning of what might be a rapid mental and physical breakdown.

No matter what he did, he was going to become unstable. The Joker's blood was going to win. He'd suffer delusions from which he couldn't break free. He'd resist as long as he could, but he couldn't fight it forever. There was no antidote for the Joker's blood. It might be a matter of hours, or days, but he would succumb.

Still, Batman hoped, he would maintain control, however tenuous, until after he stopped Scarecrow. Saving the city was all that mattered now.

And when he was done, when it was over, he'd make sure this new Batman–Joker hybrid, or whatever he was supposed to become, would never happen. He would not allow himself to become the madman who destroyed Gotham City.

He activated the comm and hailed Alfred.

"I've been worried about you, sir. I've called repeatedly, but didn't hear back."

"I'm okay now."

"Sir, what about Scarecrow? Or this... Arkham Knight character? They've got tanks and missiles. Their forces are all over the city."

"I'm sorry, Alfred. There have been, umm, complications."

"What is it, sir?" As if sensing a moment of fear in Batman's voice, Alfred responded. *"What's wrong?"*

"There was an explosion. My suit tore. A small tear, but enough to let in some of Scarecrow's toxin. I've been exposed."

"My God, sir. Are you all right? I still remember what happened in Arkham Asylum when Scarecrow—"

"Alfred, it's okay," Batman said, his voice firm. "I had a reaction, but it's over now. And I need you to know I'm not sure how long it will be before—"

Darkness.

Explosions.

In the void a distorted white face. Blood red lips. Oily green hair. Mad, insane laughter.

"You want to know how long it will be before you go mad?" that hideous voice said. "The short answer is, it's already done. You're already there. Welcome to the loony bin."

"You're not here," Batman said. "You're dead."

"You know, I've really got to hand it to Scarecrow. I've never been a fan of his concoctions, but this new batch... it's intoxicating. It brings out the 'me' in you."

"I'm not you. I'll never be you."

"Yet you're talking to me like I'm really here. And in a way I am. You can't leave me behind, or escape me now, because I'm in you. *Inside* you. Kinky, huh? I'm flowing through your veins. Wherever you go, you take me with you. I had you at first blood. You getting my meaning yet?"

"Sir. Master Bruce. Sir. Speak to me." Alfred's voice shook through Batman's thoughts, shattering the visions. *"Sir! Master Bruce! Wake up, Master Bruce. Wake up."*

"Alfred?"

"Yes. And, sir, perhaps it's time to come home."

"I'd like that, but I can't. At least not now. I have to see Gordon at lockup."

"I know I can't change your mind, sir. God knows I've

tried and failed when the stakes were high. But I want you to think of me whenever you see anything out of the ordinary. Think of me. Think of your parents. Think of being normal.

"I'm not sure what that feels like. Never been down that road before."

"You have, sir. You just don't remember it."

"Think of you. Got it. And if I can I will. Thank you, Alfred. For everything."

There was a long pause. Then, finally, Alfred spoke.

"No, sir. Thank you."

Batman hung up and realized that the Batmobile was only a block away from the G.C.P.D. lockup. *Good.* The sooner this ended, the better it would be for everyone.

On the other end of the call, Alfred breathed in deeply, sat down, then did everything he could not to cry.

19

The nightmare hadn't been real.

He hadn't brought Gordon to Panessa, hadn't shown him the prisoners. But when he saw the commissioner standing by the Bat-Signal, waiting for him, he felt a twinge of guilt. But he shrugged it away. To save Gotham City, he needed to know how Scarecrow's toxin worked. Isolate that, and he might develop a cure that would save the millions who had yet to be contaminated.

He might even be able to save part of his own soul.

"Jim," he said as he approached, dreading what was to come.

"When you contacted me I thanked God. The explosion at Ace Chemicals... I knew you were there, but I had no idea if you..." He stopped. Batman was alive, but Gordon had known him long enough to know when something was bothering him. There was something he wanted to say.

"What is it?" he asked. "What's wrong?"

"Barbara," Batman said suddenly. "Barbara's been kidnapped by Scarecrow."

"That's impossible," Gordon insisted, but a flash of dread began to take hold. "She left Gotham City. I spoke to her hours ago, and she told me she was on the bus."

Batman nodded. "I know that's what she told you. It wasn't true."

He could see Gordon trying to sort it out, to figure out what the hell he was talking about. And he knew he had no choice. The floodgates were open. Gordon had to know the truth. All of it.

"I need you to come with me. I'll explain everything once we get there."

"Get there? Get where?" Gordon said, his voice growing louder. "No. No way. I'm not going anywhere until I know where you're taking me."

"Jim, do you trust me?"

Gordon paused before answering. His eyes seemed to grow dark with suspicion.

"I don't know. I used to, but now I'm not so sure."

"Well, you have to trust me. One more time. One last time." Batman opened the door to the roof and headed to the stairs. "The Batmobile's parked in front," he said. After a moment more, Gordon followed.

They drove in awkward silence. They'd been good friends for years, but now Barbara's shadow stood between them.

He'd spoken to her. She said she was on the bus. Why would she lie to him? What was she doing instead of leaving the city?

Why would she stay behind?

Barbara was a librarian. Beautiful as her mother. Intelligent. Alive with energy. But ever since…

Gordon let the thought fade. Barbara had been confined to that wheelchair for years now. What could she be hiding? Why wouldn't she leave when he told her she had to? Gordon stared at Batman. Without knowing why, he had something hateful swelling in his gut.

The Batmobile pulled to a stop. Gordon looked out and knew where they were.

"The Clock Tower building? Why the hell are we stopping here?" The Tower only housed Gotham City's richest. Even on a Commissioner's salary, he couldn't hope to afford its smallest apartment. There's no way that Barbara…

Batman opened the door and started to get out.

"Jim… Commissioner. I know you want answers, and without any more delays. But I have to ask you to wait, if only for another few minutes. I want to make sure the penthouse is… I want to be sure there was nothing left behind." He got out of the car and was about to shut the door behind him, but instead he leaned in close. "Please. Wait here another minute."

He slammed the door and entered the building, leaving Gordon with that growing angry feeling at his core.

He'd been to the Clock Tower a thousand times, but never like this. He opened the door and entered, saw Barbara's overturned wheelchair and gently picked it up. Her files were scattered everywhere. Monitors were shattered. Batman stood absolutely still in the middle of the room, staring ahead.

"Oh, my God. What is this?"

The voice came from behind. Gordon hadn't waited. He stepped out from the freight elevator and entered Oracle's office.

"That's Barbara's wheelchair—she was here," he said. He turned to Batman, still not understand what he was seeing. "Crane did this, to get to me, didn't he? What was she doing here?"

"This isn't your fault, Jim."

"Of course it is. I should have been here. I should have made sure Barbara was on that bus."

"You don't understand, Jim. Barbara's strong. Stronger than you realize."

"What do you mean? She's not like us. Batman, what the hell do you mean? Quit playing your goddam games and tell me."

Fear joined rage in the pit of his stomach. Gordon was standing in the Clock Tower, but he was in another time, as well. He hadn't been in the Clock Tower back then, but he'd seen all the pictures. He knew every second of the terrible massacre.

Barbara was drinking tea. Earl Gray. The doorbell rang. Probably Colleen from across the street. This was their yoga night.

The doorbell rang again.

Barbara went to answer it.

The Joker pushed his way in, flanked by a couple of his goons. He wore a wide-brimmed hat and a blue aloha shirt. A camera hung from a strap around his neck. He was holding a gun.

"Candy-gram," he said, laughing.

Barbara stared at it, at first not quite understanding what she was looking at. But then, before she could register shock or horror, he squeezed the trigger and shot her in the stomach.

Gordon flinched. He was part of Barbara's agony. He grabbed his gut and collapsed as she crumbled to the ground screaming in pain. Unable to help the daughter he so loved, he could only cry.

The Joker stepped over her as she grabbed her bloody wound. Her eyes were wide and afraid. She was fighting unconsciousness. The Joker leaned close to her face and whispered softly to her.

"Don't pass out yet, Barbara. C'mon, show a little spine." He laughed, then moved even closer to her. "Show some spine. You see what I did there? It's a joke because I can see spine, right there through your open wound, and I can see bits and pieces of it strewn all over the floor.

"It's funny because it's true."

The Joker took the camera from around his neck and powered it up.

"By the way, if it isn't too much of an inconvenience, I mean with the shattered spine and all, do you think you can smile for the camera. You know, like you're a good sport and all."

He took the photos. Dozens of photos. Each more

gruesome than the one before. Then he leaned into Barbara, on the floor, barely conscious as the pain overwhelmed her. "Just wait till your father gets home. He is going to be so furious about all this mess.

"Tee-tee-eff-en," he chuckled as he exited.

Barbara had been left behind, unconscious in a pool of her own blood. For a long time the doctors weren't sure she'd survive, but once they realized she was too stubborn to give up, they altered their prognosis. Barbara Gordon would live, but she'd be paralyzed for the rest of her life.

Suddenly Batman was there, in the house where it had all happened.

Barbara was lying unconscious on the floor, face down in her own blood. Batman looked up and saw the Joker grinning, as always, his hands covered with Barbara's blood, scrawling a message on the wall.

This is what happens when you drag your friends into this crazy little game of ours.

He tried to turn away, but couldn't. The Joker tipped his hat, walked past his transfixed nemesis, through the door, and shut it behind him.

Long after he'd gone, Batman could still hear the fiend's demented laugh.

"Batman!"

He looked around the bloody room, but aside from the unconscious form of Barbara Gordon, there was nobody else there.

"BATMAN!"

The voice called to him again. Who was it?

"Wake up, Batman. *Snap out of it.*"

He shook his head, clearing away the illusions. He wasn't standing in Gordon's old apartment. Barbara wasn't lying dead on the ground. But he was standing in the Clock Tower. James Gordon was next to him, shaking him, trying to snap him out of the fever that had taken him again. Gordon's eyes were wide, and angry.

"What the hell is going on here, Batman?" Gordon demanded, a growing fury in his words. "Where is Barbara?"

His thoughts were again under his control.

"There's something I need to show you," Batman said, moving toward a Shakespeare bust that sat on a nearby table. He flipped the head back and a small camera inside it scanned his face.

"*Identity confirmed,*" a mechanical voice said. The Clock Tower's clock face transformed. Lasers created a holographic display that surrounded the two. Batman stared at the display, his thoughts going back in time. Gordon stared, as well, but there was no comprehension in his expression.

"Monitoring equipment?" he said. "All of Gotham City's on that grid map." He looked at one of the displays. "Barbara has been working with you, hasn't she? For how long, Batman? *How long has she been doing this?*"

"Jim, she used to be Batgirl."

Gordon closed his eyes trying to make sense of what he was hearing. When he opened them again, the insanity was still there.

"Batgirl?" he said. "*The* Batgirl? No. That's impossible. Batgirl disappeared years ago. How the hell could she have been…" He stopped as he put together two and two— Batgirl's disappearance coincided with the attack that left Barbara paralyzed.

"No. That would mean she'd been lying to me for years. That you've been lying to me, too. How? Why? Why didn't you tell me?"

"It wasn't my truth to tell, Jim," Batman replied. "That was Barbara's decision. She thought if you knew you'd try to stop her."

"Damn right I would've. My God, I've trained for this. You have, too. But I know Barbara's history. She was a librarian, for God's sake, not a soldier. She never fought anyone, not even in school."

"She believed in your cause, Jim. Our cause. She wanted to be part of it. And she was good. She was very good."

Gordon stared at Batman as if he couldn't believe what he was hearing.

"She was good? That's supposed to explain why the hell she became some kind of goddam vigilante? She was *good*?" For a moment Gordon forced himself to calm down. He looked again at Batman, and gestured around the Oracle room. "And this? How did this all come about? Wait. Wait. Wait. Tell me she was paralyzed. Tell me she wasn't lying about that, too. Because if she was lying, I'll never know if I can believe anything again.

"Please, for once, tell me the truth."

"She was paralyzed, Jim, and still is," Batman said softly. "That wasn't a lie. After the Joker's attack, after she recovered, she was angry. She wanted to prove that even confined to the wheelchair, she couldn't be kept down. She asked me to help set her up. I knew she'd be safe here, in the Clock Tower, off the street.

"Using the cameras spread across the city, she was able to monitor Gotham City and report to me whenever anything was amiss. For the past few years she was Gotham City's guardian angel. And because of her, a lot of crimes were stopped before they got out of hand."

"I… I don't know what to think," Gordon said. "Wait a second—you said Scarecrow kidnapped her. Is that because she was this Oracle? Or Batgirl? Was she kidnapped because of you? This is your fault?

"This is all your fault?"

"Jim, I swear to you I don't know why he took her. But I don't think it's because of who she was. I'm the only one who knew."

"Yeah. Right. Only you. Not her father."

"She's an adult, Jim. And she told me not to say anything. She made her own decisions. I chose to accept them. But you don't have to worry. I'll find her."

"You're telling her father not to worry about his only daughter? Meanwhile, she's been working for you for goddam ever, and you never thought, not once, to tell me. To warn me that my only daughter was risking her life every night I thought she was safe in the library."

He swung at Batman, hitting him hard in the face. But Batman didn't react—just took the punch.

"Goddam it, I thought you were my friend," Gordon said. "How *could* you?"

"I am your friend. But I'm also Barbara's friend…"

"Shut up! *Shut the hell up.* I should never have trusted you." He felt as if he would explode. "I'll find Barbara on my own. I don't want to see you ever again."

Gordon started to leave then turned back.

"Stay out of my way. And when I find her, stay out of Barbara's way, too. Stay away from my family. You and I are done."

Batman was alone in the room. He wanted to go after Gordon and try to justify what he had done, the decisions he had made, but he knew there was nothing he could say that could adequately explain to a father why his daughter was missing.

Instead he tapped his comm and contacted Alfred— told him what happened. Alfred listened and waited for Batman to stop.

"Master Bruce, I sympathize with both of you. But I fear there might not be a way to smooth this over. At least not until Ms. Gordon is found and safely recovered, if that's even possible."

"So what do I do?" He felt uncertainty, and it was an unwelcome thing.

"There's not much you can do, sir," Alfred replied. "Forgiveness will either come in time, or it won't, but whatever the commissioner decides, it's out of your hands now."

"He's one of the best people I've ever known, Alfred," Batman replied. "To disappoint him... it's crushing."

"And for him, as well, I'm sure," Alfred said. "I'm so sorry about this, but the commissioner is a man who believes in truth and justice, and yet he's learned that those he trusted most have betrayed him. Add to that the realization of the fact that the daughter he cherishes has been taken by a madman."

"I have to make things better between us. I can't let this fester."

"That may be what you feel you have to do, but now's not the time. Do your job. Find her. Stop Scarecrow. Save Barbara Gordon. Then whatever will happen will happen."

"Holding back's not going to be easy, Alfred."

"I know, sir. But when has anything worth accomplishing ever been easy?"

20

Alfred was right. He always was right, even when Batman couldn't bring himself to admit it. He needed to push beyond his fight with Gordon and get back to work. The rest would take care of itself.

The Arkham Knight had been here, in the Clock Tower. Batman had seen it on his comm link. The Knight took Barbara, but left her wheelchair behind, as if to prove a point. She was unconscious and even if she wasn't she still couldn't walk, so that had to mean the Knight or one of his men carried Barbara to a waiting vehicle.

"Computers," Batman said. "Show me the security camera feed from the last two hours."

"Which cameras shall I activate?"

"The ones facing the access ramps. Show me the rear cameras on monitor screens one and two, then the sides and front on monitors three through nine. Play everything at once. I'll keep track."

"Accessing."

He was too impatient to sit, so he stood and paced the room, sweeping his eyes back and forth between the monitors. As the footage was revealed everything seemed normal.

"Play it at two times normal speed."

Still nothing out of the ordinary appeared. With the exceptions of residents who lived on the lower floors, comically speeding in and out of the building, there was nothing that surprised him.

At the seven-minute mark the rear camera picked up a shadow. A moment later a small truck pulled into view.

"Computer, play at normal speed."

The rear doors opened and a moment later the Arkham Knight and four gunmen climbed out. Batman watched the Knight laser through the security lock, wave at the camera, then hurry inside. The Knight knew Batman would be going over the video.

Who the hell is he, and how does he know so much?

"Computer, access interior security cameras, same time frame. Focus on the private elevator."

"Accessing."

The holo flickered. He saw the Knight walk into the elevator and glance up at the cameras, knowing exactly where they had been hidden. *How?* He waved again, then leaned against the back wall as the elevator slowly made its way up to the Penthouse suite. The Knight took out his gun and waved it for Batman to see.

"Computer, access penthouse security cameras, same time frame."

The image switched to the interior of Barbara's penthouse. The elevator door opened and the Knight and his men rushed out. Barbara was ready for them—she must have been warned when the elevator was breached. Her tasers took out three of the four mercs, but the Knight's armor protected him and he rammed into her. Unable to fight back, she spilled out of the overturned wheelchair.

The Knight looked up to the cameras—once again he knew exactly where they'd been placed—then stepped back so Batman could watch him taser Barbara into painful submission.

He then hefted Barbara and carried her back to the elevator. Before he got in he turned to the merc who was still standing and gestured. The merc nodded as the elevator door closed behind the Knight.

"Computer, show me the private elevator on monitor one. Show me the exterior of the building on all other monitors. All the same time frame."

"Accessing."

The armored figure carried Barbara to his truck. The camera's position enabled Batman to see what occurred. The Knight placed her in a rear passenger seat, secured her there, then once again waved. A few minutes later his men climbed into the back, three of them still needing the fourth to help them, and closed the door behind them.

The truck took off.

"Computer, tag the truck then feed the information to the city's street surveillance computers. I want to track where it's going."

"Gotham City street surveillance is no longer functioning. System failure occurred. Cannot access information."

"Not functioning? When did that happen?"

"Accessing. Unable to determine exact time of system failure." Yet Batman knew when it had occurred.

"It was when the Knight got into the truck. He wanted

me to see him take Barbara away, but he also wanted to make sure I couldn't follow him."

"Awaiting further instructions."

Batman didn't answer. He stared at the monitor, replaying Barbara's abduction. He saw the truck move off to the corner then turn right, out of sight.

By now he could be most anywhere.

"Awaiting further instructions."

He replayed the scene, again and again. "Computer, tighten the image on monitor six. Zoom to three hundred percent."

"Accessing."

The Knight could be out of the city by now. Batman wished he had demanded that Barbara leave Gotham City when she called to say she was staying.

"Computer, tighten to four hundred percent on quad four."

"Accessing."

"Computer, freeze. Print it out and send me a digital copy."

"Complying. Awaiting further instructions."

He stared at the screen and saw a unique set of tire treads moving off and rounding the corner. The truck was built for hauling heavy equipment and required special reinforced tires for that purpose.

"Computer, scan those tire treads into your database. I'm pretty sure I know what they are, but let's be one hundred percent certain."

"Accessing. Tires are Amertek D60s. Awaiting further instructions."

"I'm on my way to the Batmobile. Upload that data to

its computer and set it to track. The Knight is clever, but he can't stop me from finding Barbara."

"*Complying. Awaiting further instructions.*"

But there was no one to give it any new commands. Batman had already left.

He kept his eyes on the Batmobile's computer screen. The tread pattern was interpreted as a green glyph that moved along the highway. The onboard computers tracked and followed as the Knight's path led south.

He hit his comm and connected to Alfred.

"We have a lead. I'm following it now. I'm going to find her."

"*I know you will, sir. But I was ruminating over your previous conversation concerning Commissioner Gordon, and I wanted to reiterate that, despite what he might have indicated, you are not responsible for her kidnapping.*"

"The Knight is definitely targeting me. He knows everything about me. He knows secrets nobody should know. So how do I skirt the idea that if he's also targeting my friends, it's not because he has some kind of vendetta against me?"

"*We cannot know why he chose to kidnap Ms. Gordon, but it seems just as likely that the source of his vendetta may be her father. He may be intending to punish the commissioner for any number of reasons.*"

"But I'm the one who hunts evils like him and punishes them."

"*No, to many criminals you're an annoyance, a vigilante*"

run amuck, yet operating outside the law as they do. The commissioner symbolizes the law. He's the one with whom they ultimately have to deal. It might be difficult for you to understand, but it's not always about you, sir."

"Maybe so, but that still doesn't help. I may have led my parents to their death. I'm certainly the reason why the Joker paralyzed Barbara. And don't forget Jason."

"Once again, sir, young master Todd was killed by the Joker. Maybe in reaction to you, but he chose his target. You did not. He made the decision to brutalize and kill him."

"Yes, but to get back at me," Batman said. "To punish me. And now the enemy is after Barbara… again."

"Sir, I must remind you that Oracle has many enemies of her own. The underworld knew before this that she existed. They knew she had eyes on them."

"They didn't know who she was."

"True, but secrets have a way of leaking out. As you say, the Knight knows too many of yours. What I'm saying, sir, is that Barbara Gordon chose to become Oracle. She chose her life. And if I remember correctly, sir, you tried to talk her out of it."

"Once Barbara gets her mind set she's impossible to dissuade."

"So similar to you. Nevertheless, you have to consider the possibility that the Knight targeted her because of what she might have done to him. Again, you're not necessarily the center of all universes." Alfred paused, then continued. *"Besides, sir, in the grand scheme of life, you've done far more good for this city than anyone else… with the possible exception of your own father and mother."*

"It's never enough, Alfred," Batman replied, a hot anger beginning to appear at his core. "Crime's gone crazy. I arrest one mastermind and five more pop up to replace him. Hell, I'm looking at the computer scroll and the Knight's soldiers are moving through the city with an armada of tanks that will make short work of anyone who tries to get in their way.

"Watch the news, Alfred. Even the cops are surrendering to him. What good am I doing here? In fact, my presence in Gotham City may be exactly what draws them here."

But Alfred refused to give ground.

"At worst, you're making it very difficult for the miscreants to win. At best, you're showing people that sometimes resistance can work. Bruce Wayne is only a man, sir. But Batman, he's an ideal toward which one strives. You need to—"

Batman shut off the comm.

He didn't want any more lectures, and he didn't want anything to assuage the guilt he felt growing out of control. Guilt that might be exacerbated by the Joker's tainted blood, or Scarecrow's fear toxin. And he didn't want to lash out against Alfred, the one man left who might still be on his side.

So instead of arguing, he settled back in his seat and let the Batmobile follow the tire tracks. Soon, Batman knew, he'd find Barbara and rescue her, and once she was safe he'd confront the Arkham Knight. If the Knight had done anything to hurt Barbara, Batman would make certain that he would never be a threat to anyone else again.

Then, with the Knight gone, he'll find and stop Scarecrow.

I will find them, and they will die, and I won't give a damn about—

Startled by the thought, Batman glanced at the mirror. For a moment it looked as if his eyes were sparkling green. Then he looked again, and they were normal.

Normal.

Good. *Something* about him was normal.

21

The truck had crashed on the highway, about nine miles north of the Gotham Bridge. Its front cabin was smashed in, leaving a tangle of twisted plastic, steel, aluminum, and torn cushions. The front airbags had deployed, but now hung limp from the dashboard, sliced through to remove the driver and passenger.

Batman tore open the rear compartment, but there was nobody back there, either. He checked the tires to make certain this was the correct truck, and it was. He leaned in close and smelled traces of pepper spray. Outside he saw scratch marks and other impressions made in the dirt alongside the road.

After the Joker had attacked and crippled her, Barbara habitually kept a small canister of pepper spray with her at all times. She could no longer fight like Batgirl, but she could still lay low an attacker.

In his mind's eye he replayed the scenario…

Barbara slowly and carefully took out the hidden canister. Perhaps the Arkham Knight had been driving, but the Knight wore a full mask, so there'd be no way to effectively use the spray on him. Yet if Batman's assumption was correct, she'd have sprayed it at the driver in order to disorient him, which meant one of the thugs was driving.

The Knight himself likely took the front passenger seat.

She'd need to check her seat belt, keep it buckled for her plan to work. The others might have been belted, too, but that wouldn't affect her. She probably leaned forward several times, making it seem like an involuntary nervous reaction. In doing so, she'd create a movement that would become commonplace.

When her captors became complacent, she would lean forward again—this time with the canister in her hand. Then when she shot the pepper spray in the driver's face, he would react instinctively. His eyes would burn, and he'd be nearly blind in less than five seconds.

The truck would bank and crash. Barbara, knowing what was going to happen, would brace herself for the crash. If all went as she hoped, the others would be incapacitated.

Immediately afterward, she'd free herself from the belt and pull herself from the back. Being unable to walk, she'd try to crawl to freedom—that would explain the marks he saw.

Unfortunately, there were boot prints in the dirt. The Knight may have been disoriented by the crash, but it had been brief. He'd made it out of the truck, too, and most likely recaptured Barbara as she tried to crawl away.

He scoured the area and found more scratch marks near a medium-sized rock, a few feet further from the truck. He pushed the rock aside and found a small mechanical device—

it was a voice scrambler not unlike the one he had used to disguise his own identity.

Barbara must have grabbed it in the confusion, and hid it as she crawled away, certain that Batman would find it. He'd deliver it to Lucius Fox to scan for fingerprints or DNA residue.

There had to be *some* clue that would lead to the Arkham Knight's identity.

"Well, I'm certainly familiar with the underlying electronics," Lucius Fox said, examining the scrambler's schematics, slowly rotating them on the screen. "*More* than familiar, considering the identical device I put together for you several months ago.

"Without the advancements I've made since then, however, this one's at least a generation behind the times. Still it's… quite impressive. Do you know where your old unit is? If you lost it, that would have given someone the chance to clone it."

"I think you know me better than that, Lucius," Batman said. "If it's so much like yours, though, does it include the same GPS capability?"

"Good thinking, and yes," Fox replied. "The same to your next question, as well—I've already accessed its data files, but they're encrypted. Which means the Knight doesn't want to make this easy. Even so, it shouldn't take long to break through."

"What would I do without you, Lucius?" Batman said.

"Not nearly as well as I'd do without you, Mr. Wayne."

"How are you coming with a cure for Scarecrow's

toxin? We've managed to identify the core elements, but that doesn't tell us how to combat them. I'm definitely experiencing more and more moments where its effects are disturbingly apparent." As he spoke, Lucius Fox seemed to peer at him a bit more intently, as if trying to read something into his words.

"I wish I had better news for you," Fox said, "but I'm nowhere near understanding how the toxin works, let alone finding a way to reverse it. I've contacted several A-list chemical specialists and supplied them with the data, but so far they haven't had any more success than I. Let me assure you, sir, that I'm not giving up."

"I never doubted that, Lucius. But I have to be at the top of my game if I'm going to stand a chance of stopping Scarecrow and the Knight, and discovering what's happened to Barbara."

"You fear that she may already be dead?"

Batman shook his head. "No, but you're asking that for a reason, aren't you?" To his surprise, the CEO looked... pleased.

"You see right through me," Fox replied. "I was hoping that your answer would give me some hints as to how the toxin might be affecting you. Had your reaction been more severe, I'd be much more concerned."

Well, there's no real reason for them to kill her. Not yet, at least. Scarecrow wants me to feel fear—he wants me to fall apart emotionally. Killing Barbara would get a one-time reaction. And it wouldn't be fear, but overwhelming anger. The desire for revenge would trump any other feelings I might experience. So on an intellectual level, I believe she's alive."

"But emotionally?"

"That's a different story. A part of me worries that he's killed her just to prove he can—that he's so insane he'd do anything to get to me, even if it doesn't advance his cause. As with my parents' death, and Jason's murder, and the Joker's attack on Barbara, my greatest fear is that because of me another good person—a person I deeply care about—will also die."

"I have a tough question then," Fox responded, "one you might not want to answer. Is your fear so great you might let yourself die, if you knew your death would save Barbara?"

"Why do you ask? I always put my life on the line, and not only to save people I care about."

"I wasn't speaking in theoretical terms," Fox explained. "I'm asking specifically. Would you put a bullet through your own head, if you were guaranteed that it would save her."

Batman thought about that for a long moment before responding.

"I don't know," he said. "I can't answer that. Does that tell you anything?"

"It does. You didn't answer with a firm no, and that degree of fatalism confirms that you've been affected. But you also didn't say yes, which means the toxin isn't yet controlling you—driving you by pure emotion.

"You're still in charge, Mr. Wayne."

The computer chimed, and Lucius removed a sheath of papers from the printer bin. He gave them to Batman.

"The scrambler's last one hundred GPS destinations," he announced. "I can go back even further, if you want, but this will likely produce the results you want. The data has been uploaded to your computer, as well."

Batman read over the list.

"Miagani Island," he said.

If Gotham City was hell, Miagani festered in its innermost circle.

The roads were all but deserted. Gotham City had become a ghost city—there were shattered facades everywhere. Few businesses had been spared. Any car that remained was a burned-out hulk, as were far too many of the buildings.

The few big chain stores and most of the shops on Jewelry Row employed automatic shutters to prevent late-night looting, and for the most part the high-tech defenses had done the job, but the smaller outfits relied on the last person out to pull down the protective grating. In the rush to escape Gotham City, few had done so.

As the Batmobile sped along, there began to be sporadic resistance. Here and there goons wearing gas masks and armed with big guns thought they'd have some fun shooting at his car. When their bullets ricocheted off its promethium-coated body, more often than not returning the bullets to the sender, the humor of the moment quickly disappeared.

Chaos of this sort was what the Joker had spread during his infamous career. He thrived on insanity, killing hundreds for no reason other than to torment the sane. He'd put into motion one brutal scheme after another, but never showed any overriding goal or objective.

What made it all the more delicious for him was that his enemies kept trying to figure out his endgame, but they never came close. When he died, he left in his wake chaos and unanswerable questions.

For much of their one-on-one combat, Batman believed the Joker fostered his insanity for a reason, even if he couldn't figure out what that reason might be. In the end, however, he was forced to accept that the Joker's madness was impossible to understand.

More than once Batman had wondered, despite all the limitations he'd put on himself, if he should have hunted the Joker down and put a bullet through his head, thereby sparing scores of innocents from becoming victims of his incoherent crimes.

Sanity could be dealt with through reason. True insanity could not.

"Some bugs need to be stepped on, Bats," The Joker laughed, grinning widely and playing with a cat's cradle. "They exist for no other reason."

Batman's eyes burned bright green.

22

"*I've narrowed the signal to Miagani's southernmost tunnels.*" Lucius Fox's voice brought Batman back to the here and now. "*If you want, I can guide you there.*"

Idiot. Batman's first instinct was to snap back. *I was born in Gotham City—it's my city. I know its every twist and turn and tunnel, and I don't need your goddam directions.*

His anger flared hotly. He pulled to the side of the bridge, powered down, and closed his eyes for a few seconds. Lucius Fox was an employee of WayneTech. More than that, he was one of the Dark Knight's closest and most valued allies.

He pulled in a deep breath, opened his eyes, and looked at himself in the mirror. He raised his mask and saw that his eyes were no longer green—had they been? He was himself again, even if he didn't know how long that would last. He didn't know how long he could fight the blood and toxins.

Content, he lowered his mask again. He was good for now.

"Thanks, Lucius," he said, each word carefully controlled and calm. "The tunnels crisscross Miagani in all directions. I've been down there before, and it's easy to get lost. Any guidance would be appreciated."

"*Glad to be of service, then. Tell you what, sir. I'm punching in the tunnel coordinates. Your GPS will guide you to it, but based on what my sensors are reporting, it might be prudent not to drive all the way there. Stealth and caution may be the operative words in this situation.*"

"Sounds good to me," Batman said, struggling against a new wave of anger—it came far too soon after the last. Then it passed and he was calm again.

The remainder of the approach went without incident. *Good,* he mused. *This needs to be done fast, before…*

Just before.

Named for the Native American tribe that originally inhabited the Gotham City area, the Miagani tunnels wove through bedrock, and remained pretty much the same as they'd been since the late 1920s, early 1930s. More recently some had been smoothed over with blacktop paving, allowing for vehicles that came and went to transport illicit goods. Criminals had long made use of the labyrinthine caverns to avoid being found.

Batman drove slowly, headlights off. He checked the GPS coordinates and confirmed that his destination was less than half a mile ahead. He saw a shadow move in the distance, where the tunnel turned right, and decided this was a good place to proceed on foot. He got out of the car and moved quietly ahead.

Soon he found a jeep—one of Scarecrow's thugs leaned back in the driver's seat, closing his eyes to enjoy the luxury of a brief nap. Without a sound Batman made certain his beauty sleep would last a helluva lot longer than he'd intended.

They don't make henchmen the way they used to, he thought, and then he laughed inwardly at his own joke.

He was considering his next move when Fox's voice crackled over the comm.

"Sir," Fox said, *"I'm picking up tanks in the tunnel ahead, maybe three hundred yards from where you are. They're drones."*

"I'm seeing them on my sensors, too, Lucius. But thanks. The fact that he's sending drones is a good sign. He still doesn't necessarily want me dead."

"I'm not quite as certain of that as you are. I think the drones are designed to lure you in further. If no lives are put at risk, Scarecrow—or perhaps it's the Knight—knows you'll keep moving ahead. Once you're too far inside his perimeter to easily get out again, that may be when he deploys his soldiers.

"The fight will become far more dangerous once those tanks have human drivers."

"What are you implying?" Batman snapped.

"The usual, sir," Fox replied calmly. *"I'm suggesting caution."*

Anger. Sweat. Hands balled into fists.

Where does he come off... Does he think he can do this better than I can? That he's smarter than me? I should fire his miserable ass. Show him who's...

"Sir?" Fox said. *"Are you there, sir?"*

He closed his eyes again and thought of the dozens of

times Lucius Fox had saved *his* miserable ass. This wasn't an enemy.

This was an ally.

A friend.

"I'm here, Lucius. I think you might be right, too. But I have to get past the first wave of tanks. They're moving in my direction, and even if I abandon the Batmobile, they'll discover it and know I'm here."

"So, your plan is to survive? I'm good with that."

"How many tanks are you picking up? I'm reading five, but one or two keep blinking in and out. I'm losing the signal down here."

"I'm picking up the same five drones you are."

"Then I'll call you when I'm done. Batman out."

The tanks were large and the Miagani tunnels, many of them built during Prohibition, were narrow, meant for nothing larger than a mining cart.

Returning to the Batmobile, he drove for a short time, then saw a glow in the distance and hit the brakes. Using the front-mounted cameras and magnifying the image, he saw the first line of defense. There was a line of tanks ahead—perhaps twelve of them.

Yet when he checked his sensors, they indicated the way was clear. Were they real, or another hallucination?

"Lucius, are you getting any readings?"

"No, sir. Everything is clear. Why?"

"Because my sensors say the same thing, but I'm looking at nearly a dozen tanks. I'm also seeing crews poring over them, getting them ready. I'm not sure what to think."

"I'd say somehow Scarecrow has found a way to avoid detection."

"This must be the Knight's doing. Scarecrow is a psychologist with a solid understanding of chemistry. But this is high-tech. Sensor manipulation is out of his comfort zone."

"Agreed," Fox replied. "And now you're dealing with human crews?"

"Which means I can't blast them to hell."

"Not unless you want to leave a lot of corpses in your wake."

"Well, I guess we're down to plan B. What did you call it? Stealth and caution?"

"Always a solid approach."

He pulled the Batmobile into a side tunnel and exited.

"Okay. The signal down here is terrible so I'm effectively sensor blind. Keep an eye out for me, and let me know if what I'm seeing is real or not. I'm relying on you, so don't steer me wrong."

"I'll do my best, Mr. Wayne. As I always try. The Knight's GPS indicates that on multiple occasions he visited a location about a half-mile ahead of you. According to the time stamp, it happened not long before Ms. Gordon was taken."

"So it's possible she's there?"

"Not enough information to know for certain, but it's certainly a good place to start."

Batman hugged the tunnel walls, moving slowly and deliberately. The narrow tunnel opened to a large cavern where he saw armored mercenaries climbing into a row of tanks, three-man crews in each one. As the first tank ground forward, he pulled himself back into the shadows and waited in silence until they passed him and left the area.

Several more followed. He waited until he could no longer see the last tank, and then slipped back into the large cavern and continued on. His immediate goal was an exit in the far wall.

"*Sir,*" Lucius's voice came over his ear comm. "*You diluted Scarecrow's chemicals. What sprayed over Gotham City after the Ace Chemicals explosion was relatively harmless. But if you already stopped his plan, what's he doing now?*"

He saw several workers scurrying around the cavern, some fueling waiting vehicles, others fitting them with replacement weapons. He had to get past them and into the next tunnel.

"We had a plan B, Lucius. He probably does, too. Either him or the Arkham Knight." He paused to peer around a corner, then proceeded. "The Knight worries me as much as Crane. We'd never met before this all began, but he seems to know more about me than anyone should. It wouldn't surprise me if he had his contingency plans already set up.

"I know I would."

"*And you still have no idea who he is?*"

Batman peered upward and found light fixtures hanging on chains from the roof. He aimed his grapple and fired. His line snagged a chain, and the winch drew him up. One of the workers turned toward the sudden sound, but Batman swung over the light fixture into the shadows on top. All the worker saw was the bright light.

"I've run through all the usual suspects," he said, "but nobody fits the bill. He knew how my armor was put together. That shouldn't be possible. He knew all its weak spots. Not even Cobblepot or Dent ever figured that out. Somehow he knows how our sensor equipment works, and he did an end run around it.

"He's someone who knows me, and knows me well, but since it's not you, Dick, or Alfred, or God knows, Barbara, I've run out of other options."

About thirty yards ahead, a second light fixture hung from the ceiling. He again fired his grapple and zip-lined over to it. One more jump and he'd be back in the tunnels.

"I'm pleased you ruled us out, sir."

"Me, too, Lucius," he said without intending any irony. "Going silent now. I'll reestablish communication after I get to the control center and access the Knight's GPS. Once I find him, I'll find Barbara."

"Good luck, sir."

23

From the cavern onward, the tunnels were strangely empty. Batman had expected to see more of Scarecrow's goons working on the tanks, preparing them to move into the city, to take over neighborhood after neighborhood. And though the tanks were sitting there, waiting to be put into operation, Scarecrow's workers were nowhere to be seen.

This must be a trap, Batman thought, *so let's spring it.*

The control room was a small area cut off from the main tunnel. It, too, was deserted, and Barbara wasn't there. But the main computer was, and it was already booted up. He fit a zip drive into a USB port, enabling Lucius to tap directly into its files and find the Knight's GPS location, wherever he went.

He checked his scanner and there still were no heat signatures anywhere nearby. Small comfort, though—he hadn't detected the tanks or their crews, and they'd been less than fifty yards away from him.

He searched the room for anything that might indicate the location of a holding cell or personnel quarters, in the hope that Barbara might be there. Batman was certain she was alive. If the Knight had wanted her dead he would have killed her in the Clock Tower, and left her body behind for Gordon and Batman to find.

No, like Scarecrow, the Knight wanted Batman and Gordon to suffer first. To know that they were helpless. This was a power play, pure and simple, and up until now the bad guys had been the ones flexing their muscles.

That was going to change.

"You and Lucius had a good idea, Bruce. What a shame it was never going to work."

Batman spun and found the Arkham Knight rushing toward him. He started to raise his hand in defense, but the attack was too sudden, and the Knight was moving too fast.

He landed a jab to the face. Batman took only a moment to gather his wits and avoid a second hit, but as he leaned down, the Knight slammed him with his elbow to the back of the neck, in the space between where Batman's reinforced cowl stopped and his cape began. He knew exactly where Batman was vulnerable.

His stance revealed that he knew how to box—his left foot was forward and his left arm extended. He held his right arm close to his body. Both arms were up, his fists close to his chin.

The Knight waded in again with an uppercut to the jaw.

"Come on, Batman. Why aren't you fighting back?" His tone was cheerful, taunting. "I always knew I'd be able to kick your ass from here to Sunday, but I expected a little resistance. Don't let me down."

Batman held up an arm to protect his face, and the Knight moved in—just as he'd expected. His rear hand crossed in front of his body and slammed the Knight with a right cross to the face. But at the last moment the Knight turned and Batman's fist grazed his cheek instead.

"Boxing 101, Bruce. Do you so disrespect me that you're treating me like some sort of amateur? I'd be embarrassed if I were you."

"Who the hell are you?" Batman said.

The Knight laughed. "Getting under your skin, aren't I? I know your tech and I know your fighting moves, too. And lest we forget, Bruce, I also know who you are. Not that it's much of a secret now, is it?"

Batman went low, then jabbed his knee into the Knight's gut. His opponent fell back but quickly regained his balance.

"Good try. Of course, I'm fully armored, something you should have always been. But you wanted the common rabble to see part of your face, didn't you? To know that you were human. It's funny, Bruce, part of you wanted to inspire fear in your enemies, but at the same time another part of you wanted to connect with people. I'm sure Crane would love to do a psychological profile."

The Knight moved in quickly, pummeling Batman with a series of hard jabs, only half of which could be deflected.

"With a partially open mask, the good guys might catch you smiling, so they'd know you were on their side. And the bad guys would see you scowl at them, then hear you speak through that ridiculous voice synthesizer. You wanted to sound so dark and growly that they'd be scared of you.

"Well, it might have worked for them, but not for me. I'm not the superstitious, cowardly kind you're used to dealing with. Your words—not mine."

The Knight dove low and drove the heel of his open

palm into Batman's nose, under his mask. He felt bone break and saw blood shoot free.

"That had to hurt. Good."

Batman lunged for him, but the Knight jumped, somersaulting over his head, then came down behind him. He slammed the back of Batman's skull with his foot and sent him sprawling forward.

Then he was on the ground, with the Knight standing over him, holding a gun.

"What do you want, Knight?" Batman asked. "What's this all about?"

"I guess it's all about seeing you suffer. Isn't that reason enough?"

"Bang," he whispered as he squeezed the trigger. The bullet struck Batman in the shoulder, between plates of his suit's armor. "Less than an inch of uncovered space, and I hit the target. I'm as good with a gun as I am with my fists."

Fire shot through Batman's shoulder and he grabbed it. Even through his glove he could feel blood pouring from the wound. The pain was sharp and growing, but he couldn't give in to it.

"Why are you doing this?" he gasped as he staggered to his feet.

"We'll get into the whys and wherefores another time," the Knight replied, putting the gun back in his belt pouch. "Yes, there will be another time. Killing you so soon wouldn't be at all satisfying. Scarecrow and I want you to know we're better than you. That you can't possibly survive against us." Without warning, the Knight waded in again, pummeling Batman's shoulder, keeping his wound open.

Batman felt the arm go limp. He needed a few minutes to regain his strength, so he backed away.

But the Knight followed. He leaped and landed a martial-arts kick to the kidneys. Batman doubled over in pain.

The Knight stepped back, then swung again. Batman raised his arm to deflect the Knight's blow, but the punch got past it, and knocked him to the ground. With an exaggerated sense of the casual, the Knight walked over and smashed him with his boot.

"Oh, we send in the mercenaries and weapons guys with orders to kill, but we know you're better than them. We know they're only sparring partners, getting you ready for the big boss fight."

The Knight stepped back again, and pulled out the gun from his pouch.

"You see," he said, aiming carefully, "we want you to fear that your helplessness will ultimately destroy the city you swore to protect after your parents were senselessly murdered. Yeah, I know about that, too. Does it scare you that I know everything about you, but you don't even know my name?"

He lined up the gun sight, then squeezed the trigger again. This time the gun didn't fire.

"Bang!"

Then he leaned in close and put the gun barrel under Batman's chin, against bare flesh.

"We're better than you, old man. And we're going to keep playing with you and proving your ineffectiveness until we're tired of the game. But we won't kill you then. We'll make you watch as we burn Gotham City to the ground and we kill everyone who ever meant anything to you.

"And then, when you beg us to kill you, too—and you will—we'll bury you on Gotham City Island with only your head showing, and you'll be forced to stare at the remains of what was once Lady Gotham, as you slowly and agonizingly starve to death."

Batman said nothing. He glared at the Knight, waiting for him to finish his speech.

Feel good for now, he thought. *Build yourself up. Your fall will be that much more satisfying.*

The Knight stood up again and started to leave.

"Goodbye, old man. The day of the Gotham City good guys has officially come to an end." He gave a quick bow, and then walked off into the dark.

24

Batman was conscious, but he lay on the cold ground for many minutes, gathering whatever strength he could. He felt his shoulder and realized the bullet had gone completely through it. He pulled off the plating near the gunshot hole and ripped the shirt he wore under it, then tied it tight around the wound. He'd have Leslie Thompkins or one of his other doctors look at it when he had the time, but until then his makeshift tourniquet would have to do.

Finally mustering the strength, he came to his feet.

The Knight said they weren't done, yet he likely wanted Batman to recover. Hubris was the man's major weakness, and one Batman fully intended to exploit.

He staggered through the caverns, retracing the route he'd taken. He passed the jeep where the driver was still unconscious. Reaching into his belt pouch, he removed a small canister filled with ammonium carbonate, popped it open, and waved it under the merc's nose.

Almost immediately the man sputtered awake, opening his eyes to see Batman's face pressed close to his own.

"Where is Scarecrow," Batman said, growling like a wild animal. He kept himself steady, and turned so that his wound was hidden in shadow. The man's eyes widened in fear.

"Scarecrow, he's making some sort of deal with the Penguin," he said. "I don't know what it is, but it's going down right now."

"Now, that wasn't hard, was it?" Batman gave him a quick smile, then jabbed his fist into the man's face. It would be hours before he was conscious again, and when he awoke he'd remember vividly why he was in such pain. It might even convince him to take up another line of work.

Although somehow Batman doubted it.

Reaching the Batmobile, he was pleased to find it untouched. Activating the ignition, he maneuvered out of the tunnels and across the highway. The night was cold, but the familiar surroundings of the vehicle brought back some semblance of confidence.

His gauntlet communicator buzzed, and he saw he was getting a call from Dick Grayson—the first Robin. The two rarely spoke, though Dick had frequently attempted to contact him before finally giving up. Now known as Nightwing, he insisted on choosing his own path—one which led him to take up residence in Blüdhaven. But Batman still saw him as the nine-year-old he had rescued when his parents—like Bruce's own—had been brutally murdered.

Regardless, he would need his allies if he hoped to stop Scarecrow. Robin or Nightwing, Dick was one of the best.

Batman was waiting on the roof of the Gotham City Ferry Terminal when the slim, muscular figure landed in front of him with a somersault that would have earned him a perfect score if he had performed it at the Olympics. Dick Grayson's parents had been renowned circus acrobats known as the Flying Graysons, and Dick had been hailed as an acrobatic boy wonder before he turned eight.

Nightwing gave Batman a wide smile and stuck out his hand.

"Been too long, Bruce," he said. Batman nodded, but kept his hands at his side.

"I heard about Barbara," Nightwing said.

"I'm handling that," Batman replied. "You said something was up with the Penguin?"

Nightwing lowered his hand, and the smile disappeared.

"Yeah," he said, all business now. "It's the reason I asked you to meet me here. Look down there. See those trucks?" He gestured off to one side.

Of all the arrogant, stupid questions… Batman thought, the heat returning. He fought it, and calmed himself. "North Refrigeration trucks," he replied. "So?"

"They belong to the Penguin. He's using them to pick up weapons he's been stockpiling in different secret locations for years now. I'm told there is going to be a war any time now, as all the different gangs vie to replace the Joker. And when the war begins, they say the city will be swimming in blood." He peered at the trucks. "With the weapons, the Penguin's planning to be the last boss standing."

Batman nodded. "Which means we have to find and destroy those weapons before he gets his hands on them."

"Exactly why I came prepared," Nightwing said, holding up a pen-sized device, which he handed to Batman. "This tracker's a prototype, straight out of WayneTech R&D.

The old Fox continues to outdo himself. Using this we can track those trucks wherever they go, then grab the weapon before he does.

"My sources also tell me Penguin's working with someone else," he added, "someone who wants Gotham City turned into a war zone; but they don't know who."

"That's because you idiots aren't paying attention. Do I have to do everything around here?"

The Joker was standing next to them, dressed in the same Hawaiian shirt and wide-brimmed hat he'd worn when he shot Barbara. He held up his hands, and Batman saw there were syringes where his fingers used to be.

"It's Scarecrow, you fool," the fiend cackled. "Scarecrow and the Penguin are working together."

"Batman, are you all right?" Nightwing asked. "*Bruce?*"

Batman shook himself. The Joker was gone.

"Bruce…" Nightwing said again.

"Dick? Right. I'm sorry, so sorry." Contrition fought with anger, but he kept it controlled. "It's been a hellish day, and an even longer night. But I'm okay. I'll be okay. I'll take it from here. I'll follow those trucks. Thanks for the tip."

"Hold on, Bruce," Nightwing replied. "This is my find. I'm coming with."

NO, he thought. *He can't come with me.* Anger gave way to concern this time. *There's no telling when or how the Joker blood will affect me. What if I turn on him?*

What if I kill him?

"I'm sorry, Dick, but my answer's firm," he said, struggling to keep his tone even. "I appreciate the information, but you should go back to Blüdhaven. I'll do this on my own."

* * *

"I know what you're doing," Nightwing argued as he walked to the edge of the building and watched the trucks drive off into the distance. "But I'm not the kid you keep thinking I am. I'm an adult. I'm responsible for myself. And I'm damn good at what I do."

He turned to argue with the man who was his mentor, but Batman was already gone, grappling across the seaport docks, pursuing the speeding trucks.

Nightwing shook his head. "No. Not this time, Bruce."

Batman followed the first truck across the city to an industrial waste park, then perched in a tree outside the gate. The truck pulled up to the gatehouse and the guard waved to the driver as the gate shook and slid open. The truck drove through and circled the storage facility to a small building in back. Four men scrambled out. One opened the rear cargo door while another took a key from his duffle bag and unlocked the building.

Batman was about to grapple in to stop them when Nightwing landed on the branch next to him.

"I told you not to come," Batman said.

Nightwing grinned. "'Not?' You said 'not?' Oh, my gosh, and here I thought you said to come and help. Without the 'not' part. Just come. Oops." Batman growled, but Nightwing continued without giving any sign that he noticed. "Anyway, long as I'm here, shall we play pretend partners again?"

* * *

The Penguin's thugs entered the small structure and found nearly three dozen large wooden crates stacked four high. The thug who had opened the door stared at them, his mouth dropping in surprise.

"That's gotta weigh at least a ton."

"Not a problem, guys." They turned to discover Batman standing by the door.

"We'll be happy to take them off your hands," another voice said. Looking up, they saw another figure, younger, sitting calmly on one of the stacks, his dark costume all but invisible in the murk.

"Batman... and... Robin?"

Nightwing leaped at him. His legs wrapped around the man's torso and he spun, throwing him across the room.

"It's Nightwing, you moron," he protested. "*Nightwing and Batman*. Robin was a little kid. Couldn't have been more than four feet tall. Used to wear stupid green shorts and a bright red vest. Not bad in summer, but sucked in the winter."

The thug's three associates froze, and he started to get up again. Nightwing did a full-body flip and hit him again, then stood over the man.

"Uh-uh," he said. "Stay down this time."

The thug decided to stay put, so Nightwing turned to find Batman efficiently taking out two of the other goons. As the second one hit the ground, Batman put a hand up to one shoulder, then let it drop again.

No jokes. No fun. Just smash and bash. Nightwing grabbed the last thug and slammed him to the floor, knocking the wind out of him.

"You have a choice, pal," he said. "I can beat you up

or I can let him do it." He gestured toward Batman. "But between us boys, he enjoys hurting the bad guys, while to me it's just a job. I don't have to do the beating up part if we can make a deal."

The thug's eyes widened with fear.

Nightwing grinned.

"Good man. All you have to do is tell me where the Penguin is meeting Scarecrow." He pulled the man closer, and gave him a grin. "Will you do that?"

"I don't know," the thug said, sweating profusely. "I swear to God. I'm a driver. The Penguin doesn't tell me anything."

Nightwing turned to Batman. "What do you think? Thumbs up or down?"

Batman pressed close to the thug. "Are you lying to me?" he growled.

"No. God, no." The man had pissed himself. "I'm not. I *couldn't*. You'd kill me if I was. I'm telling you the truth."

Nightwing gave a look that said he didn't believe the man.

"Maybe you should kill him anyway," he said to Batman. "You know, for giggles."

What did you say? Batman thought, his anger spiking. Before he could say anything, however, the man screamed.

"I don't know about Scarecrow," he said, almost incoherent. "I swear. But I know where the next truck is heading. I know where the next cache of guns is. Is that good enough?" He looked from one captor to the other.

"Please?"

* * *

The thug told them everything he knew, which wasn't much. Nightwing pumped his fist as he turned to Batman.

"And that's how you do it Nightwing-style."

"Too much chatter," Batman said as he handcuffed the thugs and sent a message to the G.C.P.D.

25

Jim Gordon read the report and angrily threw it in the trash.

The phone rang.

If that bastard wants to defy the law, let him get shot to hell for all I care. He stared at the trash can while his phone continued to ring. Finally he picked up the call. Then another. Then another.

Trouble in McKean Park.

Gunfire at the Simone Tunnel.

Tanks rolling through Crime Alley.

The Novick Tunnel from Bleake Island to all points north had been bombed and had collapsed. His men—the few who had the balls to stay behind in this madhouse—were hopelessly overwhelmed.

He thought about Barbara, and how much he loved her.

Protecting his daughter was his most important job, and he had failed her for the second time. The report in the trash reminded him of Batman, and the lies he'd been telling Gordon for God knows how long. He could never forgive him for that.

I won't.

More urgent phone calls—situations needing immediate

action. Dixon Dock, stretching from the Southside port, had been set on fire. Explosions ripped through the Gotham County underwater rail tubes, and the tunnels were under four feet of water. The Kane Memorial Bridge had collapsed into the river. Tanks were blasting their way through the city. Eighteen policemen had been killed in the first skirmish.

The report in the wastebasket seemed to glow in the room's fluorescent light, begging his attention.

Tanks were leveling the already crumbling tenements in Old Gotham City. His men were doing their best, but they might as well be fighting a war using peashooters.

He grabbed the wastebasket and shuffled the report back in order. Batman and Nightwing had confronted the Penguin's thugs at the industrial waste site and managed to stop them before they were able to retrieve weapons their boss had hidden there. *Thank God for small victories.* They followed Cobblepot's men to three other sites, and were able to stop them there, too. In each case they retrieved weapons that otherwise would have made it onto the streets.

Gordon's anger grew. Batman had always been a miracle worker, but he could no longer be trusted. That ship had sailed.

Sergeant O'Hara of the Fifth Precinct dropped another set of papers on Gordon's desk then hurried back to join his men on the streets. O'Hara was a good man and a trusted ally. The new report he'd brought revealed that Batman and Nightwing had engaged in a final confrontation with the Penguin and his men. This time they not only secured the weapons cache, but captured the Penguin, too. Better yet,

Cobblepot agreed to talk—but only to Gordon, and only if the police protected him from Scarecrow.

As much as he would have preferred to throw that stuffed turkey out with the rest of the trash, Gordon reluctantly had to agree.

"I'm here, Cobblepot," Gordon said as he entered the interrogation room. "So what have you got for me?" To his relief Batman wasn't there. The Penguin was sitting in an oversized chair, chomping on a huge cigar. Gordon continued to stand.

"Please, Commissioner, I prefer 'the Penguin,'" the disgusting mobster said. "You know, because of my walk. It's not like I have any choice. One leg's three inches shorter than the other. But I got used to the slings and arrows I suffered through early school, and with time I embraced my true nature. It doesn't hurt that my favorite meal is fish."

"Cobblepot, the point."

"Of course, Commissioner. I'd like to level a charge against Batman and Nightwing. Breaking and entering. Assault and battery. They think they can enter a man's home, beat him within an inch of his life, then drag him off to prison without a shred of proof. Is that not injustice? Are you not shocked that such unfairness exists, nay, *thrives* in Gotham City? Now, I'm not a lawyer, but I've tortured enough of them to know something about the law. I don't think Batman's following it."

"I wouldn't doubt that," Gordon said, glancing at his watch. "And I'll be looking into the problem—but we're not here to discuss Batman, are we?"

"Oh, no. Of course not. Ahem! As you know, I see myself as a businessman. My nightclubs, my racing parlors, my massage studios…"

"You mean your drug dens, gambling rooms, and houses of prostitution."

"Neither you nor Batman have ever proven that, have you? When I consider opening a new concern—always legal and aboveboard, I remind you—I write out an extensive business plan and offer stocks to those interested in investing. Until it's confirmed otherwise, I insist you acknowledge that my businesses are strictly legal."

"We know the kinds of businesses you're talking about," Gordon said, "and when you say 'investment,' we hear 'extortion.'"

"Po-tay-to, po-tah-to," the Penguin said. "But I am a businessman. Scarecrow, on the other hand, is an insane nutjob whose mad schemes are hurting my businesses, and badly. I would love to see you take him down. After all, my tax dollars pay your salary."

"Remind me to send a thank-you note," Gordon said as he sat down and tossed several papers to the Penguin. "If you hate him so much, why were you planning to sell him those weapons? And before you deny it, here's the bill of sale. Signed by Crane, and countersigned by you."

The Penguin swatted the papers off the table without looking at them.

"First of all, those weapons were my legal property. My lawyers will forward you our licenses. I'll expect to have them returned before the day is out or before Gotham City implodes, whichever comes first.

"Second, what kind of businessman would I be if I didn't sell him my product, especially when the fool was willing to pay even after an absolutely... reasonable markup? Profit makes for strange bedfellows, you know."

"A lot would depend on whether or not you knew what he was going to do with those weapons," Gordon replied. "If you did, you're Scarecrow's accomplice. And if I can prove it, I promise you will never see the light of day again."

"Easy to say, impossible to prove," the Penguin countered. "But no, I had no idea what he was planning to use my weapons for. Truth is I didn't ask, and he didn't tell me. And since Batman and the brat heisted the weapons before they ever got to Scarecrow, whatever's happening on the streets has nothing to do with me."

The Penguin took another puff from the cigar then crushed the stub into the styrofoam cup sitting on the table.

"Anyway, for my concerns to grow and prosper, I need Gotham City to be relatively at peace. Chaos is not a good atmosphere for business. But, and here's the real reason for this powwow, you might ask the same question of Simon Stagg. I think you'll get a totally different answer."

"Stagg? The industrialist? What does he have to do with Scarecrow?" Simon Stagg was known to walk life's gray area, but as far as Gordon knew, he had never crossed over to the dark side.

"Hell if I know. But I *do* know Scarecrow was going to see Stagg on one of his airships. He's probably there right now. Which, of course, is what I already told Batman, as well."

"How did he react?"

"Exactly as you'd expect. Abrasive. Macho. Threatening.

Big and self-important. But he turned me over to the Nightwing kid and took off like a, if you'll excuse me, bat out of hell. Now, that kid I like. He's got none of Batman's ridiculous angst. He makes me smile.

"So what exactly are you going to book me for?" the Penguin continued. "Weapons legal. *Check.* Bill of sale. *Check.* Taxes paid. *Check.* You'll never Al Capone me. And I believe my indecent exposure charge has now exceeded the statute of limitations. So, if you can't find a charge that will stick longer than it takes to get a personal-sized anchovy pizza delivered here, when can I go? I do have a business to run."

26

Batman glided to the rooftop overlooking Wayne Plaza. Lucius Fox was patiently waiting for him. He was running a few minutes late, but Fox had been following his progress, and dealing with the Arkham Knight's tanks had taken longer than expected.

Fox felt a gust of cold wind wash over him and he buttoned his coat for warmth.

"Pleased to see you made it through the, umm, traffic, Mr. Wayne," Fox said.

"You know how things get in Gotham City during rush hour," Batman said, almost smiling. "You have the new synthesizer?"

Fox handed him a small pen-shaped device. "Complete with Simon Stagg's voice. The man has given quite a few speeches in the past few years, so I was able to cobble together rather a large dictionary. You should be able to say most anything and get a fairly decent Stagg simulation."

"Thanks, Lucius," Batman said, fitting the synthesizer into the side of his mask, an inch from his mouth. "Any idea which airship Stagg is on?"

"Of course. That was the first thing I investigated when

you texted me. I've pre-programmed your GPS to take you to it."

Over the years Stagg Industries spent a small fortune introducing Gotham City to the idea of environmentally safe dirigible travel. In the beginning it had been considered a novelty and a thrill for the very rich, but the idea of traveling the city without having to deal with gridlock made it increasingly popular with businessmen rushing to their appointments. Stagg now had more than seventy ships crisscrossing the sky, and nearly a thousand landing pads, and to date there had not been a single mishap.

Fox reached back into his coat pocket, took out a small plastic case, and opened it to reveal a small computer component.

"I brought a new dongle for your communicator. It's stronger than your previous one, should you be required to go underground again. It will hop onto any location's electrical system and connect through that to the WayneTech system. It also interfaces better with your sensors, so you won't have to scroll through different screens." He gave his employer a mischievous smile. "There's an extremely large commercial possibility for its architecture, as well. I'll expect a very generous Christmas bonus."

"You've more than earned it."

"I couldn't agree with you more, sir."

Batman stood for a moment on the edge of the roof and waited for the wind to pick up again. When it did, he launched himself into the sky, and began to fall, but then his cape unfurled into large bat wings. Hidden struts gave the wings rigidity, allowing him to catch even the most insignificant breeze and use it to propel himself back up.

He loved gliding over the city, because it looked so serene from this high vantage point. The breeze rushing against his face was inviting, invigorating. There was no crime here—there were no enemies, and nobody wanted him dead.

Threading through Gotham City's brick and steel canyons like a hawk on the wing, he felt at peace with himself. The bat was definitely his avatar. Up here it was just him, the night, and nature.

He soared around WayneTech and activated the pumps he had built into its tower. They gave him another boost, which in turn allowed him to coast up toward a pair of identical airships that hung in the air over the skyline. He veered toward the one that had "Stagg-1" airbrushed onto its hull. Once he was in position, he fired his grapple and connected to the dirigible's landing struts. He made his way across the hull and found its emergency entrance door, then activated his new voice synthesizer.

"Open the emergency entrance," he said in Stagg's gravelly voice. This was where Fox's device would either work, or he'd find a dozen armed security thugs waiting to deal with an unwanted trespasser.

A moment later an iris portal spun open. He climbed inside and shut the door behind him.

Lucius would be getting that bonus.

He activated his comm and checked the airship schematics that Fox uploaded to him. Dozens of red dots appeared. His enemies were all over the ship.

"Lucius, I'm inside," he said, "but you can see my problem."

"Indeed—too many sheep and no hint of the shepherd. But not to worry, we have a sample of Simon Stagg's DNA. Despite his reputation, he's actually quite civic-minded. His company sponsored a blood drive after the earthquake and he was the first in line to donate." A pause, then Fox added, *"I'm isolating it now and feeding the results into the sensors. It should pop up on your screen in three... two..."*

"I see a green dot," Batman confirmed. "Thanks, Lucius—your upgrade works perfectly."

"I'll stay at the monitor, sir, in case you need anything else."

He made his way through the first level, easily avoiding Stagg's thugs. No point in alerting the entire force until he had no choice.

Three red dots were moving around in the room ahead. He grabbed his Batarang and somersaulted inside, pitching it at the closest thug. Landing on his feet and spinning, he kicked the next one in the throat, dropping him to his knees. He then dived to where his Batarang fell and spun it into the third thug.

"How long did that take, Lucius?" Batman asked, his voice firm despite the pain he felt where he'd been shot. *Nothing I can't manage.*

"Slightly less than eighteen seconds," Fox replied. *"Not bad, sir, but not nearly a record."*

"And you can do better?" Batman said, damping down irritation.

"We all have our areas of expertise, Mr. Wayne. Given time, I might perfect cold fusion. You excel in, well, more physical activities."

"Can't argue with that. I'd like to, but I've got work to do."

He scooped up the Batarang as he again checked his sensors. The green blip indicated that Simon Stagg was in a room on the deck directly above him. A hallway led alongside the room he was in, and there was a stairway not far away. Two thugs were moving in his direction, and he waited for them to pass. Then he darted out into the hall and sprinted for the stairs.

Reaching the next floor, he quickly located the room in question. The door was locked, so he sprayed explosive gel on the bolt and set it off. There was a sharp *bang*, the door swung open, and Batman saw Simon Stagg…

Inside a small prison cell.

Stagg was relatively short, no more than five foot five, in his mid-fifties, with the squat face of a bulldog and a wild mane of thick silver hair that seemed to fan up at the sides. He looked like he could be a short-order chef at a greasy-spoon diner, but Stagg was in fact a multi-billionaire. And where Bruce Wayne inherited much of his fortune, Stagg's various self-created enterprises supplied him his wealth. It had yet to be determined how legal some of those enterprises were.

But despite his wealth and power, Stagg was now a prisoner on his own ship, locked inside and chained to the bars. The moment Stagg saw him he screamed and pulled frantically at his chains. He slammed his head against the bars and cut open his forehead. Blood poured out.

"You're a monster," he shouted. "Now Scarecrow's sending monsters at me. Leave me alone. I swear to God I won't let you turn me into a monster, too. I'll fight you. I'll fight *all of you*. Keep away from me. *Keep away*." His voice was becoming more hysterical with each sentence.

Stagg's eyes were glazed over. He'd been drugged—most likely poisoned with Scarecrow's fear venom.

"Stagg, I'm here to help you," Batman said, keeping his voice calm and even. "Scarecrow is making you see me as a monster, but I'm not. I'm your friend."

"Nonononono. You *are* a monster. Your face doesn't have flesh. I can see your skull where the skin should be. Your eyes are on fire. You want to burn me with them, but I won't let you." He lowered his voice to sound menacing. "I have soldiers here, you know. With weapons. And they'll put you down like the damned monster you are. They won't stop until you're dead."

There was no easy way to calm him down. Batman needed to try a different tack.

"All right, Simon. You've got me. I am a monster. But Scarecrow turned me into this. Scarecrow hates me like he hates you." He shifted his tone to conspiratorial. "Maybe the two of us can work together, and defeat him before he turns you into a monster, too. What do you say to that, Simon? Do you want to help me defeat Scarecrow?"

Stagg stared, and all at once his fear was replaced by giddy confidence.

"You hate Scarecrow, too?" he said with a gleeful madness. "You want to hurt him for what he did to us?"

"I do, but I need your help," Batman replied. "Tell me

what happened. Why did he put you in this cell? Tell me, and I'll let you out."

Stagg nodded vigorously. "Yes, yes. I'll tell you. He lied to me, you know."

"He lied to me, too, Simon. All he does is lie. But we'll make him pay. Go on."

"We were supposed to work together," Stagg said angrily. "My company *built* the Cloudburst machine. It was going to be used to seed clouds over deserts. To bring rain to areas that needed water." Stagg pushed his face close to the bars and held his hand up, partially covering his mouth. "I was trying to be a good man, a helpful man, but he decided he wanted the Cloudburst for his own reasons. He wanted to buy it from me.

"In the beginning I said yes—after all, what he wanted to do with it sounded like a hoot, but then I changed my mind. I didn't want to sell him my machine. I changed my mind because I'm a good man. Not like him. He's a very bad man."

"Yes, he's a very bad man. What was he going to use it for, Simon?"

Stagg's fingers nervously scratched at his chin, cutting into his skin, but he didn't seem to notice.

"He said he had some kind of gas—I can't remember its name." He balled his hands into fists and started hitting his head with them. "Damn, damn, damn. Why can't I remember? I should know the name of that gas, he bragged about it to me so many times. What is its name? What is its name?"

"Simon," Batman said, trying again to calm him down.

"Stop hitting yourself. That's what he wants you to do, and we're here to fight him."

"Right." Stagg stared at Batman and lowered his hands to his side. "Yes. We can't let him win, can we?"

"No, we can't, Simon. Let me ask you, did he call the gas his fear toxin?"

Stagg leaped for joy. "Yes. Yes, that's it. Fear toxin. He said he wanted to use my machine to disperse it over Gotham City. To make everyone afraid. But I didn't have the full picture until later. That's when I said to him '*no way.*' If anyone was going to turn Gotham City crazy, I told him, it would be me—but I'm all about money, not fear. There wasn't enough profit in it for me. So I told him no."

"And how did he take that?"

"He was *livid.* He sent his soldiers after me and they threw me in here. You know what that bastard said to me? He said he was going to leave me here to die. He's a bad monster, not like you."

"Thank you, Simon," Batman said, convinced that if there'd been more money involved Stagg would have let Gotham City go to hell, the same as Scarecrow. They both deserved whatever happened to them. "Simon, I'm going to stop him. But do you know where he is now? I checked, and he's not on this airship."

"Oh, he wouldn't be. The Cloudburst machine is on *Stagg-2.* That's another of my airships. They're probably tethered together, so it should be floating real close to here. That's where you can find him. He would be there."

Batman started to move out of the room.

"Monster? Where are you going?" Stagg said, his voice rising again. "You said you were going to free me."

Batman turned back to Stagg and smiled. For a moment Stagg's fears seemed to lessen and he smiled back.

"You're right, Simon," Batman answered. "I said I was going to free you. But did you forget? I'm a monster. I lied. Bye, Simon."

He shut the door behind him, but he could still hear Simon Stagg screaming at the top of his lungs.

Good. He deserved it.

Batman made his way to a large circular door marked "Emergency Exit," opened it, and saw *Stagg-2* floating about three hundred yards away. The two ships were tethered together, as Stagg had said. Without hesitation he jumped, and his cape once again unfastened into wings.

He saw a flash of light explode on *Stagg-2*'s undercarriage. Then twin missiles circled the airship and rocketed for him. Stealth ceased to be an option— Scarecrow's men had reported in. They must have been waiting for him to show himself.

Batman tightened his grip on the wing struts and forced them down. He dropped as the missiles flew over him, missing by inches. They made a wide arc and targeted him again.

Wonderful, Batman thought. *Heat seekers.*

As the missiles approached again, he zoomed up and let them pass under him. The missiles arced back almost immediately, learning his moves and adapting to them.

He had no choice. He dove toward *Stagg-2*, luring the missiles along with him. There would be no time to steer out of the way—everything depended on whether or not Scarecrow realized what was about to happen.

He was closing in on the airship, and the missiles were still on his tail.

If Scarecrow didn't act immediately, they would hit him and detonate, so close to *Stagg-2* that the airship would explode, as well.

Batman landed on the airship's hull and grabbed hold. He closed his eyes and waited for the explosion. It was a massive game of chicken, and it looked as if Scarecrow wasn't going to blink.

Until he did.

The missiles veered off at the last moment, rocketing up and away from the ship, only to explode once they could no longer do any damage.

Batman crawled along the skin to the emergency door and used the voice synthesizer. It was only after the door slid open and he scrambled safely inside that he finally let himself exhale.

Even so, they would know he was there.

His sensors revealed a cluster of red dots, all gathered in a small room at the rear of the airship. Using the schematics, he made his way through the hallways until he reached the door. He kicked it in and entered.

Scarecrow's soldiers were standing in the back of the room, weapons at the ready. Scarecrow was closer, with his back to the door, staring at a computer screen. Barbara's face was on it, but as Batman entered, Scarecrow grabbed a bat and shattered the screen.

"Barbara?" Batman said. "Where the hell is she, Crane?"

Scarecrow backed away, behind his soldiers, giving them a clear shot.

"Where you'll never find her." He turned to his soldiers. "I'm afraid my schedule has changed. You boys know what to do."

They raised their weapons to shoot, but Batman became a blur of motion. He dived low and took out the first goon, then, without pausing, leaped to his feet, grabbing the head of the next closest thug and smashing it into the face of another. Both went down fast. A fourth merc—the last—lunged at him. Batman grabbed his wrist, pulled him in tight, and slammed his elbow into the back of the man's head.

His wound twinged, reminding him that he had placed additional armor there to support the shoulder and prevent further damage. So far it was doing its job. He turned back to Scarecrow and spotted a small machine behind him—most likely this was Stagg's Cloudburst device.

"It's over, Crane. Your toxins and your plans. Now tell me where you're holding Barbara Gordon."

"Don't talk to him, Bats. Beat him up until he's nothing more than pummeled meat. That is the best way of tenderizing tough cuts, you know."

The voice came from behind him. He didn't have to turn to know who it was.

27

The Joker was standing there, again dressed in his wide-brimmed hat and aloha shirt. His fists were covered with boxing gloves and he stabbed at the air as if sparring with an enemy.

"Don't talk him to death, Bats. Beat him to death. Smash in his face. Cut open his chest. Remove his heart, show it to him, then squeeze it until the blood runs dry. C'mon, pal. It's all you and me now."

"Get away from me," Batman shouted. "You're not real. You're a lie."

"And you're not? Only one of us wears a mask, pal. And it's not the guy with the chalk-white face. With me, what you see is what you get."

Batman whirled and grabbed at the Joker, but he was already gone.

"I'm here," the voice said from behind. He reached out again, but Joker had already moved. "You need glasses, Bats? I'm right here."

The Joker was standing in front of him again, arms spread wide, fingers splayed. Batman jumped at him.

"You're dead. Your ashes were flushed into the river. You can't ever come back again. You're *dead*."

Then he stopped.

The Joker's blood was making him madder than he should be. It was trying to take control of him. He needed to fight back, but he wasn't sure how.

"You're right, Bats. I *am* dead. A figment of your hopes and dreams and failures. And judging from your reactions, you've got a load of them. But Scarecrow's not a fever dream. He's real. I may have crippled the Gordon bitch, but he's the one who's having his way with her now."

"Shut up, the Joker," Batman muttered. "Shut the hell up."

"I can't. I'm nothing but a sick blemish on your head, which means you're the one who's actually doing all the talking. You're the little meat puppet, mouthing the angry words. But he, he should be your target—not me. And you should kill him the way Gordon killed me."

"So what are you waiting for, Batman? Kill him."

"I don't kill."

"Yeah, keep telling yourself that. But we know better. Your greedy demands killed your parents. I hope that movie was worth it. You got popcorn and jelly beans and all it cost you was Daddy and Mom."

Batman thrust a fist at the Joker, but the clown evaporated at his touch then appeared again behind him.

"C'mon, pal. You're not an idiot. You know I'm not really here, so you're wasting all that energy when you should be using it to kill him. C'mon over to my side, old friend. You'll see how much fun it is."

It was the Joker's blood talking, and Scarecrow's toxin was only making it worse. Batman was unable to shut out the voices shouting in his head. If there was only one way to stop him from talking, Batman had to take it.

He turned against Scarecrow and hit him.

It felt good.

He hit him again.

"Tell me where Barbara is and I'll stop. For God's sake, Scarecrow, tell me." But Scarecrow didn't answer, so Batman hit him again.

He slammed his fist into Scarecrow's face, kicked Scarecrow's legs and heard his knee bones snap and shatter. Suddenly, Scarecrow seemed to be in tears, begging for Batman to stop, but he didn't.

The Joker laughed and leaned into the figure, bloody and beaten.

"Relax, Crane. The fun's just starting," the Joker said.

Batman punched Scarecrow again.

"Relax, Crane. The fun's just starting," Batman said.

"If only you knew how liberating this is," the Joker said.

"If only you knew how liberating this is," Batman repeated.

"Look at me, Crane. I'm amazing. And this body… you wouldn't believe how strong I am. Though I suppose you're getting a good idea, aren't you?"

"Look at me, Crane," Batman said. "I'm amazing. And this body… you wouldn't believe how strong I am. Though I suppose you're getting a good idea, aren't you?"

"What's wrong, Crane?" The Joker cackled. "Are you scared I'm going to kill you? Well, news flash… I am."

"What's wrong, Crane?" Batman echoed. "Are you scared I'm going to kill you?

"Well, news flash. I… I…"

Batman fell back, staring at the broken, bloody figure of Jonathan Crane, lying in a pool of his own blood, gasping for breath. Pleading for life.

"I—I can't… I can't… I won't…" he said, and he stared at his own hands. Something was wrong—they weren't bloodied. He looked to the floor. There was no blood anywhere. He looked around him.

Scarecrow was gone.

What the hell is going on?

He felt a sudden pain to the back of his head, gasped in surprise, and fell to his knees.

Scarecrow was behind him, a steel rod in his hand, and he hit Batman with it again and again until Batman could barely see him, let alone think.

"Let me help you, Batman," Scarecrow said. "You're afraid of dying, aren't you? But you're not dying—even if you wish you were. My toxin is filling your lungs, drowning you in your greatest fears." He raised the steel bar over his head and slammed it down again.

The bar hammered Batman's face, smashing him back to the ground, but he refused to scream. Scarecrow stood over him, placing his foot on his opponent's throat.

"What can you see?" he demanded. "A city engulfed in fear? Your life betrayed by those you trust the most? Your darkest secrets revealed? *What can you see?*"

The Joker leaned in close to Batman and laughed.

"He doesn't know it, but he's talking about your parents' deaths. That's still our little secret. Oh, and your next greatest fear, turning into me. Well, sorry to tell you this, but that ship has sailed. You're already ninety percent there."

"*NO!*" Batman shouted. "I'm not you. I'll never be you."

"Who are you shouting at, Batman?" Scarecrow asked. "What fears are you experiencing that are agitating you so? Actually, it doesn't matter if I know—not as long as you do. So as I tear your mind apart, Gotham City will watch. And when everything is ready, I will cut that mask from your face and the whole world will see the fear in your eyes. Then they, too, will understand what I've always known. You're not their savior. There is no savior."

"And there will never be a savior."

He brought the rod down again on Batman's face and this time Batman was unable to stifle his pain. He screamed, and Scarecrow hit him again.

"Now we're making progress, Batman. Pain releases fear. And fear makes you mine."

"Kill him, Bats," the Joker shouted. A second Joker appeared behind him. "You can't let him kill you. That's my job. Kill the 'Crow." A third Joker joined the chorus, then a fourth. "KILL THE 'CROW!"

Suddenly, Batman felt he was gripping metal. There was a gun in his hand.

"I've provided the weapon," the Joker said gleefully. The rest is up to you. *Kill him!*"

"No," Batman said. "Murder is the last act of desperation. I don't kill. I don't kill."

"Yes, you will," the Joker said. "Because it's the only way you'll get what you want. And you want to find the girl. Squeeze that trigger, and I'll make sure you do."

"This gun isn't real. None of this is real."

"If it's imaginary, then why do you care if you shoot him

with it? This is only a test anyway. I want to see what it takes to make the kettle boil over."

"No!"

"Come on, Bats. Finish him," the Jokers shouted. "Do it. Do what you know you want to do."

Four Jokers surrounded him, and all of them were shouting the same thing.

"Kill him.

"You want to find Barbara Gordon?

"KILL HIM!"

Batman's finger tightened on the trigger.

"No. I won't."

"Oh, for God's sake. Will you look at him? He's no better than the creep who killed your parents. You need to do something. You need to stop him."

"No."

"Then girl Gordon dies."

"No," he said again, his finger squeezing the trigger. He saw his reflection in a steel strut. His eyes were burning bright green.

"Do it," the Jokers ordered. "He deserves to die as I deserved to die. So kill him and make everything right again. Kill him and you'll know where he's hiding Barbara Gordon. *Kill him and the world will make sense again!*"

"No," Batman said again, but his voice cracked and his will disappeared. He turned the gun to Scarecrow. "I won't. I won't," he kept saying.

"KILL HIM!"

Batman squeezed the trigger, and the gun fired.

"Well, about frickin' time," the Joker laughed.

* * *

Then Batman woke up, drenched in sweat and fear.

The Joker wasn't there, urging him to violate everything he had ever believed. He looked at his hands. He wasn't holding a weapon. There had never been a gun. He hadn't killed Scarecrow. It was another Joker-blood-induced nightmare.

But he had *wanted* to kill his enemy. He knew that, even if it was only in a dream, he did squeeze the trigger. And he knew his fear was very real—he was all too capable of killing.

He was no better than the villains he battled.

Batman looked at the steel strut again, and saw his face reflected. He thought his eyes were still glowing green, but he couldn't be certain.

Scarecrow was there, holding Stagg's device, watching Batman like a lab rat. Then he started to move. He backed away.

"Something's changed inside you, Batman," he said. "There's something different. Imperceptibly different, but still different. Your fever dream... What did you see in it? Tell me."

Batman was still weak, but he wasn't going to let Scarecrow take advantage.

"You're trapped, Crane. There's nowhere to run."

Scarecrow smiled then stepped to the back of the room—the rear of the airship. A ring of explosions detonated immediately in front of him, separating the front section of the airship from the rear.

* * *

Batman watched helplessly as the compartment disappeared into the sky. He struggled to where the separation had occurred, then saw that the rear compartment was attached by cable to a twin-engine helicopter, carrying it away from the dirigible.

Scarecrow had his toxin-dispersal machine. Batman felt another fear growing inside him—greater than all the others. Scarecrow was going to win this fight, and nothing could be done to stop him.

Even if it was a fever dream, the moment he killed Scarecrow, Batman lost the war.

28

The copter and the airship section disappeared into a cloudbank that hung low over the Gotham City islands. Sometimes it seemed as if the city was always covered by clouds that blanketed it in a perpetual sense of hopeless gloom. But it also provided many areas for the police to reflect the Bat-Signal, alerting him to any impending crises.

Given Gordon's anger, there was no telling how long the signal would be allowed to stay.

Gordon… Barbara? That screen shot of Barbara.

Batman turned and saw the computer Scarecrow had used. Crane had destroyed its monitor but its hard drive could still be accessed. He used a USB cord to connect it to his gauntlet, and downloaded the computer's contents. All of the data it contained might prove useful, but his primary focus was that picture of Barbara.

His gauntlet holo revealed a series of images. Batman quickly swiped through them. He found the one of Barbara, and realized he knew where she was being held. She was in one of the cells in Scarecrow's Chinatown penthouse—the same makeshift prison Ivy had been in before Batman freed her.

* * *

He landed on the Chinatown roof. Without hesitation he pushed through the door, then made his way inside. No one was there to slow him down, and the room where Ivy had been was still empty. Batman checked his sensors and saw a single heat dot thirteen feet south of his location.

In the next room.

This door was locked. He sprayed it with explosive gel and set off a small, controlled explosion. The door swung open to reveal Barbara sitting, slumped over in a chair, unmoving. A table was next to her, with a pitcher of water sitting on it. Behind the pitcher he could see a gun.

There was a bank of blank monitors on the opposing wall, but otherwise the room was empty. Barbara was also in a cell, but unlike Ivy's prison, this didn't have steel bars to keep her inside—it had been constructed as a large transparent box. There were a few air holes drilled into it to keep her alive, but otherwise there was no way in or out. Even its seams were fused together.

Batman walked around the glass, tapping the window but getting no response from the lifeless figure. The Joker was suddenly walking beside him, also tapping the glass while humming a tune from Leoncavallo's *Pagliacci*.

"What? We hurry all the way here, and Crane's already killed her?" The fiend shook his head. "That really sucks. The man's got no sense of occasion."

Batman scanned the room, looking for some sign of Scarecrow.

"Crane, I know you're watching this," he said. "You don't

have to do this. You have me. Leave her alone."

The bank of monitors behind the cell suddenly flickered with life. Scarecrow's face filled all the screens.

"Oooh, Batman, do you see the twisty needle-finger man?" the Joker mocked. "I am soooo scared."

"That is enough, clown," Scarecrow said. *"Fear is theatrics, so permit me the indulgence of putting on this show."*

How can he see the Joker? Batman wondered. The barrier between reality and illusion was becoming more fragile with every passing moment. Yet he had no choice but to allow it to play out.

The Joker bowed in fake acquiescence. "Maybe I got Bag-Face wrong. Go on with the show. I'm waiting. But make it good."

Suddenly, Batman heard the hiss of gas and saw Scarecrow's toxin flood into the chamber from a vent in the floor. Then Barbara's eyes opened—she'd been unconscious, not dead.

"Wh-what's happening?" she asked. Her voice cracked, and she was almost unable to speak.

"Barbara!" Batman yelled to her, but she couldn't hear him. Her eyes widened, and Batman knew what she was seeing. Like the patrons in Pauli's Diner, she wasn't staring at other human beings, but at demons—or in this case, a single demon. It was more than her toxin-controlled mind could take, and she screamed.

Scarecrow's voice came over Batman's comm, but he was talking directly to Barbara.

"Do you see the horror behind the glass?" he said. *"The monster that will be your doom? You know he wants to use*

those claws to tear you apart.

"He wants to feast on your blood and viscera, and watch you die. But worst of all, he wants to turn you into another monster. Another creature of the damned. You're not going to let that happen, are you?"

Batman called to her, desperate to get her attention.

"Barbara, don't listen to him. It's me."

But she still couldn't hear him.

"No!" she shouted. "You won't kill me. I won't let you. Scarecrow, please don't let him…"

"You have a way out, Barbara," Crane said. *"You know what to do, so do it."*

Batman saw Barbara reach for the gun behind the pitcher of water. She held it up, waving it at him.

"Get away from me."

"Don't," he said. "Barbara, don't do it."

"It's too late, Batman," Scarecrow responded with murderous glee. *"You bring death to everyone you love."*

"Crane's right, Bats," the Joker said. "You *are* a real downer."

"Barbara," Batman said frantically, "I'll leave the room. I won't come back. Put the gun away. Please, for God's sake, don't use it. I promise I'll leave you alone."

"I don't believe you," Barbara said as she put the barrel of the gun under her chin.

She squeezed the trigger, and fired.

Batman stared as she fell to the floor, dead, then dropped to his knees and cried. He had failed Barbara Gordon… again.

"Now that was truly cold, Batman," the Joker said, sitting

on the chair Barbara had occupied only moments before. He held up his index finger to his temple. "Pow! Wham! So very cold. Not even I ever went that far."

A second Joker walked back and forth in the cell behind the first one.

"Now, if only you hadn't broken in here the way you did, all monster-like and growly angry, she might be alive right now. But no. You had to prove your major-league macho-osity, didn't you?"

A third Joker appeared, leaning over the body, smearing his finger with Barbara's blood then using it like ink to write on the walls.

"I've got the perfect epitaph for her tombstone. 'RIP Barbara Gordon. How many times did Batman let her down? In how many ways did he destroy her?'" He turned to Batman and laughed. "You know, if I actually gave a damn about her, I'd be crying real tears right about now."

The first Joker walked to the transparent wall and leaned against it, blowing hot breath to form a layer of fog on its surface. His finger drew a happy face in the haze.

"But the good news is, my death—and now maybe hers—has emboldened the common Gotham City gutter rats. They're *all* embracing their crazy." He walked through the transparent barrier. "It's enough to make me proud."

Batman lurched at the Joker, but the hallucination faded even as his hands closed around his neck.

"More nightmares. Nothing but nightmares," he muttered to himself. He stood up straight, looked again into the cell and saw that it was empty. Nothing, not even that single chair, had ever been there.

Barbara might, in fact, be dead, but Batman was willing to bet his life on the slim hope that Scarecrow wasn't yet done with her. If he wanted Batman to suffer, there would be more.

He made his way back to the Batmobile, collapsed in the front seat, and called Alfred. His shoulder throbbed.

"Sir, did you find her? Ms. Gordon?"

"Crane's playing games with me. He made me see Barbara. She was locked in a cell. I watched as she killed herself. But after… Alfred, she wasn't there. She was never there."

"So she might still be alive, sir?"

"I don't know. It's gotten to the point where I'm not sure if anything I see is real, or another of his damned hallucinations."

"I am so sorry, sir. I wish to God I could be there with you now."

"Me too, Alfred. I need to look at a friendly face. Staring into nothing but hell… it's corrupting. And the Joker's blood mixed with Scarecrow's toxin only makes worse everything I see and do. But if she's gone, I now know it wasn't because of anything she or her father did. If she's truly dead, she was killed because of me."

"You can't assume she's gone, sir. There'd be no reason to kill her, sir. Dead, she's useless to him. But alive he can continue to use her… and perhaps control you."

"Hey, Bats, you know you look like twelve kinds of crap." Batman turned to see the Joker sitting next to him, strumming a ukulele.

"Maybe if you went away and gave the asylum over to the lunatics, there'd be nothing left to tax you. You could lie on a beach in Hawaii, order a few mai tais, and soak up the sun. And tell you what. I'll even give you the shirt off my back," the Joker said. "It's soiled with a few bloodstains and such, but after a while you forget all about them."

Batman closed his eyes and shut out the noise. When he opened them again, the Joker was gone.

"Sir? Sir? Are you there?" Alfred was calling to him.

"I… I am," he said. "I am."

"The people of Gotham City need you."

"For what? To fail them as I've failed everyone else I care about?"

"Sir, you're not sounding like yourself, so you've got to listen to me. You need to focus."

"On what? The villains? You know how many there are out there right now, all dedicated to murdering everyone they can? Or maybe Scarecrow's scheme. Or the Joker's, or… Do you get it, Alfred? I fear for the first time since I put on this mask that I'm simply overwhelmed. There's too much to do and no time to get any of it done."

"That's where you're wrong, sir. You've always said you focus on one thing at a time. Get that done, then move onto the next, then the next after that. So for now you need to find Scarecrow's Cloudburst machine. It's only a matter of time before he finds a way to trigger it. So perhaps we should put Ms. Gordon's fate aside and put our minds to solving only that."

The Joker patted Batman on the shoulder.

"Wondering if you can live with yourself, eh? Well, imagine how Daddy Gordon must feel. First he sees me shoot his little girl, crippling her. Now they'll make an internet sensation out of her. He'll see the video of you frightening the living hell out of her, until she blows her brains out. You know, maybe I should send him a few wallet-sized pics of that, too. For giggles and grins."

"Master Bruce," Alfred said, unwittingly interrupting the Joker's monologue. *"Ms. Gordon may very well be alive. So if you want to save her you've got to start... now."*

"Your butler's a dolt, pal. You can't bring her back. Tell you what, let Uncle J. take charge. I'll make everything wonderful all over again."

"Sir? Do you hear me? Please, sir. Talk to me."

"Alfred?"

"Thank God," Alfred breathed. *"You're all right, aren't you?"*

"No. But you're right. As usual. My first mission is to find the Cloudburst machine. Try to hone in on its particular field. It's worth a shot if there's any chance we can find it."

"And what will you be doing in the meantime?"

"I'm assuming the worst, Alfred. Let's say the machine does as advertised, and the city drowns in his fear toxin. I need to find a way to immunize the people against it."

"I see where you're going, sir, but I question whether or not she can be reasoned with. After your long and troubled road together, will she help you?"

"She doesn't have a choice," Batman said. "The only person who can help us save Gotham City is Poison Ivy. And come hell or high water, I'll find a way to make her do just that."

29

The G.C.P.D. officers guarding the main jail were down to a token force, and no one was ready to argue with Batman when he came to release Pamela Isley, also known as prisoner #40732. Gail Moench, the poor desk sergeant on duty, was more than happy to get rid of her one and only charge.

Moench's only thought now was how to get the hell out of Dodge.

Batman drove Ivy to the botanical gardens. The last time she had been there the plants were lush, thick, and thriving, a living canopy of colors that covered and protected the greenhouse. But now the greenhouse was patched over with growing brown spots. Ivy's glorious roses were gone. So were her hydrangeas, lilies, and lavenders. Her spice garden had been viciously uprooted and sage, rosemary, mints, thyme, and more lay torn in the dirt.

Her children were dead or dying, and Ivy was in tears.

"He did this, the meatbag!" she wailed. "Didn't he?"

"You have to help stop him, Ivy," Batman said. "Or this will just be the beginning. He'll make sure every plant in this city will die."

She turned to the trees. Some of them were still trying to cling to life. She heard her favorite eucalyptus call to her and beg for her warm touch. She held the dogwoods and oaks, and they seemed to tremble with delight.

"Can you still do it, Ivy?" he said, urgency in his voice. "Create the antidote?"

She was on the ground, petting the roots of a frail magnolia. She glanced up at him, tears in eyes that flashed with anger and hate.

"I can, and I will. These are the oldest plants in Gotham City. They'll tell me what we need to do."

She held onto the magnolia root and leaned in to kiss it. "Look at her," Ivy said. "She's been here since before man walked this land. Even weak as she is, she still holds great power."

"She'll help you then?"

"She wants to, but she's been poisoned by decades of pollution. She won't be able to fight Scarecrow's toxin— not on her own." Batman saw the roots tremble. Ivy held it tighter but it still shivered in her hands. "You don't get it, do you?" she snapped. "There aren't any left like her. Not anymore."

"What happened?"

"What do you think, Batman? You cut them back. You built over them, you stopped them from reaching the sun."

"If I can locate her deepest roots, would that revive them?"

Ivy laughed. Batman was smart, for a human, but compared to nature he was such a fool.

"They're lost. Buried beneath this concrete monstrosity.

There is no way."

"I'll find one," Batman said as his gauntlet buzzed.

Alfred's face appeared a moment later. "Good, I was about to call," Batman said. "This might sound strange, but it's urgent. Ask Lucius to pull together as many Wayne Construction personnel as he can, have them dig up the concrete surrounding Ivy's botanical gardens. And they need to be careful."

"Is there a reason for this, or are you trying to cause more of a mess than already exists out there?"

"Over the last century we've covered over ancient roots," Batman explained. "We've got to expose them again, and help Ivy revive them. They may be our final line of defense against Scarecrow's toxin."

"Very good, sir. I'll get right on it. But I called you for a reason. Henry Adams, your detainee at Panessa, says he needs to speak with you."

Batman nodded. "Somehow he's immune to toxins, and now Ivy's trying to find an antidote. One might be able to help the other. Patch him through, Alfred."

Adams' face appeared in the holo. He was visibly frightened, and his words gushed out of him almost too fast for Batman to make sense.

"The film studio was attacked," he said desperately. *"There's soldiers everywhere, and they answer to the Joker's girl. What's her name? Holly? Hayley? Helen?"*

"Harley," Batman said. "Harley Quinn."

"Yes. Yes. That's it. Harley Quinn. She was here. She is here. With the Joker's madmen. They broke into our cells

and they let out all the others. They're still infected, Batman. They'll infect others, too."

Batman started to reply but suddenly heard a gurgle of surprise and Adams fell from view. A moment later Harley Quinn's grinning face peeked into the camera. She was splattered with red. Before she could speak, Harley looked off to the side as she rubbed the red from her cheeks.

"Now, boys, pull back the camera," she said mockingly. *"I want the big, bad bat to see the whole scene."* She turned back to Batman and grinned. *"It'll be worth it, I promise you. This'll be the opening scene of my brand-new movie,* Harley Quinn Sends Batman to Hell. *Written by me, directed by me. Starring me. And you.*

"And Mr. Adams here. You see him?"

The camera pulled back to reveal Henry Adams, slumped awkwardly on his chair. Harley leaned in again and showed off her baseball bat, its barrel and end cap covered with blood.

"Well, look who's too late to save the day... again. He squooshed up real good, didn't he?"

Batman lost control, and shouted at her. "You sick, demented—"

"Now, now, watch your language, Batman," she said, cutting him off. *"Kids may be watching this later. I'm so gonna put it on the new social-media site for sociopaths, wannabes, and of course their victims, too. My Puddin' came up with the whole idea while he was waiting to be oven roasted, and I promise you, Bats, it's gonna be bigger than all the others put together."*

The camera jerked up and Batman saw Harley sitting on

Adams' chest, legs crossed, using her finger to draw smileys on his face with his own blood.

"Anyway," she said, *"I wanted to get a clip showing your reaction to your latest loss, and your look of shock and horror didn't disappoint. So catch you later, procrastinator, and remember, feel free to add your own videos, whenever you want."*

"I'm going to find you, Harley," he gritted. "And this time you won't get free."

"Oh, come on. You know better than that. The Puddin' and me, nothing holds us for long. Not even being deep-fried. By the way, I looked around this little prison of yours and I saw you're growing a whole new generation of Jokers for yourself. But they're mine now. I do like me my fresh puddin'."

"You can't let them go free, Harley," he said, striving to keep his voice steady. "They're not stable."

Harley Quinn laughed. *"They're not stable? Oh, Bat-brains, have you taken a long look in the mirror yourself? I think you'll be in for a big surprise. Anyway, this is Harley Quinn, over and—"*

The holo went black and retracted into Batman's glove. If she was to be believed, the night was about to get even worse. He turned back to Ivy as she held the vines close to her, petting them tenderly. Somehow they were responding to her touch.

"That fleshpot tried to exterminate my family," she said. "He'll pay for this, Batman. I swear to the great Mother that he will pay."

30

Robin was leaning against a wall when the Batmobile pulled up to Panessa Studios. Tim Drake was the hero now wearing the Robin mask and uniform, and he'd been Batman's partner for a couple of years.

His predecessor was Jason Todd. Batman first encountered him when he was little more than a penny-ante thief, then brought him into Bruce Wayne's home for rehabilitation. It seemed to work, but Jason rebelled whenever Batman gave him direct orders. His unwillingness to follow the rules led to his abduction.

The crowbar swung down, smashing apart flesh and bone. The Joker had killed Jason Todd, and Batman promised himself that there would be no more partners. He wasn't going to put anyone else's life on the line. For more than a year Batman kept to his promise, but then a teen named Tim Drake forced his way into Wayne Manor. Having seen footage of Dick Grayson from his Haly's Circus days, then footage of Batman and Robin in action, he had figured out that Dick Grayson had been Robin.

That meant Bruce Wayne was Batman. He was armed with evidence Bruce couldn't dismiss. A *teenager* had figured out who he was, when Gotham City's greatest criminal minds had failed.

Drake spent a year investigating Dick Grayson and his guardian, Bruce Wayne. He read all the news reports that said Wayne's parents had been murdered when he was nine. During his investigations, the first Robin struck out on his own as Nightwing.

Nobody knew for certain if the Joker had actually killed the second Robin. The Joker had said he would if the citizens of Gotham City voted for the boy's death. But Batman knew the vote was a charade. However it went, the clown planned to kill Jason anyway.

In the end, however, the public never saw the actual killing. Their attention turned to the next scandal or hoax. Nobody saw that crowbar swing down again and again, ending a young boy's life. Only Batman knew Jason Todd was dead—the Joker filmed the act as grotesque proof of what he had done. Only Batman realized there was nobody else who would mourn his passing. He kept that awful pain to himself.

After Robin's murder, Batman's behavior became increasingly erratic. He seemed angrier and—if possible—more vicious than before. Tim realized how dangerous the situation had become. Batman needed to control his emotions, and not let them control him. He needed someone who could root him in the real world.

He needed a new Robin.

A new, young conscience.

And Tim was determined it would be him.

It took almost a year for Batman to accept Tim's presence, but the boy's persistence paid off. He became the new Robin and his job was more than to help protect the city. He had to protect Batman's sanity, as well.

Robin arrived at Panessa only moments ahead of his partner. When Batman arrived, Robin glanced at his wrist as if he was checking his watch, and gave an overly dramatic yawn.

"You stop for a burger?" he asked. "I've been waiting, like, forever."

"Or at least two minutes," Batman said, smiling. "That was you I saw swing over as I pulled up, wasn't it?"

"Well, it felt like hours," Robin replied. "Anyway, I read the data. We're looking for the folks the Joker infected, right?"

"Four innocent people were mistakenly given a transfusion of his blood," Batman said. "It's slowly turning them into him."

"That's not good."

"You ready?"

"I got my *bō* staff. How much more do I need?" Without waiting for a reply, he turned and darted into the studio lot.

Batman heard someone approaching from behind, and turned. The Joker was standing there, dressed in a purple jumpsuit, holding a rusty crowbar in his right hand, impatiently tapping it into his left palm.

"You may as well get lost, Joker. I know you're not real."

"Says the man who is talking to himself. Remember this crowbar, Batman? It's still smudged with blood. Jason Todd's blood. But I wonder how much of Tim's blood I'd have to spill to cover it over?"

"You're not real," Batman repeated. "I'm not listening to you," he said, charging into the studio behind Tim.

But he knew he was.

Nearly a dozen thugs with rifles were stationed in the first building, in a small room that made their weapons difficult to use without accidentally killing one of their own. Batman and Robin took advantage of the close quarters, moving quickly and making certain they were always surrounded by the unwilling human shields.

Robin dived under the legs of the closest merc and used his *bō* to jab up quickly and painfully, taking him down while the guy yelped uncontrollably.

This guy's gonna be disappointing women for the rest of his life, Robin thought, chuckling to himself. Sliding past, he kicked him into another merc, startling both of them long enough for Batman to grab the man's weapon and smash it across his face.

Batman held onto what was left of the rifle and began using it as a fighting stick. He brought it down hard and fast, snapping the kneecap of the other merc, dropping him to the floor. Then he took out a merc who, at six foot seven, towered over him. Robin grabbed yet another thug by his collar and forced him to the floor. He leaped over his head, and then slammed his *bō* into the back of the merc's neck, leaving him unconscious.

* * *

The Joker walked casually through the crowd, still slapping his open palm with the blood-covered crowbar.

"Things didn't go well for Robin number two, did they?" he taunted. "Gosh, them surely were the good ol' days. You remember 'em, Bats?"

Suddenly they were there—the last place on Earth Batman wanted to be, that long-abandoned wing of Arkham Asylum. Through the airducts Batman could hear the moans of suffering inmates pleading to be free, knowing full well they would never be.

Jason Todd was there. He had no idea he would soon be dead.

Panessa Studios. Another soldier leaped on Batman's back and shoved his pistol to the back of his head. Scarecrow's reward money was as good as his.

But then Batman fell back, smashing the merc into the wall behind him, loosening his grip. He pried himself free, spun, slammed him with an uppercut to his gut, and let the man drop.

Three mercs charged toward the two heroes. Batman laced his fingers and Robin launched himself into the air, landing on the interlocked hands as Batman hefted him over the three assailants. Robin twisted in mid-air, and slammed all three with his feet. As he landed, he used his *bō* to knock the closest merc's legs out from under him, then he smashed his elbow into the man's face.

* * *

That horrible pit deep in the bowels of Arkham Asylum. Inside, two giant men who looked strong enough to take down an elephant. But there was fear on their faces. They were scared of the third man who walked out of the dark. Small. Slim. Long, thin face marked with a wide, twisted mouth. His skin was pink, but it didn't look real.

Panessa Studios. There were only four mercs left and they were afraid. Batman and Robin had taken down most of them without raising much of a sweat.

One of the mercs decided the hell with it. He was going to kill those two even if it meant shooting his own men. He shoved a new clip into the gun and let loose, firing the entire magazine. Batman dove and the bullets speared over his head and into one of the other opponents.

Now there were only three.

Arkham. The man with the long face and the false pink flesh. The pink-faced man held a gun on Jason while the big men grabbed and beat him. Face. Stomach. Again. Again.

All the while the Joker laughed at a joke nobody else could understand. The men parted and the Joker walked closer to the boy, playing with the crowbar in his hand. He paused before Jason and smiled tenderly to him.

"Showtime," he said.

The Joker smashed the crowbar down on Jason's head,

splitting it open. Then he swung it again, this time to his neck. Then again to his face, the back of his head. Batman still watching, helpless to fight a mirage. He couldn't stop them. He wasn't there, but he witnessed every moment of Jason's murder.

Every.

Damned.

Second.

Panessa Studios. The merc wasn't giving up. He fired again, this time at closer range. Four bullets hit into Batman's chest and imbedded themselves in his reinforced armor. He stopped for a moment as if he expected Batman to drop, but instead Batman stood and jumped at him.

The fear on his face said it all. *The rumors were right. The Bat is some kind of demon.*

Still holding his gun, he backed away, waving it in front of him. While he concentrated on Batman, Robin cartwheeled in behind him and pushed him forward. Batman slammed him with a roundhouse to the man's stomach, and he fell gasping for air.

There were only two mercs standing now. Batman held out his hand, palms up.

"You don't really want to fight, do you? You honestly don't believe you can beat us. So here's the deal. If you're still here at the count of three, you won't be leaving here standing up.

"One…

"Two…"

The last two mercs bolted from the room.

The hell with Scarecrow.

Arkham Asylum. Jason was left to die on the floor. He didn't see the Joker's men leave the hellish pit. He didn't see the Joker himself hoist the crowbar over his shoulder, then saunter out of the room. He didn't see anything.

Except for the dynamite on the floor.

Timer set to go off.

He reached for the locked door knowing he couldn't even crawl there, let alone open it in time.

Then the bombs stopped ticking.

As he died he heard the Joker's laugh fade into the distance.

And then there was only silence.

Forever.

Panessa Studios. Tim Drake was close, but now he had to leave, to get out of there before the Joker did to him what he had done to Jason.

Everyone Batman knew. Everyone he cared about. All they did was die on his watch.

His watch.

31

A television monitor blinked on, and a grinning face filled the screen. The banner underneath identified him as Johnny Charisma, one of the victims who had been infected with the Joker's blood.

The camera pulled back, revealing that he was standing on a game show stage. He was grinning the largest grin possible, happier than anyone had any right to be.

He was at home on the stage—born for entertaining and making people laugh, and his green eyes sparkled with joy.

"*Batman,*" he said in his best sing-song voice. "*If you're still playing our game, I've got good news for you. You've made it to the bonus round.*" An electronic audience applauded and cheered. "*So c'mon down, Bats, because the best is yet to come. But we do have rules, and that means your little pal Robin can't come with you.*

"*Sorry, kid. State gambling laws. Adults only.*"

"Batman, don't do it," Robin said, pleading. "It's a trap."

"Of course it is," Batman replied. "It's *always* a trap. I'm still going in. But first…" He leaned close to Robin and whispered in his ear. He gave Tim a quick smile, and then headed to the next room for whatever insanity was waiting for him.

He opened the door and stepped inside. Everything was black. He held his hand out in front of him and couldn't see his fingers. Johnny Charisma's voice echoed in the dark.

"Welcome to the room of crappy memories. Other game shows are designed to make you smile. Ours makes you so miserable you'll want to kill yourself. Good times."

Suddenly, a spotlight bursts into life, drenching him in light. The rest of the room is still dark, but something lurks there. Another spotlight ignites, and lights up another figure.

He's living each moment as it's happening. All together. All at the same time. Bruce Wayne at eight years old, in a theater, watching that damned movie again. At the end, his parents want to go out the front door, to their waiting limo, but Bruce convinces them to go out the back.

To the man with the gun.

It isn't quite the way it happened, but it's the way he remembers it. It has to be in his head, he realizes. Neither the Joker nor Scarecrow knows his innermost secrets, so it can't be their doing.

Another spotlight shows him as a ten-year-old. Alfred is teaching him how to study, and how to fight. Then he falls into that old well which he thought had been covered over. A million bats claw their way past him.

He's an adult in the Himalayas, being taught how to kill. Then he's a young Batman, fighting crime alongside the first Robin. Dick Grayson is a boy, and then he is a young man. He wants to quit college but Batman won't let him.

Dick throws a ball of crunched-up red and yellow clothing into the incinerator and leaves.

Robin isn't coming back.

At least not this Robin.

Another spotlight, and he's in a large room, looking at the back of a huge clock in the window.

Not again…

He sees Jim Gordon sitting on the couch, reading a newspaper. Barbara Gordon gets up to answer the doorbell. Her joy turns to horror as lead shatters bone and she falls to the floor, never able to walk again.

There's another Robin now. That Robin dies. His death is not pretty. Another spotlight highlights the Batman from a few minutes earlier. Entering a room that contains a large glass box. Inside the box is a crippled woman. She has a gun under her chin and it's pointed up. She squeezes the trigger, and her head explodes in a shower of gore.

Batman turns from the hallucinations.

"Those aren't real, Crane. Nothing I've seen here is real. But this promise is. I will not let you hurt anyone ever again. And nobody will die because of me."

"Oh, Batman, you loony tune, you are so wrong," Johnny Charisma says. The fact is, everyone here is going to go boom in exactly three minutes, unless you comply with everything I tell you."

A new spotlight reveals a game-show soundstage. Johnny Charisma is there.

"Batman, come on down," Charisma says, laughing. "I have a song to sing to you, but not as me. It'll be the me I'm about to be." The Joker blood continues coursing through him, burning hot in his veins, and Johnny Charisma disappears. In his place the Joker is standing in front of a microphone, wearing his show-biz best, its glitter nearly blinding.

"Ladies and gentlemen, boys and girls," the Joker says. "I've got a sweet ditty I've been saving just for you. So sit back and relax while I entertain you with a little song I call 'The Asylum Blues.'" He nods offstage to an unseen orchestra and the music begins. He waits for his cue, and then he starts the song.

> *"Take me on home to the asylum.*
> *Never alone in the asylum.*
> *Anarchy ruled, it was wild.*
> *But through it all, you never smiled.*
> *Joke's on you, I'm in your head so*
> *Look who's laughing now!"*

He sweeps across the stage to a coat rack that wasn't there a moment before, then takes it in his arms, dancing with it like he's Fred Astaire. Batman tries to reach for him, but is unable to move.

> *"Remember in Arkham City,*
> *I killed your girl, so pretty.*
> *That was the night you let me die.*
> *But when I looked you in the eye,*
> *That's when I knew we'd be together.*
> *Look who's laughing now!"*

The Joker releases the coat rack and it twirls to the back

of the stage where it falls into the dark, then disappears. He ignores the clatter as if it hasn't happened and continues his song.

> *"I'm stuck in your head and I'm laughing!*
> *I filled you with dread and I can't stop laughing!*
> *Your parents are dead and I can't stop laughing!*
> *What else can I do?*
> *Now I'm part of you."*

A gun appears in his hand. He laughs hysterically as he shoots twice, aiming offstage. A moment later two stagehands stagger in, bullet holes through their heads, and they fall face down on the stage. A pearl necklace falls to the floor, the pearls scattering in all directions.

Batman stares, but can only stand and watch—he still cannot react. There's more electronic applause and cheers for their realistic death scene. Then the Joker is Johnny Charisma again.

"Bravo," he exalts. "Bravo.

> *"I am the Clown Prince o' Crime*
> *And we've had a hell of a time.*
> *You're part of me, I'm part of you,*
> *And now there's nothing left to do.*
> *I just can't wait till I'm in control.*
> *Who'll be laughing then?"*

Harley Quinn dances onstage, dressed in a beautiful red and black gown. She daintily puts out her hand, which

Charisma—no, he's the Joker again—takes as he leads her in their dance. Her pirouettes are perfect, until she trips over her long, ruffled train. She falls and doesn't get up. The Joker dances around her until the two dead stagehands rush on stage and drag her away. Before she disappears behind the curtain, she gives a smile and a wave to the audience.

"The other blood crazies and I will be back soon," she cries. "So don't you go away. There's plenty of fun ahead.

"Back to you, Puddin'."

The Joker turns back to his audience of one, appearing morose, then brightens and continues his song.

"I drove you round the bend and I'm laughing.
I'm with you till the end and I can't stop laughing.
I killed all your friends and I can't stop laughing.
What else can I do?
Now I'm part of you."

The spotlights go dark, plunging the room into blackness. Then a single beam of light illuminates a small part of the stage. The Joker steps out of the dark and into the beam, then pours out his heart as he sings the final chorus.

"Think I can taste your fear
Now that my time is near.
I'm in your blood, I'm so alive,
I only wish you'd let me drive."

The music ends and the Joker falls to his knees. Electronic

applause and cheers go on forever, repeating as if on a loop.

"Thank you," the Joker says in his best Elvis, as congratulatory flowers are tossed to the stage. "Thank you very much. The Joker now blows up the building."

Batman stands watching, still unable to move as the Joker leaves the stage. He's going to get away, and nothing can stop him.

32

Hiding offstage, Robin heard Johnny Charisma begin singing.

"Take me on home to the asylum. Never alone in the asylum." He had said the studio would "go boom" in three minutes—which meant he'd planted bombs, and was going to detonate them, presumably after he completed his song.

That left two minutes forty-seven seconds to carry out Batman's whispered orders. He activated his comm. Instantly Lucius Fox was on the other end.

"We've got a lunatic who's wired the place with explosives," Robin said, keeping his voice low. "We need to locate them before he can set them off. Any ideas?"

"Do you still have the GPS chips I gave you last week?" Fox asked.

"To tag the bad guys so we can follow them later? Of course," Robin whispered.

"Excellent. Switch one on. I'll perform remote adjustments that should enable it to track the radio signal that triggers the explosives." Robin did as instructed, and within moments the global positioning system registered a hit.

"I've got the coordinates, Lucius. On the move now."

* * *

On stage, Charisma was still singing.

> *"Remember in Arkham City,*
> *I killed your girl, so pretty."*

Less than half a minute later Robin located the first device, and uploaded its picture to Fox.

"Any special instructions, Lucius?"

"None—this device shouldn't present any surprises. We've trained with this sort of explosives at least a dozen times. You'll do fine."

Shouldn't…? Robin thought. "Thanks for the vote of confidence. Of course, if it explodes, you're miles away."

"Then I strongly suggest that you don't let it explode."

"Now why didn't I think of that?" Robin replied as he removed a portion of the mechanism. "Like you said, no surprises—this one's defused. Going to look for number two now."

Under the spotlight, Charisma started his next chorus.

> *"I'm stuck in your head and I'm laughing!*
> *I filled you with dread and I can't stop laughing!"*

"You have two minutes nineteen seconds, and the GPS shows three more bombs to deal with. Better get a move on."

Like I didn't know that, Robin thought irritably as he

Raced through the darkness to his next target. The shadows that kept him hidden also made it difficult to find his way, no matter how well his eyes adjusted.

"Found the second bomb, Lucius. This one looks a bit different. Uploading a photo now."

"Got it. Ahhh. Not to worry. This comes from a different manufacturer, but it's essentially the same model. Follow the same procedure as before."

"Thanks." He opened the casing and quickly found the chip. "It's done. Down to one minute fifty-one seconds. Honing in on the third bomb now." Rounding a corner, he pulled open the door of a closet. "Found it. Damn. I think this one's *very* different. Let me know."

There was a pause as Fox studied the downloaded photo.

"Good call, Tim. It's got a completely different architecture. You remember what the radio chip looked like in the other two bombs? Well, if you remove the same one here, you'll find another directly under it. Remove that one without letting it touch the connections that led to the first chip—that would be bad. Then immediately refit the first one. And do it fast. Understand?"

"Yeah. Think so."

"Don't think. Do."

"Thanks, sensei. Got the first chip off. Removing the second."

"Hurry."

"You're not helping. Okay, got the first one back in place. This is all digital, so there's no ticking bomb to hear. You picking up anything?"

"I think you succeeded," Fox replied. *"Good work, Tim."*

* * *

Harley Quinn, dressed in a ball gown, danced onto the stage. Charisma started dancing with her like it's *Ballroom with the Celebrities*. But he didn't stop singing...

> *"I am the Clown Prince o' Crime.*
> *And we've had a hell of a time."*

Robin was off and running. Moments later he located the fourth device. This one was identical to the first, and he removed the radio chip by pure reflex.

"One bomb to go."

Checking his sensor, he saw that the final device was across the stage. He had twenty-two seconds to find and disable it.

Damn...

Charisma was almost done with the song.

> *"Think I can taste your fear*
> *Now that my time is near."*

Then he was thanking his audience, and moved to leave the stage.

Time was running out, and this one was unlike the others.

Seven seconds to go. Not enough time for Lucius to

explain what he had to do, and still leave time to do it. He had to make his own choices.

Five seconds.

There were three chips stacked atop each other. One had to be removed, but most likely the others needed to stay in place. But which was which?

Three seconds. The lower two chips were shiny, as if untouched. They'd been placed in position by machine. He could see part of a fingerprint on the top chip. That one was added later on.

He breathed in, held his breath…

One second.

…and removed the top chip.

Zero.

No explosion. He'd chosen right.

There was no time to celebrate. He ran past the immobile Batman, still standing under the spotlight, and saw Johnny Charisma outside the stage door, running toward the street. He was moving at a pretty good clip, but not nearly fast enough.

Robin caught up with him and tackled him to the ground, then cuffed his hands with plastic ties and dragged him to his feet.

"This is for your own good, Johnny," Robin said. "If we can cure you, you'll thank us later." Charisma just laughed. *Might as well explain physics to a gopher*, Robin thought.

He returned to the soundstage. Batman was still standing under the spotlight.

"Batman, I've diffused the bombs. I've got the Joker or Charisma or whatever he's calling himself now. We have to find Harley and the others who've been infected with the Joker's blood."

Batman looked dazed, unsure of where he was.

"Why?" he asked. "Wouldn't they all be gone by now?"

His hesitation was unnerving. Robin activated his comm and talked to Fox.

"Something's wrong with Batman, Lucius," Tim said. "And Harley said the others infected by the Joker blood are still in the theater."

"This is Harley Quinn you're talking about, Tim," Fox reminded him. *"I'm not certain she'd recognize the truth if she fell into a vat of it."*

"Normally I'd agree, but I think she was telling the truth. This time at least—she didn't have any reason to lie, and every reason to get us here. But Batman's acting as if he didn't hear her. Look, I don't know if it's Scarecrow's fear toxin or what, but I think he'll only slow me down when we need to move fast. Any ideas?"

"Whatever happened to him, beneath it all he's still the same man. If we want him to cooperate, we have to present a logical argument." Fox paused, then added, *"At least it needs to be logical to him."*

"Got it," Robin said, watching his partner intently. "And I've got an idea. Just hope it works."

"Harley Quinn is still somewhere in this studio," Robin said to Batman, and he pointed to the sensors. "I have an idea to rout her out. You okay with that?"

"Okay," Batman nodded, barely listening. "I'm okay. A little tired, but okay. You're Tim, right? Not Jason.

"Jason's dead."

Robin frowned, then made himself smile.

"You're right. I am Tim. I'm Robin. Your only Robin now. So listen, you said you're tired, right? So I think you should rest a few more minutes. While you do I'll find Harley and I'll lead her to you. You're the trap we're going to spring. Are you okay with that?"

Batman's thoughts began to clear, and with that came realization.

Robin thought of him as a hindrance. But it was true— he was tired. Too tired to go after Harley Quinn and stop her. Whatever Tim was trying to do, he could use the time. And Tim's approach made sense.

"I'm okay," he said. "I'm good with that. Where should I wait?" As he spoke, Robin lifted a grating embedded in the floor, exposing an underground passageway.

"Right here," he said. "You'll be able to follow her wherever she runs and she won't even know you're there. So we've got a plan?"

"We do." He moved to enter the tunnel, then stopped. "And, Robin…"

Tim Drake paused, looking uncertain.

"What is it, Batman?"

"Take care of yourself. You're important to me. And I care deeply for you."

Robin smiled. "You're important to me, too, Batman. And right now, you're the most important man in all of Gotham City. We'll fix the city. You and I.

"See you in a few."

33

Robin locked Johnny Charisma in one of the booths on soundstage 37.

"Hey!" Charisma shouted. "C'mon, kid. You know you wanna hear another song. I got a thousand of 'em, each better'n the one before."

Robin left without responding.

He thought about his next move. Henry Adams had been viciously clubbed by Harley and was probably dead. That left two others—Al Rogers and Christina Bell. Robin hoped they could still be saved.

There was the mysterious final victim, whoever he or she might be. Batman had never revealed the identity of the person. Robin had never seen him, but if Harley had taken three prisoners, there was no telling how many still survived.

He found Rogers hiding in the theater wing. He must have watched the Johnny Charisma show from this box high above the stage. He tried to resist, but Robin calmly sprayed him with sleep gas. Rogers was a victim, not a criminal. Unless there was no alternative, Tim wasn't going to hurt him.

He found Christina Bell hunkered in the Panessa

commissary, sitting on the floor behind a counter, leaning against its massive triple-sized ovens. In its heyday this commissary had fed hundreds of employees, actors, and studio bosses. But those days were long gone. The gas line into the studio had been shut down more than a decade earlier, and now its ovens and refrigerators were little more than slabs of rusted metal.

When Robin found her, Christina was using a plastic knife she'd picked up from a counter and was busy trying to cut into her own wrist. He found slice marks up and down her arm, most of them bleeding, but fortunately she hadn't yet penetrated a vein. To protect her, he tied her wrists together behind her back, then locked her in a cell down the hall from Rogers. He didn't know if they could cure her from the Joker's blood infection, but at least she wouldn't be causing herself any more harm.

So now he just had to find Harley Quinn.

For many years Harleen Quinzel was a psychiatrist at Arkham Asylum, considered by most to be the best on their staff. Extraordinarily empathetic, she strived to fully understand her troubled charges by imagining herself in their place. She spoke their language, and her patients very quickly came to trust her.

But she was then assigned to find a cure for the Joker's madness, and her life changed forever.

His particular brand of insanity wormed into her mind, and then her heart. His love for violence became her own. She'd spent a lifetime trying to help those people who had been hurt, some time in their past. The Joker convinced her it was far more fun to hurt them even more.

Harleen Quinzel disappeared, and in her place there was Harley Quinn, a clown, a jester, a harlequin, and above all, a remorseless murderer. If her mentor was deemed irrevocably insane, she wasn't all that far behind him.

Harley held onto the bloody baseball bat Batman had seen her use on Henry Adams, gripping it tightly with both hands when she heard Robin enter the studio's power room. She knelt behind one of the massive generators that had been used by film productions so many years ago.

Everything went silent, which meant Robin was standing inside the doorway, probably trying to figure out where she was hiding. *This way, boy,* she wanted to say, but the Joker always told her it was best to hide in silence. *Don't give them any warning before you bludgeon them to death.* Harley liked that word, "bludgeon."

It sounded so messy.

She heard footsteps coming her way, and tightened her grip again. *The stupid brat won't know what hit him.*

But then the footsteps stopped. She waited for them to start up again, but they didn't.

What are you waiting for, boy? I got a bat, you got a head. It's time they said hello to each other.

Silence.

What do I do? What do I do? He had to be only a few feet away. She could jump out and start smashing everything in sight, and if she was lucky she would take him out. Of course, it might also give him a chance to fight back, but a good bat to the face had a way of stopping most people. *Certainly a brat like Robin.*

Hell, Harley laughed silently. *He isn't even the first Robin. He's, like, the third. How good could he possibly be?*

Harley leaned out, but couldn't see past the generator casing. If she leaned out any further he'd spot her. So she backed up again and waited—held the bat over her head, ready to bring it down hard if the brat saw her.

No movement.

No shadows.

Nothing.

This isn't fair! She was beginning to sweat. *You gotta be there. So let me kill you and get on with it. I mean, everyone gets to kill a Robin eventually. And today it's my turn.* She held her breath and waited some more. *Maybe he left the room? Maybe he thought I wasn't here. Maybe I'm hiding for no reason. My bad if that's true.*

Harley craned her neck but still didn't see him.

He left. I've been hiding and he isn't even here anymore. Gosh, I'm almost happy my Puddin' is ashes. If he saw this he'd take the bat to me.

She was nervous and her hands shook, but she eased her way out from behind the generator, ready to spring and kill the kid fast as she could.

But he wasn't there.

She stepped out of hiding, relieved, and lowered her hands—they were covered with sweat. She put down the bat and rubbed the sweat on her leggings.

Then she saw his shadow, on the ground covering her

own, growing larger. He was above her and coming down fast. He'd crouched on the generator, waiting for her to move, and he jumped the moment she rested.

She grabbed the bat again and swung it without thinking. It hit Robin under the chin and sent him flying back. She thought about using it to smash in his face, just for frightening her, but if he regained his footing she'd be no match for him in hand-to-hand fighting.

So she ran.

Robin cursed himself and followed. He'd thought he had her, and allowed himself to get too cocky.

She ran through the kitchen, puffing loudly as she passed the front entryway, heading toward the soundstage. From there she'd find the door that led outside. Her car would be waiting, and she'd be gone. They'd have lost her.

He followed her and hit the message key on his comm.

She's headed your way

Robin prayed Batman not only got the text, but was ready to act.

Harley Quinn made it to the soundstage, and headed for the exit door that was on the other side, against the brick wall.

Crouched under the grating, Batman watched as she ran toward him, constantly checking behind her and looking very worried. Robin had to be close. When she was less than three feet away, he pushed up the steel grate and held it firm. Still checking behind her, she ran straight into it, and fell back in shock.

Robin came sprinting into the room, but by the time he reached them, Batman had tied her wrists behind her.

"It's time to talk, Harley," he said. Time had been to his benefit—he felt steadier, and was pleased to note that his voice reflected it.

"I got nothing to say to you, freako," she spat back. "My lips are mum."

"Have it your way," he said. They marched her toward the cell room where Robin had put Charisma, Rogers, and Bell. Just outside the closed door they saw Henry Adams slumped in a chair, holding his chest, blood still seeping from it. A long smear of blood stretched across the tile floor, indicating where Adams had crawled.

They walked toward him, and his eyes flickered open.

"Thank God. Thank God. You found the psycho," he said, his voice weak and shaking. Robin extended a hand and helped him to his feet.

"We'll get you to a hospital," he said. "You're gonna be okay." He turned to Harley. "You keep trying to kill people, but you keep failing. Maybe you should take up another line of work. Arkham Asylum could use a good librarian."

"Kill him?" Harley tried to twist free. "Hey, he was one of my Puddin's chosen. Why would I kill him? Hurt him, sure. But kill him?"

"Shut up, Harley," Batman said. "We're tired of listening to you jabber."

Harley laughed. "Me shutting up, and you saving

Gotham City, two things that'll never happen, Bat-freak."

"Robin, open the door to the cells, please," he said. "But be prepared." Robin opened the door, and gasped. Christina Bell, Johnny Charisma, and Al Rogers were sprawled on the floor, lying in pools of their own blood.

They weren't moving.

Harley Quinn gasped. "Oh, no. No. No!"

Batman turned to her. "Interesting," he said. "That was genuine. You didn't know."

"Know what?" she asked. "What are you talking about?"

Batman calmly turned to Henry Adams. Robin was still helping him to stand.

"You killed them, didn't you, Henry?"

Suddenly Adams grinned broadly, then snapped his fingers. Harley stared at him incredulously. Recognition dawned. She jerked free from Batman, and ran to his side.

"You recognize me, even in this bodybag, don't you, Harley?" Adams said.

"Hey, I'd recognize that smell of homicide anywhere. But Honey-Puddin', why'd you bash 'em? They're your soldier boys. They'd do anything you wanted."

Henry Adams' face began to change. His smile widened. His lips seemed redder. His wide face appeared to contract and hug his skull tighter. His hair was starting to take on a bright green tint.

He was becoming the Joker, with all his twisted memories intact.

"Sometimes, Harley," he said, laughing, "a man's gotta kill what a man's gotta kill." He wiped the blood from his neck and chest, and used it to paint a full Joker smile on his face.

"Honey, I'm home," he said, and he laughed loudly. Harley squealed in delight. Then he took out a gun and twirled it on his finger, like a movie cowboy. Abruptly he stopped, aimed it at Batman, then Robin, who tensed and looked as if he wanted to spring. "Don't. I'll be killing you soon enough. Like I killed that brat. That's how I'm going to kill everyone in your life. You down with that, Bats?"

"Adams, you're not the Joker," Batman said. "You don't have to be him."

"Au contraire, Batman. The other guy led the way, but he was more interested in sparring with you than having fun. I'm gonna show him what a real lunatic can do."

As he stared at Batman, he gestured his gun toward Robin.

"Go. Join your little friend over there. By the way, he's wearing long pants now? Good move. Those itty-bitty green shorts were getting a bit long in the tooth, if you ask me." He gestured again. "Now *move.*"

As he began to comply, Batman saw Christina Bell shaking. She wasn't dead—not yet. So he turned to Adams and called to him, hoping to distract him. If she was alive, there might be a chance he could still protect her.

"Henry," he said loudly, "you were infected with the Joker's blood. It's turning you into him. But it doesn't have to. We can find a cure. We can make you *you* again."

"Now why would I ever want to be that boring waste of flesh?" Adams said, still holding the gun on them. "Been there. *Sooo* done that. He was weak, so weak. But you know how it is in nature. No matter how many obstacles get put in the way, it's the strongest who always survive.

"Hence me."

He started to glance back at the cells, but Batman called to him again.

"The Joker was always after me. I'm your prisoner. Let them go. You have what you really want."

"Oh, Batty, Batty Bats—that was *so* one body ago. You're much too low on the food chain for the new, improved me. Anyway, what was I saying? Oh, right: The strong survive." He circled Batman and stepped back toward the cells.

"Still, you know what they say about evolution?" He kneeled by Christina Bell and placed his gun to her head. "Even amoebas evolve." Before anyone could move he pulled the trigger and her head exploded. "By the way, Bats. Good try. I saw that little twitch, too. This should teach her a lesson she won't soon forget."

34

Harley screamed in surprise.

"What are you doing?" she cried.

Adams grinned. "Purifying the gene pool."

The Joker appeared beside Batman, once again wearing the wide-brimmed hat and his aloha shirt. He glared at Adams and smiled, then turned to Batman.

"I never truly realized how amazingly handsome I am," he said, pointing at Adams. "Not until now. But did I hear him insult me? Obsessed with you, Bats? Me? *Really?*" He turned to Adams, who still held his gun at the ready.

"I am not obsessed with that flying rodent, you third-rate copy," he said indignantly. He turned back to Batman and smiled. "Can you imagine my confusion here? I've always enjoyed sparring with you, but I must admit what he said bothers me. *Gosh oh tooti.* I don't know which side to root for."

Adams moved closer and put the gun to Batman's forehead. His finger played with the trigger.

Robin tensed again, but Batman motioned him not to move. Frowning, Tim obeyed.

"Well, at least it's been educational," the Joker said.

His eyes went back and forth. "Adams. Batman. Adams. Batman. Who to cheer? Who to mock?" He turned to Batman and laughed.

"I've changed my mind, Bats. I've seen the light." He looked at Adams and shouted at him. "Kill him, pretty boy. Kill. Kill. *Kill.* Do it. Do it. Do it!"

Adams pressed his gun against Batman's left temple. Then he saw Batman's face begin to change, even as his had, and moved back a step. Batman's lips curled into an involuntary grin. Then he began to laugh—but his laugh was louder than Henry's, more obscene.

Adams lowered his gun. "Now that's unexpected." He turned to Harley with a look of surprise. "Did you see that coming?"

"Puddin' pie, what's going on here?" Harley reached out to Adams and took his hand in hers.

Adams grinned. "Don't you get it? I'm not the alpha Joker. I mean, I knew Bell, Charisma, and Rogers certainly weren't. At best they were stooges. So I thought, well, *I've* got to be the alpha, the one intended to take over the family business.

"But I see I'm wrong. Very wrong. It should have been obvious. But, *duh*, my bad." He studied Batman, who was still laughing without reason, then he stepped back and bowed to him. "You are going to be spectacular." Turning, he gave Harley a kiss on her forehead. She beamed at him.

"Knowing you was the best thing about today, Harley," Adams said. "But with the alpha in place, there's certainly no need for a lowly omega." Suddenly Harley tried to grab his hand, but she was too slow. He held the gun to his own head and fired.

His face exploded as the rest of him spun to the floor.

"No. No. No. Not again," she cried. Harley was in tears and she fell beside him, cradling his dead body. Batman took her hand and smiled to her.

"I'm your Puddin' now."

She stared at him, trying to decide what to do. She wiped away her tears then smiled at him, and gave him a hug.

"You sure are, pretty boy," she said, and she grinned mischievously, all else forgotten. "So tell me, exactly when can I take a peek at that incredible six-pack of yours? Skinny was real good to me, but you and those abs are really a turn-on."

Batman returned her smile, pushed her into the last empty cell and locked the door behind her. "When hell freezes over," he said."

Robin stared at Batman, unable to hide his shock.

"Your eyes. You, you're—"

"The last Joker? I know. I've known for a long time. But before I'm unable to control my instincts, I need to stop Scarecrow. Once I'm done, though, I swear I'm locking myself away. Or you'll have to do it for me. Tim, I won't let myself be a danger to anyone."

"But what if you fail? You'll be too dangerous. I won't be able to stop you."

"I've trained you to stop evil any way you have to. I

expect nothing less when I'm the one being stopped."

"*No. No. No.*" The Joker stood next to Batman. "Now that I'm finally you, I won't let you put us behind bars."

"If you don't want that, maybe that's exactly what I need to do." Batman walked into one of the empty cells and closed the door behind him. "I'm still in command," he said. "You don't control me."

"C'mon, Bats. Get out of that cell. Can't you see how much fun you and I will be? My demented mind. Your steroid-enhanced muscles. We're a match made in chemical heaven. 'Sides, you won't be able to refuse me forever. I'm going to be all over your free will any time now. So just give in to me. It'll be so much easier on both of us."

"Not going to happen, Joker. I will never be yours."

"The only thing that 'never' applies to, Bats, is your ability to fight destiny. Oh, and my tainted blood. There's no cure. No hope. No stopping me now."

"There are other ways I can stop you."

"Sure, there's always the Henry Adams way. And I have to admire that—it took guts. His guts. But here's something you need to think about. You put a bullet through that bullheaded brain of yours, and then what happens to Robin the third? Who's gonna protect him? I mean, without you, he goes the way of guess who?"

Jason Todd. He was there, on the floor in front of Batman.

The Joker was standing over him, crowbar in his hand. He raised it, brought it down with a brutal impact, again and again. Then he turned to Batman and used the back of his hand to wipe the sweat from his brow.

"Now Timmy's made of sterner meat than Toddy, but even he can be tenderized."

Batman stared at Jason, dead on the floor. He blinked his eyes and he was gone. He was still standing outside the cell, Robin at his side. It was another damned hallucination.

He was losing all control.

He turned to Tim, who had no idea what he was seeing.

"Tim," Batman said, his voice almost whispering the name. He grabbed Robin's hand and pushed him into an empty cell, then quickly locked it. "I'm so sorry. But this is for your own good. I've got to protect you... from me."

"Batman, what are you doing?" Tim shouted. "Let me out of here. Batman!"

The Joker walked over to Batman and put his arms around him.

"A man after my own heart," he said, and he giggled. "And once you fully change, you'll have that and everything else. By the way, I brought you a present."

And there was Jason Todd again, sitting on the floor, a spotlight shining on him as if from heaven itself. He was alive, but tied up in ropes. A gag prevented him from talking.

"Jason? But he's..."

"Dead?" the Joker said. "In the real world, maybe. But not in your head. Go. Talk to him. Reminisce about the good ol' days, when both of you were sane—more or less."

Batman started to untie Jason when the Joker pushed him away, a crowbar suddenly appearing in his hand.

"That's long enough," he said mockingly. "We don't want things to get mushy now, do we?" He swung the crowbar like a baseball bat, slammed Jason with it, and knocked him out of the light. The Joker laughed and followed, but the spotlight moved with him. A sheet appeared in front of him—he pulled it aside with a flamboyant tug. Jason was under the sheet, straining at his bonds. The Joker leaned into him and gestured toward Batman.

"I'm not the villain here, you know. Batface is.

"Speaking of faces," the Joker said, and he held out his hand. A branding iron appeared in it, glowing red hot. He twirled it, then slammed it onto Jason's face, burning a vivid "J" into his cheek. Jason screamed and writhed while Batman could only stand and watch.

"Oh, quiet down, Toddy," the Joker laughed. "If anyone asks, you can always say the 'J' was for Jason. If they're stupid enough, they might even believe it." He looked at Batman and shrugged his shoulders. "Who'd think getting your initials branded into you would cause such a ruckus."

Jason was holding back his screams even as his flesh was still sizzling.

"You know, I actually meant to ask you a question first, and use the branding iron later, in case I needed an incentive," the Joker said. "But I got it backwards. Being dead and having your ashes flushed into the Gotham River has played havoc with my attention span. I do apologize."

Jason was writhing on the ground. The ropes were gone, and his hands were free. He was whimpering in pain. Batman wanted to go to him, help him, but he couldn't move.

"Anyway, what's done is done. So, if you don't mind my doing this out of order, I'll ask my question now." The Joker leaned closer and whispered conspiratorially.

"What is Batman's secret identity?"

Jason lowered his hands and glared at the Joker, but all his fight and rebellion were gone.

"B… Bru…"

"Oh, I don't really care." The Joker laughed as he put a bullet through Jason's head.

Robin called out, grabbing his cell bars, trying to pull them loose even while recognizing that was impossible.

"Batman. Wake up! Whatever you're seeing, it isn't real. Let me out. I can help you."

But Batman couldn't hear him. He walked to the door, opened it and left. The Joker followed behind.

"Who shall be next? The good commissioner? The faithful butler? The gruff but dedicated scientist-slash-CEO? I'd name more friends, but you don't have any others. Still, I'll kill them all, and for extra fun, I'll shoot all your casual acquaintances, too."

Batman wasn't listening to him, either.

He walked through the corridor, knowing he had locked away Robin to save him. He feared for Tim's life, afraid that he'd share the same fate as Barbara or Jason. Whether or not it was Scarecrow's toxin, it was a justified fear. What had happened before could very well happen again.

What's past, as Shakespeare wrote, *is prologue*.

He walked past more than a dozen bodies lying on the studio floor, but didn't glance at them. He found the exit and walked outside into the cold. It was a moonless night and everything was dark.

Batman preferred it that way. No one could see him.

He returned to the Batmobile, its window open wide, and climbed inside. In the distance he could hear the screams of those in need. He rolled up the window and the screams were gone. If only it was really that simple.

He closed his eyes and let his thoughts wash over him. Everything was changing—that much was obvious—and not for the good. Jason was dead. Barbara was probably dead, too.

For the moment Tim was safe, but locked up in a cell with crazies everywhere. And Tim was good. He'd soon pick the lock and escape. If Batman had taught him well, he'd make it all the way back to Wayne Manor. Then he'd be with Alfred, and almost nothing could stop those two.

So many fears, and though Batman realized they were being generated by Scarecrow's toxins, it didn't mean they weren't real.

Well, he thought, if this was his last mission, he was going to go out fighting. He needed to go to the botanical gardens and find Ivy. She was his last chance to find a cure. He took a deep breath, held it for a long while, then exhaled and started the car. One thought was foremost in his mind.

Nothing can stop you when you know you're going to die.

35

Jonathan Crane was pleased with the way things had worked out.

He had manufactured far more fear toxin than was needed for Gotham City—the supply Batman destroyed was a backup produced in case his main stockpile was damaged. At worst he had been slowed down, and marginally at that. Once Gotham City turned on itself, he would simply produce more.

Then he would begin planning his next attack. He was trying to decide between spreading his fear in Metropolis or Central City. He tried to picture what the results would look like if a fear-crazed Superman or Flash were suddenly released on their cities.

Imagine that destruction.

More than ever, Crane was obsessed with the nature of fear and how it drove sane men to joyously commit acts even the insane couldn't conceive. His experiments proved that all men possessed dark thoughts, but had, over many millennia, learned to control them.

"Civilized" man had seemingly discarded his savage beginnings, and so mankind indulged those unable to lift themselves out of the mire, yet that veneer of civilization was a mistake. Man was given savage urges for a reason. In nature, only the strong survived. The most powerful always got to feast on the weak. Those who gave in to fear were meant to serve those who would experience it fully then rise above it.

The weak took advantage of the strong, sucking them into the abyss. Before it was too late, mankind had to rid itself of the shackles that dragged it into the depths.

And now the fear toxin would fix everything.

Yet how to test a man's worth? Certainly everyone suffered from phobias—no one could long hide from their nightmares. But some people were able to push past them, while others succumbed. How a person dealt with the irrational would show whether they were the wheat or the chaff. If they gave in to their fears, they were feeble and deserved to be purged.

Learn to turn them against others, and you prove your strength, Scarecrow knew. *Your value.* He was the only one who could lead the way to mankind's reawakening. And he was more than up to the task.

But first there were a few messy details with which he needed to deal.

"Scarecrow!" The Arkham Knight's voice came over his communicator. *"Everything's in place."* The Knight was in command of the lead tank—the one that held Simon Stagg's Cloudburst machine.

"She has to be destroyed," Scarecrow said.

"She will be," the Knight replied, *"as will her plants.*

Nothing will survive. Neither here, nor in Gotham City."

"Somehow her ancient spores are able to counteract my toxins," Crane said. "Poison Ivy spouts her gibberish, that Mother Nature will save the world. But I've proven that if left uncontrolled, nature will only bring us all to the brink of self-destruction. She's failed us time and time again. Now man needs to take over."

"I'm outside the gardens, powering up the weapons. The pavement has been torn up, and it already looks like a war zone out here. But we'll get through. It won't be long now."

"You've done a good job, Knight. Your master is pleased."

"Gotham City will soon be yours, sir," Arkham Knight said. *"But remember, Batman is mine.*

"Knight out."

Alfred Pennyworth's voice came over the comm.

"Sir, we've located the Cloudburst device," he said. *"The good news is, it's less than a thousand yards from your current location."*

Batman looked at Ivy, cradling one of her plants, coaxing it back to life. She saw him watching her and gave a warm smile.

"And the bad news?"

"See for yourself, sir. Patching you in now. That's a satellite view of the scene showing the immediate area surrounding Ivy's gardens. The red dot you see is the Cloudburst's power source—it's on one of Scarecrow's tanks. You can't see him now, but a moment ago you could see the driver. I'll rewind the feed."

Batman watched as the image scrolled backward. The

tank hatch opened and a man peered out for a moment, then burrowed back inside, closing the hatch behind him.

The tank commander was the Arkham Knight.

Batman turned to Ivy.

"We need to leave," he said. "Scarecrow's men are outside, and you represent a serious threat to him."

"I can't go, Batman." She held her plant, hugging it close to her. "They need me."

"Sir," Alfred said, *"our instruments show that they're powering up their weapons. I strongly urge you and Ms. Isley to vacate immediately."*

"Ivy, we can't wait," Batman said. "We have to go... *now.*"

"You go. I'm staying."

"Sir, there's no time."

Batman grabbed Ivy's wrist and pulled her away from the plant. She cried out to him and the vine writhed, echoing her emotions.

"No, Batman. Please don't do this to me." She struggled in his grip. "I have to stay here. A mother never leaves her children behind."

"You're not their mother, Ivy," he said, ignoring her tugging. "They're just plants. Come on."

"Just plants?" she echoed. "I thought you were a good man, who understood me—but you're as bad as they are." She clawed at him now, trying to scratch through his armor with her nails, which she had dipped in plant poison. But he firmly held her wrists.

"Sir," Alfred called out again, *"there can be no further delay."*

"We'll sort it out later," Batman said to Ivy. "We're going now."

Then the world exploded.

A sphere of pulsing blue energy crashed through the greenhouse wall, then suddenly erupted with devastating effect. Instantly, shockwaves spread through the gardens, ripping through stems, flowers, and leaves. Their primary and secondary root systems dried up and crumbled. Bright red azaleas turned brown and withered, their petals crumbling to dust. Black-eyed Susans, ancient Damasks, and Gallicas simply disintegrated, their ashes swept away by the pulsing energy waves. Alba heritage roses, which had bloomed as far back as the middle ages and were used for medicines, were gone in a single instant.

Ivy tried to launch herself toward the enemy tank, which was firing a second wave of energy, but Batman maintained his grip and forced her to the ground. Then he lay on top of her, shielding her.

This sphere was larger, more destructive, and was centered outside of the greenhouse. Once again the energy wave oscillated in all directions, spreading from the blast site. The greenhouse wall was ripped into uncountable shards, and even the Batmobile was lifted by yet another pulse. Batman watched as it disappeared from view, then moments later heard its crash.

"Ivy, we have to get to your tunnels," he told her. "Where's the closest entrance grate?"

"Do you have children of your own? Would you leave them now? Would you leave Robin to die?"

"God forgive me, but I already may have."

* * *

He heard the thumping before he looked up.

The Joker was standing in front of him, laughing as he hammered the long-dead body of Jason Todd.

The laugh persisted even after Batman could no longer see him.

"There's nothing we can do to help them, Ivy. We have to go underground."

Scarecrow's fear gas appeared in a noxious cloud, and the shockwave spread it everywhere. Seeing it, Ivy finally nodded and led him to a hatchway.

The shockwave tore through Gotham City's streets and bou-levards, constructed when the city was rich and prosperous and wanted to show off its splendor. Towering trees, planted in the 1920s to line the shopping plazas, were obliterated—reduced to crumbled bark and splintered wood.

Even hiding in the tunnels, Ivy could hear her children's screams as one by one they died around her. She was crying and she was angry, but when she looked at Batman, she was also determined.

"I understand now, Batman," she said, her jaw clenched with fury. "Unless you terminate those evil people, *all* of my beautiful plants will die. I have to stop the fear toxin… and I know how."

Grief-stricken, she ran through the tunnels, not looking where she was going, but guided by a presence Batman could never see. Still, he followed her.

"Ivy, where are you going? What are you doing?"

"What you wanted me to do, Batman," she answered without turning. "The only thing I can do." The tunnel system wound its way under Ivy's gardens, then suddenly came to an end. She looked up, past a grating that was directly above, and pointed to a small, leafless stub of a tree. It looked like the witch's tree from *The Wizard of Oz*, its branches twisted like arms that clawed at the sky.

"That's the bristlecone pine," she said. "It's the oldest tree in the world. Did you know it comes from here? Not Africa, nor Asia, but *here*. It comes from California. Isn't that a miracle, Batman? The oldest tree in the world was born right here in the United States. And it's also the tree from which those spores came. The ones that countered Scarecrow's fear toxin."

"Ivy, it's too late to make an antidote," he said. "The only thing we can do now is stay down here and let the fear gas settle."

She just stared at him for a moment.

"Batman, you're so good at hitting people, but when it comes to nature, you are naïve." She turned back toward the grate. "I think you should stand back now. Let me do what I have to."

"No!" he said "Talk to me first, Ivy. Tell me what you're doing."

"Why? You'd never understand. Just watch. Please. I have to save my babies." With that she pushed open the grating and walked to the plant. Its lowest branch seemed to turn to her and take her hand. "She understands what's happening, and she's ready." She looked back at him. "And so am I."

She nestled in the tree's branches and let herself be

covered by them. Smaller branches sprouted from larger ones, and wove a cradle that surrounded her.

"She speaks to me," Ivy said. "We can absorb the toxins already in the air, but you'll need to stop their machines from creating more."

Batman moved to pull her away, but a tree branch swiped him back. With every passing second she was becoming more a part of the bristlecone, and he could see drifts of fear gas rushing toward her.

"Ivy, don't," he said. "You'll die."

"I can't die, Batman. Nature is forever."

"IVY!" he shouted, and he launched himself at her again, but the tree kept pushing him back. Her voice came from somewhere within the tangle of new bristlecone growth.

"You know what to do now," she said. "Protect my babies still to be."

Then she was gone.

But she was right. He knew what had to be done. Simon Stagg had built the Cloudburst machine.

Now he'd tell Batman how to destroy it.

36

Simon Stagg was hanging upside down, held just outside the airship's emergency exit, the ground nearly two thousand dizzying feet below him. He had no choice but to look down.

He was not a happy man.

"You're sweating, Simon, but there's really no need to worry," Batman said, gripping Stagg by the ankles. "It won't hurt for more than a second or two. You'll barely feel the impact."

"What the hell do you want?" Stagg screamed. "I'll give you anything. You want money? I've got *billions*."

"You've seen some of my toys, Simon." Batman smiled at him, hoping the effect would be disconcerting. "The car. The plane. The weapons. And they're all paid for. I don't need money."

"Then what do you want? Please, tell me."

"Okay. I want to know how to stop the Cloudburst machine."

Stagg didn't answer immediately, and Batman wondered if he had passed out.

"Scarecrow will kill me."

"Maybe. Probably." Batman let go of Stagg's right ankle,

keeping a tight grip on the left, but letting it seem unsteady. "Unless I put an end to him first."

Stagg screamed again. "Don't drop me, man. I'll tell you. I'll tell you *everything*. Just bring me back inside. Please."

Batman didn't move. "I think you have that backward, Simon. Tell me how to stop the Cloudburst machine, and then I'll bring you back inside. But I'd hurry. You weigh quite a bit, and my arm is getting tired." His fingers loosened around Stagg's ankle, and he allowed him to slip. "Very, very tired."

"Okay. *Okay.*" As Batman gripped the right ankle again, and steadied his grip, Stagg gave him the information. Once he was done, Batman hoisted him up and into the emergency exit.

"Thank you, Simon," he said. Bracing himself on the floor, Stagg grabbed his ankles and massaged them.

"You've hurt me," he said angrily. "I should sue you."

Batman shrugged. "Do what you have to, Stagg. But a word of advice. Unless you want to go through that all over again, I suggest that you stay out of my business."

Stagg Industries designed the Nimbus power cell to mitigate the effects of their Cloudburst machine, originally conceived as a means of alleviating drought conditions.

As the corporation had learned many years earlier, however, it was financially and legally prudent to build fail-safe functions into all of their devices—especially ones designed to have lethal aspects.

When their oil pipeline unexpectedly ruptured and

polluted Lake Erie, the federally mandated cleanup cost Stagg nearly fourteen billion dollars. For an additional nine million, they installed a series of shut-off valves that prevented the problem from repeating when the next rupture occurred.

The Nimbus power cell, once it was fitted into the Batmobile and powered up, would filter Scarecrow's toxins. Much of the city would be spared. Now all he needed was a Batmobile.

He tapped his gauntlet comm and Lucius Fox appeared.

"Ah, I was about to call you. I've got a replacement ready—it's parked outside Wayne Tower. And by the way," Fox continued, *"you won't need a key any longer—your fingerprints and retinal scans should suffice."*

"Thank you, Lucius. I think we're very close to putting a stop to this madness."

"I certainly hope so. Gotham City has never teetered quite this far into the abyss. More than ever before, a hero is needed."

"I'm not alone out here," Batman said. "You, Alfred, Robin, the police who've remained. Gordon, too, though he won't speak to me. If we win this, it won't have been the result of an individual."

"It takes a village, eh? Well, that is *the way of civilization."* He paused, and added, *"I know you don't believe in it, but good luck, Mr. Wayne."*

Batman's holo retracted back into his glove. With the Nimbus tucked under his arm, he left Stagg and headed to Amusement Mile and his new Batmobile.

* * *

A thick cloud of Scarecrow fear gas hung low over the river, as well as the park. It was continuing to spread. He opened the car's hood and lowered the filter into position.

"You sure you really want to do that, Bats?" the Joker said, standing behind him, watching him splice the first of all too many wires into place. Batman closed his eyes for a second, regrouped, then continued working on the installation.

"You *know* what's happening to you," the Joker said. "You're my alpha. You're going to become me, you lucky bastard." Nothing could drown out the Joker's cackling voice. "You're already changing. My goodness, locking poor Robin in that cell? If that isn't embracing the dark side, I don't know what is. I do hope you've told either Fox or Alfie where to find him. I'd hate to see him starve to death in there."

"Shut up, Joker," Batman gritted. "Tim's a professional. He's probably broken out of the cell by now."

"Probably. Maybe. Coulda, woulda, shoulda. Well, one way or another, he's either alive or he's dead. And if he's alive, once you become me, he'll be dead soon anyway. This wonderful world of ours will never run out of good crowbars and young brains to bash in."

"Get out of my head, Joker. I will *never* become you."

"And yet you're still talking to me, as you have been since this all began," the Joker gloated. "You're a detective, Bats. Analyze the evidence and accept the truth."

Batman slammed his hands to his ears, but the talking didn't stop.

"If I'm right—and being you, I have to be—my blood and the fear toxin have taken over about seventy or eighty percent of your psyche. Your last bits of sanity will be gone pretty soon. With that coursing through your veins, you should be starting to get really tired about now, too.

"Lie down, flip that filter into place, and let me take you over while you sleep. One minute you're a man of logic, the next, not so much. Go to sleep, little Bats. Accept the inevitable."

"SHUT UP!"

"I can't, Bats. That's the beauty of it. I'm inside your mind. You're the one *making* me talk. Come on. We've fought back and forth for years now. And as you once said, our little duet will end with one of us killing the other. You were so close to winning. Instead, this will end with one of us *becoming* the other.

"And since I'm dead, that leaves you. I can see it—you're getting very, very tired now. So close your eyes, go to sleep, and let me do what I do so well."

Batman *was* tired. He could barely look up at the Joker, hovering in front of him, a mocking grin plastered across his face. He closed his eyes hoping the Joker would disappear, but he could still feel his presence, closer than ever.

"Please… go away…"

"I'll help you sleep, Bats. C'mon, cuddle up to me. In a manly sort of way, of course. Stay calm, take deep, slow breaths. Deep, slow, breaths. Let me sing you asleep as my mother did for me so long ago, just before I killed her.

"Rock-a-bye Batsy, I'm getting free.

Soon you'll be the one trapped inside me.

So keep taking breaths, great lungfuls of fear.

Soon Bats will be gone, and I will be here."

"Shut up. Shut the hell up." Batman reached out to the

Joker to stop him, but his hands went through the mirage.

"You want more? Of course. One last ditty, then it's really off to bed.

"Hush little Batsy, listen to me sing.
When the Joker takes over you won't feel a thing.
And once this gas has set me free…
I'm going on a Bat-family killing spree.

"Ready for sleep now?" the Joker asked. Batman's hands were pressed against his ears, but he could still hear every word. His eyes were closed and he counted silently to himself.

One—you don't have to listen to him.

Two—you can resist him.

Three—he doesn't control you.

Four—you can control him.

He counted to ten, one number at a time, each accompanied by a factor that would help him reclaim his thoughts. Each number reinforcing that he, not a dead man, was in control.

"Let Uncle Joker tuck you in, sweetums."

Batman opened his eyes. He reached out, calmly this time, and ran his hands through the Joker image that hovered in front of him.

"I will never be yours," he said. "Go away and never return." He turned from where the ghost had been and walked off, without bothering to look back to see if it was still there, waiting for him.

The Joker didn't follow him—he was gone.

But for how long?

37

James Gordon tightened the strap on his re-breather then stepped into the chaos. He had sucked in a single lungful of the fear toxin before securing it, and prayed that wouldn't be enough to turn him into one of... *them*.

Them.

The citizens he had pledged years ago to protect and serve. Even in an asylum like Gotham City, most of them had been good, solid people. Some believed in God, others in justice, but the only thing most of them wanted was to live their lives in peace. To take care of those who depended on them, and perhaps to be taken care of in kind.

Most days they quietly boarded the Gotham City railways and sat reading the morning papers. Many brought a container of coffee or tea, which usually remained hot for most of the trip to midtown and work. Some stood and offered their seat if a pregnant woman or an elderly straphanger boarded the train.

Not many smiled as the trains bumped their way through the city, but they weren't unhappy. Work was work, and whether it was their calling or a job, it was a means to an end. Rent would be paid. Food could be bought. Clothing could be kept new. Children would be cared for.

But today was different. For him, today they went from being one of "us" to one of "them." Today there was a reason nobody was smiling or offering help to those who needed it.

Today was the day the city went insane.

Today was the day Gotham City became Arkham.

And today was the day Police Commissioner James Gordon realized he could no longer protect or serve.

They were running all around him, shouting, screaming, crying. All of them were afraid of something, and if they had a weapon in their hands, they would use it believing they were protecting themselves from the monsters or the serpents or the dark ones with the fiery eyes who were slithering through the sewers.

Everything in the world was out to hurt them, including their loved ones, but they knew they could save themselves. They would lash out first, before they could be attacked, and kill those damnable… *things*.

A numberless pile of bodies littered the Gotham City streets like so much garbage tossed in the dump. Gordon saw his men, cops he'd known for more than a decade, dressed in what had been their finest blues, but now were torn and bloodied. They thought they were doing their jobs, shooting the monsters, but they were just adding more corpses to the piles.

He called out to stop them, but they turned on him as they turned on all the stray beasts. He ducked into an office building and for a long time hid in a supply room. His city was dying and he wanted to cry. But until and unless he was taken over, too, he had to do everything he could to help.

But how do I do that without being killed? he wondered. Unfortunately, he didn't have an answer.

He braved his way through the building, took the elevator to the twenty-third floor, and stared out through a large window at his city. Even from up here, the city scared the shit out of him.

He heard every scream. He watched helplessly as men and women fell to the ground, never to get up again. Cars careened through the crowded streets, aiming at pedestrians, running them over. The drivers thought they were saving the city from hell unleashed, never understanding the God-awful truth.

Gordon thought about Batman, and as much as he hated that lying, pointy-eared freak, he wished he was with him now. But shouldn't he hate Barbara, too? She was the one who told Batman to lie. She was the one who hid away in that tower, serving as eyes and ears for the Batman.

But she's dead now. He couldn't hate the dead.

He also didn't want to hate the Batman who had saved his life so many times, who had risked his own so many more times. But he did hate him.

His re-breather beeped. He had fifteen minutes of unpolluted air left, and wondered if that one whiff of fear gas explained why he was so angry, so filled with hate. Was the fear toxin the reason why he despised his own daughter for lying to him?

Or was that his own baggage?

Ever since Barbara was a child, he was always so busy with work that he rarely spent much time with her—let alone any quality time. In their family, Gotham City always came first. Maybe he was the reason his son James grew up to become the psychopath he was. Gordon knew his fanatical devotion to Gotham City had been the reason his wife left him.

She told him as much.

And now Barbara. The love of his life. The perfect child. She'd been lying to him for more than a decade. She was Batgirl. *She was freaking Batgirl.* Fighting crime, playing superhero alongside the damned Batman, risking her life every day, every night.

And she couldn't stop playing those games after the Joker crippled her, humiliated her. From Batgirl to Oracle—both names a mocking reminder that the daughter he so trusted had continually betrayed him.

All this, Gordon thought as he tried to block out the screams coming from the street below, was her fault. She was the witch. And if she really was dead this time, then goddam it, she deserved to—

He stopped.

Even if he was under Scarecrow's control, he still would never condemn his own daughter. He loved Barbara more than his own life, even more than he loved Gotham City. James Gordon knew he had to fight his fear. Barbara was his daughter, and no matter what she said or became, he would always love her.

Gordon leaned against the window and took several deep breaths, clearing his mind, restoring his reason. He'd fight this fear, and then he'd go downstairs again, and whether he'd make it through the night or not, he'd do everything in his power to save his city.

He may have lost one love tonight, but he wasn't going to lose another.

38

Lucius Fox double-checked the data, then with the satellite uplink he uploaded it to the Batmobile's GPS, locking in the coordinates. Normally this would be an automated function, but Scarecrow's assault had interrupted their satellite connections, and played havoc with navigation.

Better to be safe than sorry.

"Intel should be in place now," he reported. "I've also got visuals on the Knight's tank, and a confirmed reading that the Cloudburst machine is onboard. Based on the schematics I downloaded from Stagg's computers, the only way to stop the signal that powers the device is to destroy it."

"I was planning to do that, no matter what," Batman replied. *"I'm less than a mile from his coordinates."*

"Good. I'm monitoring the situation in the city, and the havoc is the worst I've ever seen. I fear for Gotham City's survival."

"We can't give in to our fears, Lucius. Certainly not now. Scarecrow can't be allowed to win."

* * *

Then he had a visual.

The Arkham Knight's command tank was ahead of him. Pilotless drone tanks flanked him for additional protection. Batman readied his onboard missiles. He was sorely tempted to take out the Knight's tank, but the explosion would kill him. Batman swore he would not succumb to the Joker's toxic blood.

Not now.

Not yet.

There had to be another way.

Twin missiles took out the drones. With them out of the way, he then switched to the grenade launcher and shot them at the command tank's drive sprockets. Its track shattered, halting the vehicle's forward movement and severely limiting the Knight's options.

But he wasn't done. Batman fired three more grenades at the tank's turret, effectively preventing it from turning, limiting the circular range of its main gun while also blasting a small hole in its hull.

The Batmobile raced up next to the tank. Its roof retracted and Batman sprung out, landing on the tank's turret. He dived through the break in the hull and discovered that the Knight had fallen on his back, knocked there by the explosion. He was struggling to stand up, and Batman had only seconds to deal with the Cloudburst machine before he would be forced to fight.

Machine first. Killer next. Sure. More than enough time, he thought, laughing inwardly. But Batman was laughing *his* laugh.

The Cloudburst machine was plugged into the tank's

engine, feeding on its power. Batman had two grenades left. He adhered the first to the Cloudburst's face. He stuck the second explosive near the cables that led to the tank's cooling line.

The Knight was almost on his feet. Batman had another second, maybe two, but the grenades were primed to explode in seven. Everything depended on his ability to delay his opponent.

Lashing out with a boot, Batman kicked him back down again, then scrambled through the break in the hull and leaped to safety. Landing, he spun to watch.

The Knight leaped through the hole as the grenade attached to the Cloudburst machine exploded, propelling him away from the tank in an uncontrolled spin. He hit the ground and rolled. A heartbeat later the second grenade exploded.

The Cloudburst machine was neutralized.

Batman readied himself.

The Knight lurched to his feet, stared… and took off.

Good move, Batman thought. The Knight had lost his advantage—the initiative was gone. There was no logical reason for him to engage in battle now except to satisfy a wounded ego. The Knight was able to hold his hubris in check.

Whoever trained him did a good job, Batman mused as he prepared to follow.

"*Batman.*" Fox's voice interrupted his thoughts. "*Satellite surveillance spotted the Knight. Two blocks from you, on the rooftop of the former Gotham City Textile Manufacturer's building. He's heading east.*"

"Thanks, Lucius. Try to keep track of him. I'm on my way."

* * *

Batman grappled to the rooftops then checked his sensors. The Knight was five blocks south, keeping to the rooftops, running in a zigzag pattern, making it harder to be followed. Piercing the veil that blanketed the city, the satellites kept a lock on him—at least for the moment. He was headed toward the seaport.

Heading south along Fourteenth Street, Batman swung toward the west-side docks. He had to anticipate all of the Knight's possible escape routes, then choose the one he believed most likely. Following him wouldn't narrow the gap that lay between them. He had to predict his course, and get ahead of him.

He fired his Batline at the wolf-like gargoyle guarding the roof of Our Lady Of Sorrows. The gargoyle had been brought to Gotham City from Venice in 1892 when the church was first built. Whether it was because of a guardian angel, or just unexpected reverence from Gotham City's lowlife, the church seemed to have been declared off limits to crime.

Batman used the gargoyle as a pivot that let him swing around the church and propel himself toward the docks, saving him at least three blocks. He affixed a second line to the flagpole projecting from the nine-story Maritime Control building, then winched to its roof, saving him another two blocks.

There he is.

The Arkham Knight was ahead of him.

He fired his grapple and grabbed the Knight's legs,

pulling them out from under him, dropping him to the rooftop. As the Knight fell, Batman was on top of him, pile-driving one fist after another into the Knight's face and gut.

He had to keep the advantage.

The Knight thrust his knee into Batman's solar plexus, knocking him back. He twisted, wrapped his legs around Batman's neck, and squeezed.

"I don't need to play any more games, Batman," he growled. "I'm going to kill you and be done with it."

Batman felt his anger rise. Without warning, it was growing out of control. He ripped off his right glove and stabbed his fingers through the eyepieces of the Knight's mask.

"I'm not the one who's going to die, killer," he shouted. Yelping in pain, the Knight grabbed his face and fell back, releasing his hold. Then Batman was on him again. He smashed his elbow into the Knight's throat, and the Knight gasped. He reached back to the mask and again stabbed his fingers through its holes, but this time to yank the mask off, to see the face of his enemy.

It came free, but the Knight rolled to his side and stabbed a knee up into Batman's face. Blood shot from torn bone, but Batman held on. He laced his hands together and smashed down as hard as possible into the soft spot under the Knight's ribcage.

"Let's end this now. Let's see who you are."

"Yes. Yes. Hurt him. Cripple him. Break all your rules and slaughter him." Batman didn't have to turn to know the Joker was behind him, probably dancing with glee every time the Batman struck the Knight with his fists.

"What are you waiting for, Batman?" the lunatic cried.

"Don't you want to know who he is?"

Batman stared.

Where the full-face mask had been a moment before, the Joker was laughing up at him.

"Surprise!"

Glancing back, Batman saw the Joker standing behind him, still dancing with joy and convulsing with laughter.

"I bet you didn't see that coming."

Then a third Joker appeared to his side. This one reached for his own face and tore it off, exposing the Knight's mask.

"How can this possibly be? I'm dead. We're *all* dead. How can we be the Knight? Bet that's a conundrum even the Riddler couldn't solve."

This fourth Joker leaned in close. "By the way, the Riddler? Really? Isn't he just a second rate version of me? I'm your first nutcase from the dawn of time. He's just a Jokey-Come-Lately."

A fifth and sixth Joker appeared. They were surrounding him, laughing at him. He forced himself to his feet and lashed out, punching each figure even though his fists could never connect with his nightmares.

"Well, this isn't getting either of us anywhere," the first Joker said. "You're fighting with figments of your own imagination, and we're getting bored watching you make a fool of yourself. So *sayonara*, old friend. We'll meet again when you rip off your own mask, and paint your pretty pink skin white. B'bye."

The Jokers vanished, and Batman looked down to where the Arkham Knight had been. But he was gone.

Batman sat on the roof of the Maritime Control building, quietly regaining control over his thoughts, looking out over Gotham City, wondering how long he'd stay sane enough to help the city he loved. His fingers were still hooked on the Knight's mask. If the Joker hadn't distracted him, he likely would have blinded the Knight for life, and laughed at the results.

His time was running out.

He had stopped the Cloudburst device from manufacturing more fear toxin, but the city was still covered in layers of it. There were still screams coming from the streets below. People were still running in fear, attacking brothers and sisters, husbands and wives, even children and other loved ones. Fear was destroying the city and he wasn't sure there was anything he could do about it.

He sat watching as the winds blew the fear gas west, toward Poison Ivy's gardens. She had merged with her plants and was drawing the toxin into her, but it wasn't happening quickly enough. So he got up and grappled his way west. There was nothing he could do here.

Perhaps he could still help Ivy.

39

As Batman walked through the greenhouse, all he saw were brown stretches of plants, dying or dead. The once oxygen-rich air was now dank and fetid, and it made Batman sick to his stomach. He checked his re-breather and tightened the straps that held it in place. The fear gas was flowing into the greenhouse, but her task was nearly done.

Pamela Isley may have been mad, but she embraced the life that allowed humans to live. Her children—and she truly believed they were her children—gave humans something to breathe. In return, they were being condemned to a slow, painful death.

Without them, Batman wondered, *how long would we survive?*

He followed the currents of the flowing fear gas and found Ivy herself, whimpering in pain, almost fully merged with the ancient bristlecone pine.

"Ivy, you're dying," Batman said. "You can stop now."

"It's not done yet, and I've accepted my fate," she whispered. "All my babies will die unless I save them." Her voice was so weak he could barely hear her. "They need their mother. They need me. But will you stay with me, Batman? Will you let me borrow your strength? Will you help me save them?"

He reached out and rooted under the bark of the old pine. Most of her was already covered over but he found the tips of two fingers and placed his hand over them.

"I'll stay with you, Pamela," he said. "For as long as you need me."

He did so as the toxin flowed into her, and he gave her whatever support he could to help with her pain. She swallowed in the poison and exhaled fresh air.

As the poison dissipated, the trees and plants closest to her were the first to sprout new buds. The brown that covered the greenhouse slowly faded as a new layer of green supplanted them. Ivy was in silent agony, no longer able to give voice, but her garden was growing.

This wasn't science, Batman thought. To a man who demanded logic, this defied everything he understood. Yet, as the bristlecone closed, encasing her, he swore to himself that when all was done, whether they succeeded in saving Gotham City or not, everyone would know that Pamela Isley had died trying to save their city.

The pine branches reached out toward him, and he forced himself not to flinch. Its leaves surrounded him, and he found that he was comforted by their touch. He thought he heard Ivy's voice, thanking him for his help, but it had to be another hallucination—like the Joker.

One of the shoots rested on his hand as his had on hers. Its thorns turned to face him and gently pricked his fingers.

He felt cold and pushed it away.

* * *

40

"Excuse the interruption," Lucius Fox said. *"It appears as if the G.C.P.D. has located Scarecrow's lair. It's in an abandoned shopping mall on Founder's Island. I've uploaded the schematics."*

"Thanks, Lucius. I'm on my way."

"You should know the commissioner is already on site. You might want to tread carefully. I don't think he's requesting, expecting, or desiring your assistance."

"Probably not, but the police aren't equipped to handle menaces like Crane. This is more in my ballpark. Besides, I have less to lose."

"What do you mean by that?"

He and Alfred don't know about the Joker's blood.

"He's already lost Barbara," Batman replied. "He's lost enough."

"Well, then, good luck. But be careful. Scarecrow has taken it to a whole new level—he's never threatened anything like this before. It scares me."

"I'm not that far behind you," Batman admitted. "It seems like each new madmen ups the ante. There will come a time when even my tricks are useless against them."

"And then what do we do?"

"What we've always done, I suppose. We keep fighting until we no longer can."

The Founder's Island shopping mall had closed its doors after Gotham City's devastating earthquake. But even before the quake brought down several of its hub stores, the mall was in serious financial trouble. Wary of driving to *that* part of town, customers decided en masse not to leave their safe homes, but to buy their non-perishables over the internet. Over a four-year span, the mall fell into a downward spiral, and finally crashed when the earth collapsed beneath it.

Batman pulled the Batmobile into the north parking lot, as close to the back fence as possible. His sensors scanned the buildings, then he called Fox.

"You seeing this, Lucius?"

"I am. The mall's been reconditioned, and a fortified gate has been built. Its beams and walls are reinforced. I'm picking up sensor alarms everywhere. It's a break-in artist's worst nightmare."

"Yet I've driven past it a hundred times and never suspected it had been retrofitted—the outside looks no different than it did the day after the quake brought it down. This is a study in *very* effective camouflage."

"Scarecrow must have been planning this for a very long time," Fox said. *"So what now?"*

"I can't drive in with the gate closed," Batman said. "But I think I have an alternative."

"At the risk of repeating myself, please be careful. Someone spent a fortune shoring up those buildings. They're not going to give it up easily."

The original schematics presented a clear picture. Odds were that its footprint would essentially be the same. Batman made his way to the exterior generators. A guard gate stood beyond that. Blocking his entrance to the mall was a reinforced steel grating. He couldn't shut down the generator for long without engendering suspicion, but momentary brownouts were common in Gotham City.

"Lucius, on the count of three, please."

"How long will you need?"

"If I can't get through in three seconds, I don't deserve the mask or the cape."

"You honestly don't expect a reply to that, do you?" Fox replied. "All right. Get ready.

"One."

The power went down. Batman's auto-ratchet undid the bolts and let him remove the gate.

"Two…"

He snaked through, replaced the gate, and fastened the bolts just as the generators turned back on and power returned to the mall.

"How long was that, Lucius?"

"You had at least a half-second to spare."

"So next time I can take my time. Maybe have a latte."

"If you decide to do that, please warn me in advance. I'd like to prepare my résumé."

"Not an option, Lucius. Your contract's iron clad."

Locating a manhole cover, he entered the tunnels.

He looked up through an open metal grating and saw Scarecrow's soldiers running past, getting ready for whatever their boss was planning next. Several hundred feet further on, Batman entered a side tunnel and found a power box that connected to the mall's phone system.

"Lucius, are you picking up any phone usage?"

"Indeed I am," Fox replied. *"Cellular. I've been monitoring them, and as yet nothing has been said that would be of any use. Why?"*

"I need to make a phone call. I saw a guard gatehouse. Can you find out if someone inside is using their cell?"

"Done and done. I've downloaded the number to your address book. And I've already reprogrammed your little toy, so it's ready for use."

"Good. Once we're in position, you'll remote pilot the Batmobile. I'll deal with Scarecrow and the Knight." Batman hit his gauntlet comm and made the call. When a guard answered, he spoke into the voice synthesizer, reprogrammed by Fox to replicate Scarecrow's voice.

"There's been a change of plans," he said, mimicking his opponent's halting speech pattern. "We've taken the Batmobile. I've arranged for it to be delivered here. When it arrives, open the gate immediately and let it pass."

"Yes, sir!"

The gate slid open, allowing the vehicle to enter and make its way inside. Once past the defenses, Fox transformed the car to tank mode. Before any of the enemy could act, he launched a missile at the closest tank, then used non-lethal weaponry on the living.

As he did, Batman made his way deeper into the fortress.

Four mercs were posted by the elevator leading to the mall's ground floor. Only auxiliary lights were on, casting the entire facility in a bizarre pattern of crisscrossing light and shadows. Distant explosions and gunfire could be heard.

Several dozen stores, long closed, crowded the perimeter surrounding an outsized promenade where large events had once been staged. Spring fashion shows packed the promenade in May only to be replaced when fall fashions found their way into the stores. October was turned over to ghosts, goblins and witches, while cover bands of seventies, eighties and nineties hit groups entertained shoppers the rest of the year.

At the moment, Santa's village filled a small corner of the space, as eerily empty as its surroundings. The rest had become a staging area for Scarecrow and his killers. Four men guarded a variety of equipment—mostly weapons.

Emerging quietly, Batman launched his Batarang at the closest merc, taking him down before he registered what hit him. Seeing him collapse in a heap, others reached for their weapons—but were too slow. A second Batarang throw brought down the next merc while Batman waded into the remaining two, dispatching them efficiently and with a minimum of noise.

He pried open the elevator, dragged the unconscious mercs inside, then removed the access panel on the ceiling. Climbing up into the shaft, he fired a grapple to a ledge and rewound it, so that it carried him to level one.

Undetected, Batman made his way through the mall.

Scarecrow and the Knight were there somewhere, and he was bringing the war to them.

Two mercs stood between him and the access corridor that led to a back hallway. It circled the mall behind the stores, enabling retailers to move merchandise in and out without customers seeing them. Slipping up in the shadows, he used a chokehold to bring one of them down, while a knee to the groin doubled over the second one.

He dragged them both through the access door, closing it quietly, and turned to the merc moaning in pain.

"Where's Scarecrow?" he demanded in a low growl. The merc shook his head.

"No way. No way. You… you'll only hurt me—but he'll *kill* me if I tell you."

Batman's eyes flashed green.

"The rules have changed," he said, and he moved in closer. "I *will* kill you. And then I'll kill everyone you've ever known." He grabbed the man and lifted him. "Tell me. Tell me *now*."

The man's eyes went wide, and Batman dropped him unceremoniously.

"Now you're showing guts, chum," the Joker said, leaning in between Batman and the merc. He crossed his arms in front of his chest and looked heavenward with delight. "My psycho baby is growing up. Daddy couldn't be more proud."

Batman fell back, shaking off his anger. But he didn't take his eyes off of the merc, who was still shivering from the threat. The man came to a decision, rose, and pointed across the mall.

"Th… the old shoe store… on level two. Don't kill me. *Please* don't kill me."

Batman paused, then drove his fist into the merc's face and the man collapsed again, unconscious. The Joker applauded as he stepped out of the way and let Batman pass.

Batman exited back into the main hallway, then grappled to the second level. The schematic located the shoe store on the opposite end of the atrium—a wide, circular area that opened onto all four floors. When he reached it, there were at least a half-dozen mercs on patrol. He grappled to a high spot, and perched thirty feet above the floor.

Off in the distance he heard another round of explosions, and the walls shook. The thugs below stopped and peered off into the distance, then resumed their rounds.

Two of the mercs walked together toward the toy store. Though it was dangling by a single cable, the old "TOYZ" sign still hung over the door. Batman estimated that it was solid enough for him to land on, and high enough for him not to be seen from the floor. Keeping to the shadows, he swung to the sign and kneeled behind the oversized Z. Then he patiently waited as the mercs passed under him.

When they started to move on, he dropped down behind one, grabbed him around the windpipe, then tightened his grip and brought him down. Simultaneously he shoved his palm into the throat of the other merc then spun, slamming his foot into the man's face. They both lay unconscious, and Batman grappled up to the sign again.

Maynard & May, the one-time high-end fashion store, was four hundred feet to the left, across the hallway. Three mercs paced in front of it, weapons ready. The M&M sign above its padlocked doors hung directly overhead. He waited for a moment when the mercs had turned away, then grappled over to it and nestled above them.

Scarecrow's voice blasted over the mall intercom.

"Attention. An intruder has invaded our premises. Find him, but be aware, I want him alive. You have your master's orders. Obey them."

The mercs below snapped to attention, then moved off in separate directions, each hoping to claim the reward. *Good.* Separating them would make this easier.

He fired a grapple line at one of them, snagged him by the collar, then pulled him up. The man shouted as Batman grabbed his wrist and lifted him to eye level.

"You picked the wrong side," he said, then he dropped the merc back to the floor. He heard a leg snap and a gasp of pain, but shock kept the thug quiet. He'd live, but he wouldn't be running any marathons.

The Joker blood was taking control and he knew somehow he had to fight it, but it was pushing him far beyond the limits. He closed his eyes, let his anger fade, then moved on.

A Batarang brought down the second of the three. The third one saw his friend fall and ran to help. A moment later Batman landed on top of him and smashed him into the stone floor.

The final merc saw him from across the atrium and fired his rifle. The bullet slammed into Batman's chest and the force threw him back. His armor protected him, but the high-velocity impact still hurt like hell.

The man fired again, but Batman was ready. He rolled

to the side as the bullet shot past, missing by inches. The merc tossed the rifle aside and grabbed his automatic. But Batman fired his grapple first. It snagged the weapon and pulled it from the merc's hand.

Then he leaped. His cape blossomed into wings, allowing him to soar across the atrium and dive into the would-be killer. He drove his fist hard into the merc's face, and the man was down.

More mercs would soon be coming, and his luck would eventually run out. As good as he was, he ultimately couldn't outrace hundreds of bullets fired at the same time. All Scarecrow's men needed was one solid hit. He lowered himself to the ground floor again, and made his way to the delivery hallway. It would offer a small measure of protection, and some much-needed time to catch his breath.

The hallway led him behind the shopping area, to the private offices as well as the loading bay. They were surprisingly empty now, which meant all the mercs were all out looking for him. The empty corridors made his job easier, and allowed him a moment's respite. He paused and leaned against the wall, then triggered his communicator to call Fox.

"It's all fun and games here, Lucius," he said, keeping his voice low to prevent it from echoing. "How's it going with you?"

"As well as one can expect, sir. The Batmobile and I have taken out at least five drone tanks, and we've put several dozen armed mercenaries to sleep. They should wake up in a few hours, with fairly severe headaches."

"I'm sure there's a drug store in the mall. We'll spring for some aspirin."

"*I'll put in the order now. We've also been causing a bit of structural damage to the buildings. To shake things up a bit.*"

"Good. Any word on Gordon? I haven't seen any sign of him anywhere."

"*Nothing. I've been looking, too. You know, Scarecrow or Knight might have found him first.*" A pause, then he added, "*It's possible they've already executed him.*"

"I considered that, Lucius, but no, I don't think so. Scarecrow wants to make me feel fear. He's given instructions to keep me alive—he wants to *break* me. Killing Gordon off-screen doesn't help his mission. I think they'll keep him around until they get me, and then they'll kill him in front of me to achieve maximum impact.

"It's sick, twisted, but it'll be effective."

"*And how are we planning to avoid that scenario?*"

"I can't allow myself to be captured, I guess."

"*Good plan.*" Another pause, then Fox said, "*Ahh, I see another tank up ahead that needs to be dealt with. I'll speak with you later, then.*"

"Later. And good luck."

"*I thought you didn't believe in luck.*"

"Desperate times. Desperate measures."

41

He followed the hallway to another tunnel grating. His schematics indicated that this one snaked its way under the mall. Just what he needed. His sensors showed three red dots about ninety yards ahead. *Why only three?* Why weren't they with the others, hunting for him?

Batman thought he knew the answer. He hurried through the tunnels until he was under a grating that let him observe two mercs standing outside a heavy steel door, guarding it. They accounted for two of the red dots, and now there was a green one inside the room.

It had to be Gordon.

He stood up carefully, keeping his eyes on the guards. They looked professional, with rifles at the ready. He reached into one of his belt pouches and removed a small screwdriver from it, then tossed it through the grating, away from the door.

The screwdriver clanked down the tunnel, startling the men. Weapons up, they ran to the sound. Batman used the distraction to lift the grating, then sprung at them, taking them down from behind.

He smashed his foot into one of the merc's legs,

splintering his knee bone. The man fell, yelping in pain. The second merc spun, already in position, about to fire. Batman arced over the top of him, and as he did so he grabbed the merc's head and pulled it down, shoving it hard into the floor.

The Joker's methods might be vicious but they worked, and they worked fast. Still, the impact wasn't enough. The merc scrambled to his feet again, aimed his weapon and squeezed the trigger. As he did so, however, Batman grabbed his wrist and forced the gun up. Its bullet blasted into the ceiling.

The merc tried to pull his hand away, but Batman refused to let go. He forced the man's hand back, until the gun was aimed at his own face. That was the last straw—the merc panicked. He opened his hand and released the rifle.

In a single move Batman kicked the gun away, then followed through and drove his knee into the merc's gut. As his opponent doubled over, Batman clasped his hands together and slammed down on the back of the man's head.

This time he was down for the count.

Batman bolted for the door.

Jim Gordon was gagged and bound to a chair in the middle of an immense chamber, broken up by a series of short walls that created an almost maze-like effect with dozens of closed-in cubicle-like spaces in which one could hide. A series of stone gargoyles protruded from all four walls just below the high ceiling, staring down on the insanity below.

Gordon looked at Batman, first with disbelief then with

elation. Batman started to remove his gag when he saw Gordon's eyes suddenly widen with panic.

Batman spun to see the Arkham Knight standing behind him, gun in hand, aimed at Batman's head.

"Should I say 'surprise?' I mean, you already know I'm here."

Batman glanced at his gauntlet sensor; there was still only one red dot in the room. The Knight saw him do it, and laughed.

"Confused?" he said. "Once you know everything there is to know about Lucius and his toys, it's easy to counter them."

"Who *are* you?"

"You really have no idea, do you, Bruce?" the Knight said as he unlocked his mask and slid it open. Batman stared in stunned silence.

Jason Todd grinned.

"I'm thinking 'surprise' is more appropriate now, don't you? And aren't you happy? I mean, the Knight's come out into daylight."

Batman stared. It had been three years since he last saw him, but Jason was looking even older than that. He once had a ready laugh, but now, even though he was relishing the moment and enjoying Batman's confusion, his laugh was grim and angry. There was no humor in his dark eyes.

"You're staring at me crazy-like, Bruce. Don't you want to say, 'Jason, but you're dead,' or something else obvious?" The entire time he spoke, the gun never wavered.

The Joker moved closer to Batman, waving his hands in front of him to catch his attention.

"Let's not have a falling out here, Bats. I might have told

you a teeny tiny little lie. But c'mon. Look at the boy. He's alive. Isn't that a kick in the *cojones*?"

He moved to the Arkham Knight and grinned. "You did good, boy. We did good. You should be proud." He then turned to Batman and laughed. "You know, Bats, if I were you—and I will be soon enough—about now I'd be trying to decide if the Todd is another hallucination or not. Hint, he's the real deal."

"I don't care what I'm seeing now," Batman said. "If Jason Todd was alive, he wouldn't have waited three years to tell me."

Jason took another step closer to Batman. "It has been three years, hasn't it, Bruce. Three years during which that monster tortured me. Lied to me, twisted around all my thoughts until I didn't know what was right any more.

"Three... goddam... years."

The Joker nodded to Batman. "The boy's right. I did it. Me. And mea culpa. I dug into his gray matter and stirred it all up until Toddy made me look almost sane. But on the bright side, screwing around with his little-kid brain was the happiest I'd been in a long, long time."

Jason stepped closer.

"So tell me, Bruce, did you even bother to check if the world's biggest liar had actually lied to you about my death, or did you shrug your shoulders and say, 'I need a new Robin. Who's next in line?'"

None of this is real. It can't be. Batman stared at Jason, remembering what he once looked like, but the man standing in front of him looked so very, very different. *You can't be here. None of this is possible. You're Joker blood mixed with the Scarecrow's toxins.*

"No, he's not, Bats," the Joker said, laughing. "Look at the boy. As we've said before, if you prick him, will he not bleed? If you tickle him, would he not laugh? If you wrong him, does he not seek revenge? And if you bash in his head, will he not die? Ummm. Actually, I guess the answer to that last one may be 'no'."

"What's the matter?" Jason said. "Lost for words? I expected more. I'm hurt."

"The Joker sent me the film. I saw him kill you."

Jason held his gun on Batman as he moved closer, putting his cowl back into place. "I know what you saw, and that's how I learned how little I meant to you. How long did you wait before replacing me with Timmy boy? A month? A week? I trusted you, and you just left me to die."

"That's not what happened, Jason."

Jason pushed the gun into Batman's chin.

"You always told me… focus on what I want to achieve and it will happen. Well, Bruce, I want you dead."

Batman nodded and allowed himself a brief smile. Then he slammed his head hard into Jason's face, shattering his mask and cowl.

Jason staggered back and gasped in pain and shock. He closed his eyes for a moment to regain control, but when he opened them, Batman was gone.

"Coward."

He reached for his shattered cowl and threw it aside,

then he assembled his gun into a sniper rifle before tearing off a strap tied to his chest to reveal the red bat symbol hidden beneath it.

"You can't hide from me, you bastard," he said as he activated a red visor that wrapped around his face. "I will hunt you down. I will find you."

While the Dark Knight's eyes were closed, Batman darted behind one of the many short walls that formed the room's cubicles, not far from where Gordon sat, chained to the chair, unable to do anything but watch the battle in play.

Gordon watched Batman crouch behind the wall even as Jason Todd shook off the pain and rose again to his feet. Jason snapped his fingers and a half-dozen guards streamed into the room.

"He's here, somewhere. Find him—but bring him to me alive. I'm the one who will kill him. Nobody else. Just me."

Jason looked up at the gargoyles, scanning each one. "He's got a thing for hiding in high places. Maybe even hanging upside down, just like all the goddam bats. Keep your eyes up. Keep your eyes open."

Batman was still crouching behind the wall, waiting. Jason carefully circled the immense chamber, moving behind each protruding wall, checking the cubicle hiding spaces, until he was less than thirty yards from where Batman was waiting. It wouldn't take long to find him, Gordon knew.

Jason moved closer, then heard a muffled sound behind him. He whirled, gun ready, but nobody was there. He continued ahead, moving quickly, reaching the wall behind which Batman was hiding, ready to fire.

Batman wasn't there.

He'd taken that momentary distraction and grappled to the closest gargoyle, then pressed close to it to avoid being seen. As Jason and his militia continued to scour the room, he grappled to a second gargoyle, once again pressing in close. He waited for them to move on, then grappled to the next gargoyle.

He waited. Jason moved past him, the militia flanking him on all sides. Batman waited for the last soldier to step beneath him, and then he dropped to the ground and took the man out with a silent chokehold.

The soldiers heard nothing, but Jason had. He whirled and fired, but Batman was already gone.

"He's here. He's targeting us. Do your damn jobs and find him." The men nodded quietly. It was clear from their expressions that they feared him.

Batman grappled to the next gargoyle, then flattened himself again as Jason opened fire on the one he'd just vacated. The gargoyle exploded into countless pieces, but Batman was nowhere to be found.

He lowered himself behind another of the militia soldiers, grabbed him across his mouth and throat. In seconds the man was unconscious. Batman fired his grapple across the room, latching onto the next level up and disappearing into the dark.

"Bruce, listen to me," Jason shouted. "I know you won't

leave until you confront me again, but that only means you're giving me more time to find you and kill you. You think I'm trapped here with you, but you're trapped here with me—and remember, I know all your secrets. I know how you think, and I know exactly how I'm going to kill you."

He suddenly turned again and sprayed the gargoyles with bullets, destroying three more, damaging all of them. But Batman was back on the ground, hiding in another cubicle, another unconscious soldier lying behind him. He nodded to Gordon, who gave no sign, but watched as Batman once again grappled to a gargoyle. Jason's bullets had destroyed half of it, but still Batman blended into the shadows, away from view.

Two more soldiers to go, and then he had to confront Jason Todd. He prayed he could convince his former partner to surrender, yet knew he would not. Batman couldn't kill him, but he was afraid there would be no other way to stop him. He wasn't sure what he was going to do when they came face to face.

Batman lowered himself behind another short wall and grabbed a soldier who was peering up at the gargoyles. The soldier went down, leaving only one more with whom to deal.

And then Jason.

"You're good, Bruce. Better than ever, but you're going to lose this war, and I think you know it." Jason stepped away from the last soldier. "Everything you care about has been taken from you. Your former friend," he said, pointing at Gordon, still chained to his chair. "He now hates you, as well he should. The Joker would never have had any reason to ruin his daughter's life if it wasn't for you.

"Your first Robin barely speaks to you. Your current one feels neglected. And you can see how you impacted on my life. I not only want you dead, I want you thoroughly destroyed. I want the very memory of you purged from the history books."

Jason stared up toward the dark ceiling. Batman had to be there, hiding on top of a gargoyle, or in the shadows of the rafters. Jason held his weapon, pivoting it right, left, up, down; Jason would find Bruce wherever he was hiding.

"Change of plans, Bats," he shouted. "You tend to win these engagements because your enemies talk you to death. Well, my talking ends now. No more witty banter. If I see you, I shoot you—and if I shoot you, you will die."

Jason turned to give new orders to the final soldier, but the man was already unconscious on the ground. A silent takedown. Batman specialized in those. He started to get angry, but pushed it aside. The soldiers were only cannon fodder. They existed solely to keep Batman busy. To tire him out.

Batman had the weight advantage and, as hard as it was to admit it, he was the better fighter. Exhausting him before the two faced off would almost make them equals.

Jason strained to listen to every sound echoing through the vast chamber. Everything reverberated off the walls—every step, every movement. Maybe it had been a mistake, luring Batman here where he couldn't easily pinpoint his location.

Maybe it was, but there was no turning back. Whatever

happened next, however the encounter unfolded, the only way it was going to end was with his former mentor lying face down on the floor in a spreading pool of his own blood.

Suddenly a shadow flashed by and Jason fired, but there was no one there. Something moved off to his left. He fired again.

Still nothing. He heard a whooshing sound high overhead, in the rafters. He sprayed the ceiling with bullets, but there was nobody there.

Jason was angry now.

Where the hell are you—?

Batman was behind him.

Jason whirled but a clenched fist slammed him back. Then a foot smashed into his arm, breaking something, forcing him to drop his gun. He scrambled for it but a volley of hard, steady punches kept him off balance. He tried to back away, to gain a moment to collect his thoughts, but a knee smashed into his groin and he yelped in pain.

He fell back, then the dark shadow moved closer. He twisted and rolled off to the side. The shadow fell on empty ground.

Jason caught his breath and rose to his feet.

"You are good, old man, but I'm ready now. Let's see what you've got."

Batman emerged from the shadows just in front of him, scarcely two feet away. Suddenly, he was on top of Jason, balled fists smashing into his face and gut.

Jason intentionally fell back and then spun. His foot slammed into Batman's neck, just where the cape was secured to his shoulders. By necessity this was an unprotected area—one of the very few in Batman's armor.

Batman tumbled back, and before he could right himself, Jason was on him, smashing a fist into his face, smashing his elbows into Batman's gut.

"I *trusted* you, Bruce," Jason screamed. "I trusted you and what did you do? You left me to be tortured for so long in that rotting cell in Arkham."

"That's not what happened, Jason. I swear. I didn't know you were alive."

"You didn't care enough to find out."

"But I know now," Batman replied, blood pouring from his nose as Jason slammed him again. He didn't bother to wipe it away. "We can work together to fix you. Let me help you. Please, Jason. Give me the chance to help."

The Joker was dancing behind Batman. "You don't honestly think he's going to let you help? The kid's a feral dog, Bats. The only way to stop him is to put him down."

But Batman wasn't listening.

Jason picked the gun up from the floor and again pointed it at Batman.

"Go ahead," Batman said. "I understand. I accepted a lunatic's word that he killed you. I believed the faked video he sent me. And if you decide, I'll accept the consequences. But I can help you… I want to help you."

"There's no way on Earth you can do anything to help me. Not now. Not ever." Jason stared at Batman, his hand trembled and he tightened his grip on the gun. "I was in his goddam prison for three years, Bruce. You have no idea what he did to me. You left me to suffer there for so long. He made me suffer for so long."

"I did. I really did," the Joker said, theatrically solemn. He pulled a long, multicolored handkerchief from his pocket and wiped his eyes. "I am such a bad man. Next time I get deep-fried, I want to push the button myself."

Suddenly Jason screamed. He dropped the gun to the floor and turned away.

"I *can't*. I want to, but I can't." He fell to his knees and wept.

As he watched Jason crying, Batman knew this was his fault, and because of him, everyone he cared about was hurt, or died. He turned from Jason and tapped his gauntlet communicator.

Alfred's face appeared in the hologram.

"Is everything all right, sir?"

"Alfred, I found him," Batman said. "I found Jason."

"Excuse me?" For a moment Alfred was speechless. *"Master Todd is—"*

"No," Batman said. "He's been alive all this time. Prisoner of the Joker. I believed that madman's lies. I should have known better than that."

"I'm so sorry, sir. But is he all right now?"

Batman turned back to Jason, but he was gone. All that was left in his place was the Arkham Knight's mask, broken and discarded.

"No, Alfred," Batman said, his voice soft and hollow. "No. He's not." He stopped talking, said nothing for a long time, then took a deep breath and pushed aside his melancholy. "I wanted to touch base with you one more time. I'm not sure what's going to happen now."

"Sir, don't do anything rash," Alfred said, and it was clear

he was struggling to stay calm. *"Why don't you come home? I think we need to talk."*

"I think I've talked more than enough. Take care, Alfred. I'm sending you instructions. See that they're implemented." He turned off the comm and the hologram retracted into his glove. Then he turned to see Jim Gordon, still gagged and bound to the chair, staring at Batman, fully aware of everything he'd just seen.

Batman removed his gag then cut through the ropes.

"What happened?" he asked.

"I went after Crane. I got caught."

"Jim, I am so sorry. For everything. Especially Barbara. Please forgive me."

"No. Don't." Gordon stood up and shook off the last of the bindings. "Let's get this over with. Look, I may be sorry for what you must be going through, but all I care about now is finding Scarecrow. And after I deal with him, you and I are done."

"I know I should have found a way to stop him before, but we can find him now. Together."

"He's on the roof," Gordon said. "Let's go." Batman followed him to the elevator. They stood in silence as it slowly creaked its way up.

"Jim, I won't let us stop being friends. Working with you has been an honor."

"No. Don't."

"I have to. You're too important to me. And even if you can't forgive me, you've got to believe I was honoring Barbara's wishes. She wouldn't have let you stop her even if you knew the truth. She was that stubborn."

Gordon gave a short laugh. "Yeah. Like her old man. You know, you see a lot in this job. A lot of pain. A lot of suffering. But I'll never forget taking a witness statement from an eight-year-old who had seen his parents gunned down."

"You were kind, Jim."

"I was thinking, I may never get the chance to tell you this. To say sorry."

"There's nothing to apologize for, Jim," Batman said. "We go back too long to fight forever."

"I'm not trying to apologize. I'm trying to explain that you and I are very much the same. We'd do anything for our family. Anything."

"What do you mean?" Batman asked. But Gordon was staring at the elevator door, waiting for it to open.

42

Gordon stepped out onto the roof, and Batman followed as the door closed behind him. Scarecrow was standing at the edge, looking over the city he had tried to destroy.

"Gotham City was so close to perfection," Scarecrow said. "But now it's like every place else. So many opportunities wasted. It's so sad."

"It's over, Crane," Batman said. "On your knees. You're under arrest."

"You did it," Scarecrow continued, as if Batman hadn't even spoken. "You know, I must admit I had my doubts that you could make this happen, but you did."

"What the hell are you talking about, Crane?"

"I'm not talking to you," Scarecrow said as he turned to Jim Gordon. "It's time."

Batman turned to find Jim Gordon standing behind him, holding a gun, pointing it at Batman.

"Sorry, but this is the only way all this can end," Gordon said. He called to Scarecrow but kept his eyes on Batman. "Get me my daughter, Crane."

The elevator door opened again and Batman saw one of Scarecrow's mercs wheel Barbara Gordon onto the roof.

She was bound to the wheelchair and tried to squirm free, but she couldn't. Then she saw her father holding a gun on Batman.

"Dad, what are you doing?"

"Barbara, are you all right?" he responded. "Did he hurt you?" He started to move to her when Scarecrow stepped in front of him.

"Close enough."

Batman stared, still not believing.

First Jason, now Barbara.

"She's alive? What's going on, Jim?"

"You assumed, Batman," Scarecrow said. "You believed things without verifying them. But the truth is, once your closest friend kills you, I will allow him to walk out of here with his daughter alive. And should he fail to kill you, then he and his spawn will die along with you. You know which choice he has to make. There is no alternative."

He looked back at the city and spread his arms wide, as if welcoming it into his life.

"You are going to die now. Your true face will be revealed for everyone to see. The fools who believed in you will then learn their savior was no heaven-sent angel, but just a delusional failure of a man. And they will realize they have no choice but to bow before me."

Gordon turned the gun from Batman and aimed it at Scarecrow.

"That wasn't our deal, Crane. It was Barbara's life for Batman's."

Scarecrow laughed. "Deals change, And if you resist me, the next change I make will be the last for you and your progeny." He turned his attention to the soldier who had pushed Barbara's chair to the roof's edge.

"Call in the transport."

"Jim, you can't be part of this," Batman said. Yet with all that had caused Gordon pain over the years—his wife, his son, his daughter's injury—he fully believed the cop would do everything possible if it meant sparing Barbara more pain.

"Why not?" Gordon said, his voice strained. "You've been lying to me for years now. Even after she was crippled you put her in constant peril. Dear God, you nearly got her killed."

Scarecrow walked over to the wheelchair and tapped it. It teetered precariously on the roof edge, but he then pulled it back, steadying it. He held onto the handle and turned back to Batman.

"I don't know why you're resisting death. After all, you and I both know you haven't got much longer to go anyway. Before he died the Joker informed me that he infected your blood. I designed a very special form of my fear toxin to bring out the Joker in you."

"He's right, Bats. We were working together. So, tick tock, your time is running out. Madness and fear is what your future's all about."

Stunned by what he had heard, Gordon stared at the gun in his hand, then turned quickly to Batman and fired twice, both bullets hitting him squarely in the chest. The impact sent him flying back off the roof, out of sight.

* * *

Barbara gasped, horrified as another of Scarecrow's mercenaries forced Gordon to the ground.

"For God's sake, Crane," he gritted, struggling against the thugs. "I did everything you wanted. Let her go."

Scarecrow leaned down until they were eye to eye.

"Gotham City will know the truth," Scarecrow said. He walked to the roof's edge and again rested his hand on the wheelchair's push handle. "And they will learn the truth today."

As Scarecrow pushed her wheelchair even closer to the edge, Barbara glared at him.

"You don't scare me."

Scarecrow laughed. "It's okay to be afraid, dear. You know what happens when you refuse to let your fears control you?

"You. Must. Face. Them," he said.

With a casual push, he shoved the wheelchair over the edge of the roof, and turned back to see Gordon screaming in horror. Then he turned to the mercenary who had wheeled Barbara onto the roof.

"Inform my tank drivers that we're good to go." He gestured toward the commissioner. "Bring the crying fool with us. He might still prove useful."

Scarecrow entered the elevator and took it to the mall parking lot where a transport helicopter waited on the uppermost level. He climbed inside, thinking Batman and the girl were both dead. Perhaps not the way he wanted, but that was no reason to be nit-picky about it. In a few days his tanks would disperse more fear gas. This time there'd be nobody to stop him.

Gotham City would still be his.

* * *

Four minutes, twelve seconds earlier

Gordon stared at the gun in his hand then turned to Batman and fired it, shooting him squarely in the chest. The impact sent him flying back off the roof, out of sight.

Gordon shot him in the bat-symbol that covered his reinforced, bulletproof armor beneath.

The hit was not an accident.

Two minutes, thirty-nine seconds earlier

With a casual push, Scarecrow shoved her wheelchair over the edge of the roof. Barbara fell, the ropes still binding her to the wheelchair. She began to silently recite her prayers as a Batclaw suddenly grabbed the chair's push bar and held it in place, dangling it many stories above the ground.

A thin line dropped next to her. A moment later Batman slid down it. He reached out to her.

"Take my hand."

Barbara held onto him as he cut the ropes. Then the wheelchair shook free and crashed below. He held onto her as he lowered them both to the ground.

"I thought he killed you," she said as he sat on the curb next to her.

"Your father knew what he was doing," he said, removing the two bullets imbedded in his chest plate, then handing them to her. A moment later the Batmobile pulled to a stop in front of them. Its door swung open and Batman lifted her up again, carefully placing her inside.

"Where are they taking him, Bruce?"

"Don't worry, Barbara. We found you. I'll find him."

The present

Gordon knew how Batman thought. He'd known him since he was a boy of eight, sharp, dedicated, and brilliant. He'd watched him grow into the man Gordon wished his own son could have been.

When he shot him he knew Batman would be stunned for at most a few seconds before his survival instinct kicked in. He'd use his grapple cable to swing to safety somewhere under the mall roof, out of Scarecrow's line of sight.

He hadn't anticipated what Crane would do with Barbara, but Scarecrow didn't leave his prisoners alive. He and Barbara were doomed long before Gordon led Batman to the rooftop. His only hope—his single prayer—was that if Batman didn't die when Gordon put two bullets into him, he would somehow find a way to save Barbara, too.

But until he knew for certain, he had to act as if she hadn't died. It gave him hope, but he also knew he couldn't give Crane even a single excuse to search for them.

43

The police had been decimated—only a token force remained behind. A few hundred cops decided on their own to stay in the city and help those who needed them. Government officials had long abandoned City Hall and fled north to safety. A half-dozen fire engines were still in service, but were hopelessly undermanned. Huge sections of the city were left to burn simply because there weren't enough personnel to put out the fires.

When the attacks first began, the federal authorities received a message. They were warned that, were they to launch a counter assault, Scarecrow would immediately unleash enough fear toxin to kill everyone within a ten-mile radius. The feds had the National Guard and the Marines ready to move in, but waited for a full assessment of the situation.

They didn't know if the Gotham City vigilante known as Batman could be trusted, but they did know he was their only contact inside the city. Even Air Force drones weren't secure against mercenaries armed with surface-to-air missiles.

Scarecrow's tanks patrolled all of Gotham City, unopposed by any resistance. The first few civilian attacks against the invaders had been met with lethal responses. In one instance an entire neighborhood had been razed to the ground.

Gotham City belonged to Scarecrow.

Batman brought Barbara to the relative safety of the Gotham City Police headquarters. The building had been abandoned, giving little reason for Scarecrow to send his forces there. He carried her to the police computer facilities, a former interrogation room that had been retrofitted with the most up-to-date tech the G.C.P.D. could afford—by 2007 standards. The computers were still running old software that had been barely functional when it first debuted.

Despite the tech, Oracle still felt at home.

"Trouble," she said after a few keystrokes. "Data's being deleted from the Clock Tower's servers. I don't have access to my intel." She looked up at him. "Wonder what took them so long."

"I can stop them," Batman said. "Do your best to delay it, but give me at least ten minutes."

As he made his way back through the G.C.P.D., his gauntlet comm buzzed and Scarecrow's face filled the holo screen.

"My tech boys said they thought someone was piggybacking them. And guess who I found on the other end of our hack? Hello again, Batman. You're certainly full of surprises. Yet I'm so… pleased you checked in. I wanted to show you something I found in the Panessa Studios trash dump."

The picture widened. Scarecrow was holding a gun, and

it was pressed to Robin's temple.

"Another of your acolytes will die because of you, Batman."

"Crane, if you hurt him..."

"Your threats are meaningless, Batman. It is only when you bow before me and acknowledge me as your master will I relieve you of your pain."

"What do you want from me?"

"Surrender to me immediately, or the boy dies."

"All right, Crane. You win."

"My victory was always assured. You just needed to accept it."

44

Darkness.

Then he woke up in an alley. But how did he get here?

He remembered meeting Scarecrow's men in front of the Gotham City Library. He let his hands be tied together behind his back. He remembered being pushed into a truck.

But nothing else.

Not until the darkness faded and he saw the washed-out sign for the single-room-occupancy hotel. That told him he was in Crime Alley, originally called Park Row until two innocent people leaving a nearby theater were attacked and murdered.

This was where it all started for Bruce Wayne. This, he feared, is where it would also end. Feared?

No.

He had to fight fear, not embrace it.

He would not let Scarecrow win.

A black shape whizzed past. Then another and another. The dark alleyway was filled with thousands of these shapes, flitting past him like… like… like the bats in that well. They were screaming at him then, too. And laughing. Laughing so loud that his ears started to bleed.

One of the shapes paused in front of him, shouted something indecipherable, then flew away. It wasn't a bat. None of them were bats. They were all shadows of the Joker—hundreds of Jokers, and they were all trying to claw their way inside him.

He screamed.

Then he woke up.

He was in a hospital van. The words "Arkham Asylum" were stenciled on the inside of the doors. Arkham on the left door. Asylum on the right. He was chained to a hospital gurney, unable to move.

Crane stood over him, fingering one of the syringes that fit over his fingers. It was glowing with fear toxin. "I've injected you with five times the necessary dose, but you show no signs of submission. Are you not human? How do you defy me? Why can't I control you as I do everyone else?"

Batman smiled but said nothing. He knew the answer but he wasn't going to share it with the madman. *Ivy did this. When her plants held me, when that thorn pricked me.*

"Whatever your secret, you cannot hold out forever. And if I cannot make you suffer fear, I will watch you die… painfully. Either way, I win."

Batman saw the Joker sitting in the back of the van, tied up in a straitjacket, his hands trapped behind him. He was happily whistling a song Batman didn't recognize. It was about losing your mind and never being able to see daylight again.

For the very first time since that terrible night in the well, Batman truly felt fear.

45

Arkham Asylum, founded by Dr. Amadeus Arkham in the early nineteen hundreds, was named after Elizabeth Arkham, Amadeus' mother. Elizabeth had long suffered from mental illness and eventually committed suicide, although legend had it that Amadeus had actually euthanized her.

Whatever the truth, Elizabeth was the asylum's first patient, as well as its first victim. Over the next century there would be hundreds of others.

For more than a hundred years, Gotham City's most sick and twisted were sentenced to Arkham to undergo rehabilitation, although none of its proprietors ever seemed to succeed in ridding their patients of any of their madness. Harleen Quinzel had served there as the asylum psychologist, and, for a short while, so had Jonathan Crane. Hugo Strange had worked with the Asylum as well as the Gotham PD, analyzing criminal behavior—when he wasn't chemically transforming his own patients into monsters.

The joke among the brutal asylum guards was if you weren't criminally insane when you entered Arkham Asylum, you would be before you broke free. It was funny because it was all too true.

* * *

Drugged into submission, Batman was chained to a gurney and wheeled down an old stone corridor to the main examination room, a dark, gloomy laboratory that wouldn't have been out of place in a black-and-white monster movie. He didn't bother struggling—even if there was a way to free himself, there was no place he could go.

He felt the Joker's blood taking control. Soon he would no longer be able to think straight. He wondered how much longer after that he would try to kill his first prey. He could not let that happen, either to Gotham City or to himself.

Arkham, in all its hideousness, was probably the best place for him to be.

A thick brace kept his neck pinned to the gurney, but he could still see Robin tied to a chair. The boy's face showed signs of a beating and there was blood everywhere.

Another damned failure.

"I'm so sorry," he stammered. "I am so very sorry." Robin was gagged and unable to reply, but his eyes showed no fear.

TV cameras had been set up and stage lights were in place, ready to light up on command. Whatever Crane's plans were, they were going to be broadcast live.

Scarecrow ran a syringe-encased finger across Batman's mask, then tapped him on the shoulder.

"You have been playing a game with Gotham City for too long. You made its citizens believe in you. Belief led to trust and trust to dependence. But you are no heaven-sent angel, are you, Batman? You are merely some foolish dilettante devoid of hope, betrayed by his best friend, and ultimately crippled with fear." Scarecrow turned to the lighting crew and nodded. A moment later five 2,400-watt tungsten lamps brought sudden daylight to the gloom.

He turned to the camera crew and three professional camcorders started up, recording the scene. Every angle was covered.

Then he whispered softly and turned to camera one.

"Ladies and gentlemen of Gotham City, I am about to show you the true face of your once much-vaunted savior." He peered into camera two and gestured for the operator to pull in for a close-up on Batman's masked face.

"One doesn't need to see the true face of the devil in order to fear him but I show it to you because you've elevated this... annoyance... to a level of adoration that only the gods should command." He circled Batman, and gently ran his needled fingers across his armor. Then, suddenly and viciously, he slapped his face.

"But he is no saint, nor is he some meta-powered divinity. I show this to you so you will fully understand that all your hopes have been resting at the feet of an ordinary man who gets his kicks wearing black armor, while pretending to be nothing more than some flying rat."

He gestured to James Gordon, struggling while being held by two of Scarecrow's mercenaries. Camera one turned at his direction.

"For those of you who don't recognize this man, he is Police Commissioner James Gordon. An upstanding man who actually believes there is a place for hope in this cruel world. Like all believers, he is amazingly naïve, but we can forgive him that. Everyone is innocent until they've been shown the truth."

The mercenaries pushed Gordon toward Scarecrow. The commissioner looked down at Batman, lying helpless on the gurney.

"Commissioner, for nearly a decade you've been this demon's closest ally. You lied for him when the city's fathers wanted to have him imprisoned. You worked with him despite his violent, illegal methods. And until recently, when you learned he'd been lying to you for all these years, you were perhaps his only friend.

"And now I want you to have the honor of revealing Batman's true identity. I want you to remove his mask, and let the world finally see the truth."

Gordon stared at Batman, then turned to Scarecrow.

"No. I won't do it," he said.

"Then you leave me no choice." Scarecrow spun and faced Robin, then casually shot him just below his ribcage. The boy screamed in pain.

Gordon's eyes went wide, and he had to steady himself.

"You bastard!" he shouted at Scarecrow. "I'll see you die for this."

"No. You lost your control the moment you cooperated with the demon. But he doesn't control you any longer. I do."

"No. Never."

"Oh, you will. Do what I say, or my next bullet goes through the boy's heart."

Batman looked up at Gordon.

"It's okay, Jim," he said, his voice weak and the words forced. "Do it."

Gordon shook his head. "It's not okay. You know what this means."

"I know," Batman said. "And I welcome it."

Gordon glared at Scarecrow, then looked back to his old friend. "If I do this everyone will know who you are. There'll be no hiding."

"Trust me, Jim. Please. Do it."

"You heard the Bat, Gordon. Do it. NOW!"

Jim Gordon put his hands on the mask and closed his eyes. He had no choice. As the camera moved in tighter, Gordon pulled off Batman's mask.

Bruce Wayne's face filled the TV screens.

It was covered with cuts and bruises, his eyes blackened by repeated beatings. He looked into the camera but didn't try to speak. His life had been exposed for everyone to see, and there was nothing he needed to add.

"Bruce Wayne," Scarecrow said, leaning into the shot. "Billionaire philanthropist, son of Thomas and Martha Wayne—murdered by some insignificant thug when their son was only eight. That event twisted the young boy, caused him to fixate on revenge against anyone who did him wrong.

"Do I lie, Bruce?"

Wayne didn't reply.

Scarecrow turned back to the camera and addressed his unseen audience. "And so a legend is now laid bare. Powerless. Human. Afraid. And that is not the stuff of heroes."

Then, in a single move, Scarecrow slammed a syringe-covered finger deep into Batman's neck. The cameras tightened on him as Bruce shouted in pain. He struggled with his ropes, but was unable to move.

Scarecrow gestured, and the image on the monitors became a split screen. The audience would see Scarecrow slowly walking around the gurney, every so often stabbing Batman with yet another syringe-finger, injecting even more toxin into him. They would witness Bruce's reactions, but they would never see the fight inside his mind, the struggle with the Joker, the final battle between the two old foes.

"I'm feeling weird, Bruce," the Joker laughed. "No, not funny weird. Strange weird. Sickly weird. Painful weird."

Then the pain stopped. The Joker looked around, again searching for Batman, but finding nothing. But now he was in front of the wreckage of the G.C.P.D. headquarters. The city behind it was in flames.

The Joker grinned. The city deserved to burn. That was something he'd always wanted but had never achieved. How odd, he thought. It took his death to accomplish his life's ambitions.

"Hey, Bats, don't know if you can hear me with all that Scarecrow toxin flowing inside you. But you know what's great? It hasn't affected me. Guess I'm toxin proof, eh? All it's done is give me everything I ever wanted. Hey, Bats? Don't you want to say something mean to put me down?

"Bats? You still there?"

No answer. The Joker could only hear a distant beating sound, like switches being flipped. With each echoing thump the city lights turned off, blanketing him in darkness. He turned right, then left, then spun and looked behind him, but there was nothing but darkness. Nothing but endless nothingness.

"If you think this is going to screw with me you're greatly mistaken, Bruce. I'm not afraid of the dark. I am the dark... but I come with my own light." He suddenly held a WayneTech rifle in his right hand. A torch beam flickered on, revealing a small, stone-walled room. "Now you're trying to screw with my mind, aren't you? So where am I? A crypt? City Hall? Maybe some old museum celebrating all the great things Gotham City used to be but no longer is. All forgotten. Like you."

A painting hung on the stone wall: Batman holding up the Joker's corpse as he exited the old Monarch Theater.

"Is this wishful thinking, Bats? Memories of better times? But guess what, Brucey? I'm still here."

He heard a sudden rattling behind him and whirled, expecting to see the city still on fire. But it was no longer Gotham City that was burning. It was him. The Joker. Lying on the incinerator mesh. Hundreds of blue gas flames, a scorching 1,800 degrees Fahrenheit, were dancing on what was left of his body. He watched as his flesh and bones disintegrated, and then he laughed.

"Gotta tell you, Bats, I outgrew that emaciated body anyway."

No answer. No reply.

No acknowledgment he was even there.

"Where the goddam hell are you, Bats? I'm here. Talk to me. No, no, maybe you are. Maybe this is all your deluded way of you trying to tell me I'm dead? Well, look at me, Brucey. My skinny little body may be gone, but I'm still here. I'm not dead. Hell, I've never been so alive."

A sound behind him. Barely perceptible. He whirled to face the painting, only it was gone. In its place was an open doorway.

"I'm supposed to go through that? Sure. Why not. You can't hurt me now."

He stepped through the opening. He was still inside the crypt but somehow outside, as well, surrounded by tombstones. He looked to see who was buried beneath them but the markers were blank. No names. No chiseled birth or death dates. No solemn declarations from loved ones.

He made his way past each stone until he found a memorial with a statue standing over it. The grave was overgrown with weeds and littered with trash and bird crap. The statue over the sarcophagus was broken, missing an arm as well as its head, but there was no mistaking who was supposed to be buried there. He saw a crow resting where his own head should have been. As the Joker approached the crow screamed then flew off.

"This is supposed to be my grave?" He laughed a nervous laugh. "No, no, no. This is too small for me—and look at it. It's a wreck. Surely my followers would be taking better care of…"

He paused then laughed again.

"Oh, I get it. You're trying to tell me my sycophants have forgotten all about me. Very funny, Bats. But that's not gonna happen." He looked at the statue again then hurried away from it. "You obviously have no clue how to be funny. Some jokes can be in bad taste. Leave the comedy to us professionals."

The Joker took another step then saw a second door to yet another room.

"So what's here, Bats? What do you want me to see now?"

A crying sound. Then Batman was suddenly behind him. "What? You?"

Not Batman. A statue. Stone. Unmoving. Silent.

"Good one, Bats. Almost funny." This time the Joker wasn't laughing. He lifted his gun and fired. The statue quietly exploded.

"See, old boy. You aren't the death of me."

Another door. The crying was coming from there. Inside were empty chairs. Row after row of empty chairs. All pointing at a pathetic-looking buffet and the half-torn banner that hung over it.

JOKER'S WAKE. THANKS FOR ALL THE LAUGHS.

The crying continued. From behind the furthest chair. Sitting on it was Harley. Harley Quinn. The only one who had come.

"Hey, Harley, where is everyone?" She didn't respond. "Wait a second. You forgot to send the invites, didn't you?"

She couldn't hear him. He leaned over to her and shouted.

"Quit crying, you useless idiot. Rustle me up a wake.

"Harley! Dammit, Harley!"

Still no response.

He laughed again. "Of course. Of course. Brucey, this is you trying to send me some lame message, isn't it? I know what you're doing. This is the toxin talking. You and Scarecrow are trying to scare me. But this doesn't cut

it, Bats. It doesn't even come close."

Another room. On a plain wooden coffee table was an old-fashioned radio. Flanking the table were two blown-up newspaper front pages. "JOKER DIES. CITY DOESN'T CARE," was the first headline. Next to that another front page. "POLLS SHOW TWO-FACE MORE FEARED THAN EVER."

"Oh, c'mon, Bats. Is this the best you've got?"

Suddenly, the radio crackled with life.

"Welcome to *Good Evening Gotham*. I'm Jack Ryder."

Then a second voice. "And I'm Vicki Vale. So, Jack, it's the one-year anniversary of the Joker's death. Any thoughts on the occasion?"

"Sorry, Vicki...? Who?"

Vicki Vale laughed. "Oh, you remember. The Joker."

"Oh, right," Ryder chuckled. "The question mark guy. He's dead?"

Vicki laughed again. "No, not him. Try again."

"Gosh darn it, Vicki. I'm clueless. Help me out."

"You know what, Jack?" Vicky laughed. "It doesn't matter. Let's forget about him and move on."

"Yes, Vicky. You're right. Let's forget about him and move on."

Vicki cleared her throat and continued with her report. "In other news, a museum dedicated to Batman and his arch-nemesis, the Penguin, opened on Bleake Island today..."

The radio faded to static, then silence. The Joker stared at it then looked up, away from the table.

"Oh, you think that's scary, Bats? When I get out of here I'll write my name in blood on every street corner. I'll carve it on every corpse. No one... no one is forgetting me." He

gave a self-satisfied *humph* then searched the room again. "Now how do I get out of here?"

The room looked bigger to him now, extending far beyond where the wall had been just a moment before. The table with the radio and newspapers seemed to vanish, and near where it had stood was another large statue of Batman, this one with flaming red eyes.

The Joker laughed then shot at the statue. "Running out of ideas already, Bats?"

More statues suddenly surrounded him. The Joker raised his gun and fired. The closest statue exploded, but instead of crumbling, a flesh-and-blood Batman stepped from it, grabbed the Joker and threw him to the floor. The Joker raised his weapon again, but his attacker was gone.

"Come on, Batman. Where the hell are you? Show me some sack, Bats. Look me in the eye. Talk to me. Let me put a bullet through you."

Silence. No Batman. No statues. The Joker was back in the room where he had started, but this time it wasn't completely dark. Through a crack in the wall he could make out a sliver of light.

He aimed his gun at it and fired.

The wall gave way, revealing an open space with a steel gantry that projected into the distance.

A way out.

"So long, Bats," he laughed. "Good try. Hell of a ride, but I'm getting off now." A switch was on the far wall. As he pulled it he could hear distant machinery whir into life. The Joker let out a deep breath and relaxed. "You know, Bats, you almost had me scared back there. Me.

Ha! I mean, what have I got to be afraid of?"

The machinery sounded louder now, like an elevator rising to his floor.

And then a voice.

His voice.

"You're afraid of being ashes. You're afraid of being forgotten. And you will be forgotten, Joker." A door appeared where there hadn't been one. It slid open. Batman was standing inside.

"Because of me," he finished, and he stepped closer even as the Joker stumbled back.

"No. Get away." Another step back. "Die, damn you." Another step. "Stop. Stop. Stay away."

But Batman wouldn't stop.

"No. Just die," the Joker begged.

Batman wouldn't die.

"I am vengeance," Batman said. "I am the night."

His voice deepened. "I am Batman," he growled.

His gloved fist lashed out and the Joker fell to the floor. Another fist slammed him along the corridor. Yet another sent him sprawling back, and back, and back. All the Joker could do was plead for his existence.

"Bats, please. Don't do this." Another fist pushed him back to the floor. "You're making a mistake. C'mon, Bats, after everything we've been through." He tried to stand but he was knocked down yet again. "I'll be good. I'll tell jokes. Nice ones. You don't have to do this."

He felt a wall behind him and he tried to use it to push himself back to his feet. The wall vanished and he fell again. "I know. I know what we can do. We can share your brain. I'll take it on weekends. Listen, listen to me. I'll leave Robin alone. I'll be nice to him."

A gloved fist smashed the Joker's face, crushing bone. He was bleeding and he was in tears. "You'll miss me. You know you will. No more dead parent gags, I swear. C'mon, Bats. You really want this to end?"

Another gloved fist knocked him backward. A heavy iron door slammed shut in front of him—he was in a cell. "No, Bruce. Don't leave me. I need you."

Batman pressed close to the bars. He was almost smiling.

"Goodbye, Joker," he said as the cell pulled back and away.

"Do you understand, Gotham?" Scarecrow said. "You have no savior. No more hope." He pointed to Bruce, who was thrashing on the cot, two of the cameras trained on him. "And no more Batman."

He leaned in close to Bruce and whispered in his ear.

"I am your master now. I have won."

But Bruce Wayne only smiled at him. "No, Crane. No, you haven't. I'm not afraid. You failed. Again."

"No. *Impossible*," Scarecrow rasped, backing away. "Without fear, life is meaningless." He saw the cameras still filming and raised his gun, aiming it at Wayne. Then he pressed the gun to Wayne's head.

"Even if you refuse to feel fear," he said, staring into the camera lens, "they will feel it when I put a bullet through your head. They'll see that if you can die, anyone can die."

"You're right, Jonathan." Bruce smiled at him again.

"Anyone can die. We're all human. Even you. Do you see it?"

Scarecrow looked at his hand, the one holding the gun, and he saw a small red laser dot centered on it. An instant later he heard the soft puff of a silencer, and the gun fell from his hand.

Bruce looked up to see someone on the balcony. The figure moved into the light, and he could tell who it was.

But Jason Todd was no longer the Arkham Knight. He wore a bright red hood over armor emblazoned with a large red bat. The Arkham Knight had been a deluded villain, but he'd been shown the lies that had warped him, and he chose to fight them.

Jason Todd was now the Red Hood.

He took aim and fired again. The restraints that held Batman to the gurney were shredded, freeing him. Scarecrow fell back as Bruce Wayne clambered off the gurney, then turned to the cameramen and shouted.

"Keep filming," Bruce instructed. "I want everyone to see this." He lunged for Scarecrow and forced him to the floor. Crane tried to crawl free, but Wayne held him firmly. Scarecrow tried to stab with his syringes, but Bruce grabbed his wrists and pushed them back.

With a powerful thrust, Bruce forced the poisoned syringes back into Scarecrow's chest and neck. He held him still for several moments as the toxin took hold.

"It's over now, Crane. And fear loses."

Wayne stood and stepped back as Scarecrow staggered to his feet.

* * *

He reeled back and forth, flailing wildly at the monsters that were suddenly everywhere. He wanted to run, to get away from them, but they surrounded him, then pushed closer until he had nowhere to run.

One by one they took their turn biting his flesh, ripping it from bone. He fell again to the floor as the monsters turned into dark shapes with blazing eyes and long talons that ripped into his armor then cut into his skin.

The bat monster was going to gorge on him and turn him into one of them. He screamed in uncontrolled horror as ten thousand bats clawed their way into him. He could do nothing but succumb to his fears.

Gordon stared at his old friend, looking confused.

"Who was he? In the red hood? Why did he help us?"

Batman stood but turned his back to Gordon.

He can't see my face. He should never see what I'm becoming.

"That's what friends do," he said.

It was almost over. Bruce watched Gordon cradle Robin, still bleeding but no longer in shock. He stood near Gordon but kept his back to him.

"Look after him, Jim. Look after them all."

Gordon stared at Batman, at first surprised but then understanding what Bruce had said.

"What's going to happen to you now?"

Bruce retrieved his mask and put it back on. Bruce

Wayne was just a man, and it didn't matter now if everyone knew it. But Batman could be anyone who believed in justice. Batman was a symbol.

"You've been a good friend. The best I could ask for. You were there at the beginning," he said as he walked toward the cameras, then past them. "And now you get to see how it ends."

46

Alfred stared out the window of Wayne Manor, and saw the endless throng of reporters packed behind the front gates. There must have been a thousand of them, sent to Gotham City by every news agency and television network. Camera crews had set up spotlights aimed at nearly every door and window, on the off chance there'd be something, anything, for them to film.

Vicki Vale stood before the gate, microphone in hand. She dated Bruce Wayne, thought she understood him, but she still couldn't accept that the supposed playboy was actually Gotham City's protector. Her cameraman aimed his camcorder at her as she began her report.

"This is Vicki Vale reporting live outside Wayne Manor following the dramatic unmasking of billionaire Bruce Wayne. There have been unconfirmed reports that Wayne would address the world and we are waiting for—"

They heard the roar of the Batwing as it emerged from the thick cloudbank blanketing the sprawling mansion. It circled over the great lawn before landing near the marble fountain Wayne's great grandfather had found in Italy in the late nineteenth century, and shipped back to the States.

"That's him," she shouted. "Are we still rolling?" The cameraman nodded. A figure stepped out of the aircraft.

"It's him."

"It's Wayne."

"It's Batman."

He stood in front of the Batwing as at least a thousand camera flashes illuminated the night. Vicki turned to her cameraman.

"Get a close-up. I want to be sure it's him."

It was Batman. He pulled back his cowl and so the reporters all knew he was also Bruce Wayne.

The front door opened, and Alfred Pennyworth walked out to greet him.

"Are you sure you want to do this, sir?"

Bruce pulled his cowl back over his head and fastened it under his chin.

"I've got to, Alfred. It's the only way to protect them."

Alfred looked out toward the reporters. The flashes were so bright they almost blinded him. He saw Vicki Vale speaking to the cameras. He always liked her. She was smart and would have made a good match for Master Wayne, if circumstances had been very different.

"You should go now, Alfred. This isn't for you."

"I'm sorry, sir. But my job here isn't done. Shall we, then?"

"Batman is Bruce Wayne," Vicki said. "My God, Gotham, this is huge. What does it mean for the future of the city?"

For a moment Alfred felt sad, then he straightened his tie and stood tall, proud and maybe a bit defiant. He held the door open for Master Wayne to enter, followed him inside, then closed it behind them.

And the mansion exploded.

The first detonation was off to one side, and allowed the press to pull back. Then there were a hundred separate explosions, beginning with the largest one set by the front door, destroying the long foyer into the living room to the left and the dining room to the right. Explosives had been carefully placed in every room.

In a matter of seconds, the once-proud manor was gone.

James Gordon sat on the roof of the G.C.P.D. headquarters. He could see the fires licking at the dark skies from more than fourteen miles away and he knew it was over. His journal was opened on his lap, and he finished writing his thoughts.

This is not the story that was leaked to the press.
This is how it happened.
This is how the Batman died.

EPILOGUE—PART ONE

Gordon was staring at the city. Months had passed, and he was still only beginning to recover from the events that had occurred. He had decided to begin a new journal, starting with strength, not defeat. It was night, and Gordon, dressed all in black, blended into the dark.

He almost preferred it that way.

"A friend once told me that criminals were a cowardly and superstitious lot. That the only way to beat them was to give them something to be scared of." He paused and lit his pipe and took a puff from it. "I understand now. As his world grew darker, so did ours."

He paused and looked at the pieces of the dismantled Bat-Signal. They had wanted to cart it to the junkyard, to bury the memory of it, but he asked them to leave it in place. It wasn't much, but it was something he needed in order to remember.

He returned to his new journal, thought for a few seconds, then started writing again.

"When his war ended, he believed our lives could begin again. So he set us free. To live… and to love."

He paused again—his phone was buzzing. An email message appeared on the screen.

From: Tim Drake
To: James Gordon

Don't forget the ring.

Tim and Barbara. Batman would have loved it, too.

He took the elevator from his office down to the street, where a limousine was waiting to take him to the ceremony. A motorcycle escort surrounded the limo as it hurried through Gotham City's streets.

He took out his pen and continued to write in his ledger.

There was an inquest, of course. Hundreds of suspects. Who killed Bruce Wayne? I guess we'll never know for sure.

So what's next? Criminals are a cowardly and superstitious lot. But what happens when they have nothing to be scared of?

Who will protect Gotham City now that the Batman is dead?

The limo passed the building that had been Gordon's campaign headquarters. The sign proclaiming "Gotham City's new mayor" still hung in the window. It passed an alleyway that had, until recently, been called Crime Alley. Two months ago Gordon had officially changed it to Wayne Way.

It was starting to rain and, as he continued to write his thoughts, he didn't notice three figures—a father, mother, and son—duck into the alley trying to stay dry under its overhang.

EPILOGUE—PART TWO

The limo moved on as two other figures followed the family into the alley. One pulled out a handgun.

The father saw the two, stepped toward the gunman and tried to reason with him. The gunman slammed the pistol across his face, knocking him to the ground. The boy hugged his mother.

"Help me," she cried. "Help us."

The thug pushed her to the wall, grabbed her pearl necklace and pulled. The chain broke and the pearls fell to the ground, scattering in all directions.

"No one's coming to help you, lady. Not in this city. Not anymore." He turned to the other thug and gestured to the father, still sprawled on the ground. "Take his wallet."

But then the gunman heard a shriek behind him. It was the woman. He turned and looked up and gasped. The other thug followed his gaze.

He was standing on the roof. A dark silhouette.

"Hey, freak," the gunman said, laughing, no longer afraid. "Maybe you missed the news, but the Batman's dead. That costume, it don't scare us no more."

The figure on the roof said nothing. But his eyes glowed

dark green, two burning fires in the night.

A swarm of bats exploded from his body, forming giant wings, spread wide as their shrieking grew louder and louder. The figure swooped down from the roof, its demonic face snarling with bared fangs and fiery eyes.

The gunman was wrong.

There was something to fear.

ACKNOWLEDGMENTS

To DC Entertainment, and the many people who have made Batman who he is. You gave birth to a legend and in doing so enriched the lives of millions.

A special thanks to Ames Kirshen, Josh Anderson, Elizabeth Seminario, Matthew Mizutani, Craig Mitchell, Ernest Zamora and everyone at WBIE for their help, encouragement and guidance. This book could not have been possible without all of you.

Thanks to everyone at Rocksteady for creating such a powerful and emotional game, and especially to Sefton Hill, Martin Lancaster, Phil Huxley, and Craig Owens for their amazing game script.

Special thanks to my editor, Steve Saffel, and all the good folk at Titan Books including Nick Landau, Vivian Cheung, Laura Price, Paul Gill, and Alice Nightingale and Hayley Shepherd.

Marv Wolfman
January 30, 2015

ABOUT THE AUTHOR

MARV WOLFMAN has written the adventures of many of the most famous characters in comic books, including Batman, Superman, Green Lantern, Wonder Woman, Spider-Man, and Fantastic Four. He was the co-creator of The New Teen Titans, Deathstroke the Terminator, and Nova, and wrote the universe-changing limited series *Crisis on Infinite Earths*. In the video-game world he contributed to *Green Lantern*, the DCU-Online massive multiplayer online game; *Superman Returns*; *Dark Knight Returns*; *Flash*, and more. His novels include *Crisis on Infinite Earths*, *Superman Returns*, and *The Oz Encounter*. His awards include the Will Eisner Hall of Fame Award, the National Jewish Council Book Award, and the Scribe Award for Speculative Fiction (for *Superman Returns*).